PARADE
ON AN
EMPTY STREET

PARADE
ON AN
EMPTY STREET

Margaret
Drury
Gane

ST. MARTIN'S PRESS   NEW YORK

Library of Congress Cataloging in Publication Data

Gane, Margaret Drury.
  Parade on an empty street.

  I. Title.
PZ4.G192Par   1979   [PR8199.3.G283]   813'.5'4
ISBN 0-312-59594-8   79-2132

To my father,
and my mother

PROLOGUE

"Mr. Gillies—"

For a moment my name doesn't register as I thumb through the fan of magazines spread on the waiting room table.

"Mr. Gillies? Mr. Biggs says he'll be delayed—he's very sorry but he had court this morning. He says would you mind waiting?"

"How long?"

"'bout half an hour?" She amends that estimate with a jutting smile. "Well, maybe just twenty-five minutes, at the most, that is." But there is an inflection of doubt.

I frown at my watch, which has stopped at 11:30. This appointment has been worked into my lunch hour, and I still have to eat. "All right, but I do have patients. . . ."

"You sure need it with lawyers," she sighs, flicking the intercom button and delivering her message to Biggs.

Obviously she doesn't know my profession. I suppose the appointment was made with just my surname, though it doesn't matter. I'm long past the time when I flaunted my medical prefix because it boosted my young ego. Today I feel a nice sense of anonymity, not having to hear *doctor* away from the office, nor having to explain my profession: *A physician? A vet? Oh, a dentist! Oh.*

1

The room is done in bland and harmless beiges and browns with orange ashtrays and a few struggling potted plants to lighten the stolid furnishings. Behind the secretary's desk hang prints of the rain-blurred City Hall and an elegant Osgoode. By Biggs' door, an original oil captures the reproving drawn-and-quartered expression of a fully-robed judge.

A door opens slowly outward from one of the three inner offices, only one more welcome diversion until something rivets my attention. Did I miss her name on the door as I came in? That *is* Shirley there, partially turned away from me, talking earnestly to a client. I turn in disbelief to check the firm's roster now printed backwards on the frosted glass: Finlay, Biggs and Upshaw. *Shirley* Upshaw.

The first sense of recognition turns to mounting excitement, then incredulity. I feel disconnected, part of no time and yet immersed in both past and present. The woman I see, one hand resting lightly on the door knob, has been changed by the years, and I know it. But her figure is still a slight, straight exclamation mark. Her face, what I can see of it, is as pale and delicately composed as I remember, though all youthful roundness has gone and the line from temple to chin has become taut, emphasizing her cheekbones. The most startling change is her hair, now darkened to a biscuit colour and cut into a classic style she's looped indifferently over one ear. When she was young, she appeared each morning with white rags wound in all directions from her head, like bandages. And when they were healed, golden corkscrew curls sprung like light, bounding in the sun. . . .

Now there's an impulse to cross the brown broadloom and ask if she remembers. Is twenty-five years too long? My self-preservation masks itself as thoughtfulness for her. I tell myself that she's obviously busy—it's entirely possible that it would embarrass her, being interrupted at work. But I'm rooted to this chair by reasons more powerful. I am afraid that she won't recognize me, that less hair and more poundage have dumped me into the mass of indistinct memory. I

2

don't think of myself as a man who leaps into view; in crowded rooms, at parties, I tend to blend with wallpaper and couches, the last to be offered the *hors d'oeuvres*. Still, would it be so difficult to get up, stroll the carpet like a lawn, and say "Keith Gillies, remember?"

Hesitation has taken the decision out of my hands. Her client has left and the door is firmly shut. Yet for a moment the room expands, the light seems quite brilliant, glancing sharply off ordinary objects; something unfinished charges the air. I didn't speak to her; now all the questions pour through me, when the chance has passed. Perhaps the disappointment shows somehow on my face, for Biggs' secretary is lowering her silvery lids quizzically in my direction. Automatically I reach for a magazine, but I can't read.

Shirley's closed door claims my mind as it always did, for she is part of my childhood, and a past we shared so strangely—far back, long before the Beatles, before the high school girls of 3B, who wore loafers and had brothers in the army, and put on crimson lipstick with a photo of Rita Hayworth propped by the mirror.

Shirley touched my life before much had made it memorable, and it is this that now comes crowding back, transforming the far-off thud of a piledriver to the sound of a ball hitting a garage door.

PART ONE

The ball I threw while playing in the park
Has not yet reached the ground.

Dylan Thomas
"Should Lanterns Shine"

1

I was eleven years old in 1939. It was in August of that year that I first saw Shirley Upshaw, when she moved into the house across the road from ours. We lived on one of those cool, narrow, tree-lined streets that struggle to exist today, while developers are levelling the landmarks all around.

The house I lived in still stands, incredibly, many gallons of paint hiding the bottle green and battleship grey I used to pick at. It was all frame, prey to carpenter ants, wood rot that crept like grave mould into fissures, and illegal little fires my brothers and I lit under the wood steps. More threatening were the winter fires my father built in the black basement, fires so intense that in the darkness I could see the furnace throbbing red, hissing, luminous and terrifying. If it fizzled out in the night, I would hear my dad crumpling newspaper, rattling the iron handles that shook ashes, scraping a shovel through the coal bin.

There was a small window in the back of the bin, hinged, thick with sludge, through which the coalman periodically dumped twelve sacks of coal. His face was miner-swarthy from carbon, and that and the filthy cap and permanently bent back made him indistinguishable from other drivers. His bill was shoved through the mail slot. *Count the bags.* And one of us would count from behind the curtains, insulting his honesty with hard eyes: "They'll give you nine or ten and keep the rest, you know."

On the day Shirley appeared, however, the bin window was smothered in zinnias and the fire was above us, simmering in a cloudless sky. Our lawn was stalked by twin crows, coal black with blue-flame heads. Above me, a second crop of baby jays squawked, tapping our maple tree for insects and moisture. Except for the birds, only the thwack of my ball against the garage door carved the afternoon silence. Women who could were napping or listening to soap operas behind drawn blinds, or sat spread-kneed on verandahs, mopping their necks.

Yesterday we had escaped the heat with a trip to the Island, where the frigid lake sent shocks to the marrow, and there were ponies to ride.

"They're all blind," my brother Doug said, full of authority. They were harnessed together with heads down, blue-white eyes and tangled manes tortured with huge flies. Around and around they plodded, while kids kicked their ladder ribs and a man picked his teeth and counted dimes. "They go to the glue factory after," Doug said, and I didn't want to ride them.

This morning I had wandered to the nearby schoolyard, drawn there out of habit and boredom, and the sight of the big dead building with all the blinds down and no fat ABC's stuck to the kindergarten window. I had gone with Don White, Pinky Yorke and some others, thinking that our regular counsellor would be there—a stocky, blunt-armed guy in the required grey drill pants. "'Nuff here for a team?" he'd ask, flipping the ball indifferently and gazing off toward the smoke shop. He'd bring a softball, a hardball, a couple of mitts and a bat, and a sheaf of papers we thought were important until he stood on them once with his big dirty sneakers. His glasses looked a half-inch think, magnifying his eyes into monstrous raw eggs; yet he could pitch a hole through you when he was in the mood. Once we got started, he'd pull Tarzan comics and a pack of cigarettes from his windbreaker, settle in a black patch of shade and leave us to play on our own. But today he hadn't appeared.

"Who the hell's *that*?" Don White said, nodding in the direction of the figure marching toward us from the side door of the school, beating papers *slap slap slap* against a huge thigh. He strode up to the straggling group and stared us down—big, bull-shouldered, neckless, a tight white shirt with Camp Wandemasedig printed on it. The temperature was around eighty, even that early in the morning. Sweat slithered and itched under my arms.

"Line up."

We stood side by side as he went from one to the other, his beardless Fosdick chin an inch from our faces, demanding names, addresses, ages.

"You?" I could smell lifesavers.

"Keith."

"*Surname*, creep, surname!"

"Gillies—" "Yorke—" "White—" down the line of dumb volunteers.

He was making quick private notes. "Okay, get this, you guys—" he'd seen *Little Caesar* because the whistle that never left his mouth was being worked over like a metal cigar "—*no* swearing, smoking, cut the cute stuff, get it?" "Camp Wandemasedig" rose and fell with the deep muscular breaths. Don White, never too sensitive to the atmosphere around him, slid disgusted eyes sideways and immediately the whistle flew front-and-centre and shrieked, sending some foraging sparrows off in a fluster of fear. "Shut up, Creep, and eyes front!" He planted turnip-fists on his hips. "Around the yard five times, full speed." We started off, passing the girls sitting under the oaks who paused in whatever they were making with needles and squares of cardboard to giggle. Two kids were batting a tetherball around the metal pole. No one was on the five baby swings with the worn wooden seats and sliding safety bars, but farther back a girl alone on the big swings had pumped herself to heady heights. The chains clanked dangerously. I kept running, one eye on the Creep, who stood in the centre of the yard, whistle poised and a grey cloth hat protecting him from the sun.

Through an opening in the board fence appeared the front wheel of a bike, and then a boy's face, innocent and curious. "NO BICYCLES—CAN'T YOU READ?" Another shrill blast. Beside me, Don's face burned and dripped. "Let's get-the-hell-out-of-here-" I nodded and jerked a forefinger at Pinky, and we took off. The boy on the bike had backed away, and the Creep wheeled in fury to belt after us. The front gate was about twenty-five yards away. Something told us that once beyond it we were safe.

The last one through, staggering in exhaustion, was Don White, a hand-span away from the lunging counsellor. We flung ourselves down on the damp lawn of the Oddfellow's Orphanage across the road, throats dry and ribs aching. Standing just inside the gate, the Creep began to tell us off, the whistle dangling uselessly on his chest.

"Don't let me catch you buggers in here again!"

"No swearing, creep!" Pinky Yorke mimicked in a winded patsy voice.

The counsellor had made a few mistakes that morning, but his biggest one was staying there too long, trying to bully us down. Something clicked in Don's plodding brain and he swaggered up on his spindly legs, his face glistening with sweat and the flush of creative genius.

"Hey, Creep, whazzat say on your sweater? Camp Wanna-See-My-Dick?"

We picked it up in a chorus like something triumphant from an opera and pelted his back with it as he trudged furiously up to the school.

So I stayed home in the afternoon, pitching balls against the garage door. The air was heavy and golden with heat. Down the street, kids in their underpants were running in and out of silver spray from the hose tied to a wooden pole on their lawn.

10

I heard the cab before I saw it and automatically turned to look, because any car was a rarity. I was astonished to see the driver pull in at the Upshaw place, right across the road from me. *Nothing* stopped at the Upshaw's, except Brown's Bakery and once in a while a black tea carriage with a huge grey horse that terrified us by snuffling the air and lipping the bit, wild-eyed. Through the open back window I saw a girl's face. Her placid grey eyes stared back at me, returning grave acceptance for curiosity. Turning in his seat, the driver made a pantomime motion of lips and then walked up to the house, leaving her behind. As he reached the porch the front door opened a little, so that he had to lean like an intruder to speak.

I was still watching, of course. Any glimpse of old Mrs. Upshaw, any light shed on her secretive and bitter life, made rudeness worthwhile. Money was placed into the driver's hand and he motioned to the girl to come. She climbed from the cab carrying an old-fashioned wicker case, a nondescript little figure in a sacky grey dress, a flat yellow hat pancaked over hair as straight and reflective as tinsel. The slight weight of the basket tilted her to the right as she walked. She disappeared into the house and the door slammed. I wondered what she was doing there, thinking that if she had any sense she'd run out and get back in the car. But nothing more happened and I turned my attention to the spokes of the cab wheels, the tarnished chrome figure perched on the hood, the running board I would have liked to jump on for a block or so. Slinging himself importantly into the front seat, the driver paid little attention to me and even less to the children who had deserted their hose and now stood gawking with their shingled haircuts plastered to their heads.

I went back to my game. *Thwack*—too low, but I caught the return in the tips of the mitt. I tucked the forefinger and third finger under into fearsome knuckles, a pitch I envied, but it eluded me because my body was growing in pieces, unevenly. Giving up, I sat down against the trunk of the

11

maple, watching Mrs. Halwick making her way slowly down the sidewalk. She kept close to the lawns and the splayed shade where the flattening sun could not reach her bony frame. A grocery bag on each hip gave her a curious, pack-mule walk.

"Afternoon, Keith. Hot." She pushed out a violet lower lip, blowing a stream of air toward her nose to underline her discomfort. "Your mother standing up to it?"

"Yeah. Guess so." I could smell the pie she was baking through our screen door, now plastered with flies gone mad. "I don't think she minds the heat." Whether she did or not, she looked a hell of a lot better than Mrs. Halwick, standing there with sweat patching her Eaton's Annex dress.

"Saw you playing ball. Don't know how you do it in ninety-two degrees. Should be up at Crang's having a swim." Crang's was an outdoor pool on St. Clair Avenue with a diving board like a hydro tower, surrounded by a high mesh fence. The liquor store was close by, a fact that we all knew appealed more to Mrs. Halwick's husband than any body of chlorinated water would. Everyone saw him weaving down Arlington Road around five-thirty, regular as a bread delivery. Going into his house with the exaggerated care of habitual drunks, he would gulp down whatever his wife carried in those burro bags and spend the rest of the evening plastered to his top verandah step in a grey undershirt.

Suddenly I felt sorry for Mrs. Halwick, slumping from one tilting brown pump to the other, talking pleasantly to me. "We-ell," she was say, as though it were possible, "*I* sure would be up there today, crowd or no crowd. Or at the Island maybe. Or Sunnyside. That would be nice, eh?"

"My mom doesn't like us to swim while the polio's around, not since John Bench got it."

Her mouth flopped open and her eyebrows met sadly over the bridge of her nose. "No! You don't say! Now that's a shame. Think he got it from swimming, do they?" She didn't wait for an answer, but swept the bad tidings away with a windy sigh in the direction of the Upshaw house. "Noticed goings-on over *there* just now," she said tightly. "A little girl, wasn't it?"

"Yeah."

"Relative, d'you suppose? Or is the old woman takin' in boarders?" Now she was talking to me as she talked to adults, and I just shrugged my shoulders, lost. "Probably is," she said serenely, shifting the groceries. "Well, I'd better be getting along. It'll soon be time for the mister, and I always say a man who earns the bread deserves to find it on the table when he gets home. . . ." *Under* the table would be more like it, my father would say.

I watched her sway away from me on vein-splotched, bowed legs. "Rickets," my mother had explained to me once when I'd wanted to know the reason for Mrs. Halwick's rocking walk. And prevention was thrust at me immediately in the form of an extra glass of milk, though I think my mother was more concerned with the drinking habits of Mr. Halwick. "Rickets are the least of that lady's problems," she'd said, clamping her lips. "Diet won't help door-mats. . . ."

At that time I shared a bedroom with Doug, who may have seemed easy to bunk with because he was the middle child, insulated from the concentration focused on George, the eldest, and the indulgent concern showered on me, the youngest. Adapting, compromising and sharing made him appear self-effacing, but he wasn't, at least not in the bedroom. There he quietly ruled, as he could not anywhere else, and his passion for cars papered the walls.

It had begun as a big room, bay-windowed on the street side, but stuffed so haphazardly with odds and ends of furniture bequeathed by bored or dead relatives that in the end the space meant nothing. A foundry smell of metal battling rust rose from our castiron beds. The prison-striped mattresses had been pounded by other people before us to thin, hard felt. There was the lingering musk of my grandfather's overstuffed armchair and our own assortment of old shoes, mildewed comic books and airplane glue. On her rare visits, my grandmother would declare that it smelled of boys, though how she detected that human scent above the others—and the harsh weapon of Lysol my mother wielded against them—I don't know.

But the mess that they disliked was simply insulation to us. Even when Doug was there he'd either be reading or surrounded by a fresh batch of car clippings, so conversations were sparse. I thought of it as my room.

On the day that the strange girl arrived at the Upshaw house, I'd gone upstairs to find Doug centring a newspaper photo above his bed—*Cobb Sets New World Record at 368.85 Miles Per Hour!*—concentrating so much that his tongue was clamped between his teeth. I didn't take my hobbies that seriously. I was in the process of making a dentist's drill of Meccano, which I intended to try out on the dumb brat up the street. There were second-hand Tom Swifts, and the only balsa model I ever finished, a six-inch *Spirit of St. Louis* floating on a string before the open window. I flopped on the bed, spread-eagled across the cool sheets, hearing our neighbour's radio crackling out *boop-boop-dittum-dottum* through the humming late-day heat. Mrs. Collins kept it on the front porch all summer long, just as she kept herself there, to absorb and dispense information.

"I don't know," I heard her sing-songing to someone, "whether it's an act of mercy or madness d'you? Little thing like that should—" I strained to hear more, but she was clucking as if calling chickens and her voice dropped below the level of the radio. I sat upright, looking for the cause of Mrs. Collins' caution through the screen. There she was, directly across the street, something right out of Grimm's fairy tales.

Through the dark green leaves of the maple tree, I saw the transformed girl on the Upshaw verandah, skinned of the drab dress and wearing something white. Ruffles flopped around her bony shoulders and along the hem. She seemed younger than I was, which heightened the oddly circumspect look she had, seated primly on the wicker chair that was never used, with her skinny ankles crossed. A book lay open on her lap, but she was glancing around the street, up, then down, as if all this was perfectly natural, not knowing how weird she looked. Her hair had been washed, sharply parted in the centre; white rags bobbed in all directions. She wore bright white shoes and unwrinkled pink socks, and there was a stiff bow on her stomach where the sash tied. Nothing like it lived on our street, and I knew I could spy on her, relieved that the distance, the angle and our old tree kept her from knowing. There were not many secret places in my life, not many things that I could do that were not pried into and exposed.

I pressed my fists, smelling of leather from the baseball, into my chin and leaned my elbows on the sill. The window frame enclosed the girl and the verandah; a blur of white, the bloody spears of Mrs. Upshaw's salvia, the fern that stood in jungle moistness by the railing.

By evening, speculation on who the girl was and what she was doing "over there" had gently crackled like bush fire from home to home. The stifling, humid summer, made worse with uneasy news from abroad, was lightened by street gossip and the simple optimism of people who could not believe there'd be another war so soon. Even though Mackenzie King was dutifully hissed whenever he appeared in *News Of The World* in movie theatres, my father decided that his dismissal of Parliament was a good sign: would he do that if there was anything to worry about?

"Of course not," he replied to his own question, spearing a grey square of warmed-over roast beef.

"There's a kid staying with old Mrs. Upshaw," I said, bored with rumours of war.

"Upshaw, Upshaw. . ." my father mused, fingering through his mind for clues. "Cody Upshaw was her only son

15

. . . and *that's* going back, because he died. . . ."

"How?" asked Doug.

My father ignored this with his usual single-mindedness. "And he ran away, too, didn't he, Mother?"

"Yes." She sent a flat look of warning which I caught but my father did not. Slowly, comfortably, he removed the elastics from his shirt sleeves, undid his striped tie and left it dangling like a dead snake over the back of his chair.

"A very messy business. Cody ran away with the Appleton girl, if I remember. . . ." He asked for the bread, but George, who was close enough to adulthood to risk direct questions, persisted.

"I heard he had to get married." George was becoming useful to Doug and me as mouthpiece in the family court, now that he was six inches taller than my dad and beyond slaps of reprimand. For a moment the statement hung in the air, carrying with it an air of intrigue, of unspeakable deeds and parents defied. I waited, hoping for added information. But my mother lit on an aspect of the promising situation that managed to turn it away, briefly, from the murky avenues George wanted to explore.

"They never came back to the house, you know, to see the old woman," she declared, the disbelief at this oversight playing on her face as though no one she knew would stoop to such rudeness.

"Who'd go back there if they didn't have to?" demanded Doug.

My father had remained silent through this, his habitually crusty leadership softened by heat and the long streetcar ride home. He looked up at my mother as though they were alone at the table.

"I'll bet that girl is Co—"

"Who would like peach pie?" my mother said loudly. "Homemade, not Christie's—" Doug bellowed with delight and sent his changing vocal cords into a spasm of indecision. I felt belligerent. There was George, grinning as though he'd unravelled the whole mystery without stirring a brain cell. And my mother had slapped her cooking over the subject just as things were really getting interesting.

"I saw the whole thing!" I yelled. "I saw the kid come in a cab this aft', and go into the house—"

"What kind of cab?" Doug wanted to know, his eyes like wheels.

"—and I saw her on the porch, too—" But nobody was listening. None of my dull facts could stand up to the frustrating hints and half-sentences that had gone before. As my mother carried the dessert into the dining room everyone forgot the Upshaws, so I gave up and lapsed into silence.

Goddam being the youngest!

2

At that time there seemed to be far more boys than girls around, a fact explained by my grandmother Gillies as being God's way of providing the right sex for an impending war. On any given summer night you could count at least twenty boys fooling around on the street, some of whom were my friends. But old allegiances occasionally shifted, and even though I started kindergarten with Don White, it was Pinky Yorke who became closer to me than anyone else. He had arrived during the previous school year, well into the spring of 1939, one of a large family who'd made the long ocean voyage from Ireland. He did not know *why* they came, though a war in the wind must have been some sort of catalyst, or the poverty in his homeland.

The brown wall phone jangled as we sat in class one day, and the teacher switched a look of annoyance to the side of his face away from us as he answered it. Nods, replies in a voice he never used with us— "Yes, certainly. Would you like me to send someone to bring him up? Fine. Yes, thanks, sir." Our ears, well-trained to subtleties of timbre, knew that the Principal was on the other end. Mr. Powell turned to catch Dicky Jackson grinning and slammed a ruler down hard on his vulnerable front desk. Reflex action was second nature by this time, and Dicky's fingers snapped back like soldiers in retreat from the steel-edged weapon.

Minutes later we were coolly appraising the stocky, tweed-clad figure of the new boy. Standing beside Mr. Powell's desk, he flipped back strangely-long, bronze hair as it slipped over his eyes. The square face seemed to have turned red under the curious assessment of the class.

"This is Eric Yorke, class," the teacher said by way of introduction, the only polite words we'd hear from him all year. He did not like interruptions, especially Irish ones who drew attention away from his soliloquy on long-division. Within minutes he had Eric Yorke seated and staring numbly at a faded copy of Arithmetic-Senior Fourth, and the numbered facts droned on.

As time went on Eric became Pinky, for we discovered that his face was always that colour. He also had a disturbing ability to rattle off right answers. Mr. Powell lost no time in pointing out his superiority in "catching on fast—something a few of *you* might try!" We would all be ditch-diggers or plumbers.

Since none of this endeared Pinky to us, he remained on the periphery of things for a time. He didn't look like us, which was suspect. A light brogue on his tongue, heavier ones on his feet. *Knitted* knee socks, for God's sake! We found all the reasons for criticism dropped right in our laps. Until the day he came up with a brilliant idea.

One morning, after seat work had been assigned and Powell retired behind the *Globe and Mail* while we did it, someone snapped a spitball from the back of the room, hitting Pinky's cheek with moist accuracy. He returned it, naturally, and it was during the second flight that Powell jumped to his feet, roaring. Angered, he looked like an outraged guinea-pig: round brown eyes, bulging slightly; spumes of unruly centre-parted hair suddenly bristling with indignation. It was not unusual for teachers to have their own straps, and his hung in listless menace from a back pocket.

"ALL the boys . . . on your feet!" We rose with military precision. Blame, like homework, had to be assigned.

"Line up!" He had taken his punishment-post by the right-hand door of the cloakroom, just under a pastel photo of the Royal Princesses. We shifted, eighteen of us, into a shambling line in front of the blackboard. There was some prestige attached to daring to be first, and the honour fell to Dick Jackson, who looked around to see if we were admiring his bravery. Swwwiiish-crack! Dick withdrew a hardball-callused hand and ambled through the cloakroom, where he had about ten feet of privacy to assemble his face into bored disdain for the sake of the girls, who were staring as he made his entrance. Pinky Yorke was next. Powell was so mad that he didn't even look up, so bright Pinky got it just as hard as anyone. He winced and jammed his lips together, clamping an Irish obscenity back down his throat. My turn. I was not particularly brave, but what is one moment in time? I shut my eyes, hearing the pitted leather cleave the air and then burn like a tong across my hand. When I began the journey past the winter Meltons and leather windbreakers, there was Pinky, grinning like a leprechaun. "Line up again!" he hissed. "He's blind as a bat and he'll never know!" I agreed, yanking Dick back with us to the end of the moving line. The idea was brilliant, and best of all, it was working!

Powell slapped away for almost fifteen minutes, until his arm gave out and the built-up violence seeped to a standstill. Finally we were ordered back to our seats, never to be lined up again.

Pinky could bask in security now. The brain we disliked rattling off right answers was on our side. "I know how he saw us, too," he confided at recess. "The bugger has a *hole* in the paper, 'bout the size of an eye." He said "oy" for eye.

"But he didn't notice all of us lined up again. . . ."

"Long-sighted," said Pinky Yorke serenely.

My own friendship with Pinky began toward the end of the school year, in June, a month that surely triggered more conflict for us than the unknown hazards of September. Only the brightest escaped the fear of final exams: for those

20

of us with average marks there was always the possibility of a mind stricken blank in the silent, sweating room. For the slow and stupid, exams became the ultimate horror that stripped away their last bits of pride and left them alone to face an ineptitude they'd been accused of all year. Weak bladders and roiling stomachs caused several accidents. Dick Jackson, who knew failure when he smelled it, vomited all over his geography paper. With borderline marks, he shrewdly decided the examiners would be thrown into a bind of indecision, giving him at least a fifty-fifty chance of passing.

By the time exams were finished, the days of June had lengthened. The air drugged us, carrying the smell of cut grass, roses, and silky winds from the west; lassitude had replaced anxiety. Anything that would liven the long, warm days had to be found in the evening, and I had discovered an intriguing way to spend a couple of hours a week. Up on Benson Avenue squatted the Church of the Evangelical Host, where a congregation could be secretly watched through a side window. They were "low" Baptists, somebody told me, distinguished from high Baptists like my parents by an exciting lack of restraint. Slapping tambourines and yelling back at the preacher, they wound themselves up to a fury of religious joy every time I watched them.

It was the contrast that drew me. Happiness wasn't a priority at my parents' church. Amber caution met them from the moment the massive oak doors swung open. Whispers— "Good morning, Mrs. Gillies, Edward" —a program of worship from which no one deviated placed into gloved hands. Muted music by Bach and Handel, or on daring days, Vivaldi. The only yell might come from a small child, who would be whisked away in profound embarrassment. After Sunday services the doors were bolted and chained against any trespassers who might want to pray in there during the week.

But almost any night there was a free-wheeling service at

Evangelical Host, which I could watch by inching sideways between the wall and a seven-foot board fence.

"WHO are we heah fo?" demanded a man in rolled-up shirt sleeves.

"Jesus Christ!" yelled the crowd in unison.

"And WHO does He save?"

"SINNERS!"

I was settled by the small window, knees jammed against my chin, enjoying the preacher's rallying cry, when I jumped at the sound of shifting gravel and turned to see Pinky Yorke worming his way toward me. At first the sight of him annoyed me, blazing hair and red face and odd clothes so obvious that I was sure he'd draw the whole damned street in after him. But once he'd got his thick body down and it seemed he'd come in undetected, I began to like the idea of a shared conspiracy. We had decided, separately and illegally, to spy on the same scene. Something else was added: a faint, chilling sense of fear, which had never been there when I was alone. It sharpened the adventure for me, feeding an imagination withered by nine months of rote learning. I shivered lightly. Outsiders who crept the black hills of Haiti must have felt the same way, peering down on a voodoo ceremony ablaze with torches, knowing the curse that would follow if they were discovered. . .*an effigy of the head, stuck with pins! A lingering, wasting illness! Things of hideous hair and bones hung secretly on the door while you shook through the dank, drumming night!*

Pinky giggled, nudging me. "Get that guy with the funny accent!"

Look who's talking, I thought, but not unkindly.

We both jumped as a strange voice called down the alley.

"You could see and hear much better inside, boys. Brother Windheimer would like it, too." There at the end of the alley, blocking our exit, stood an angular man in a drooping grey suit.

Pinky summed up the hopeless situation. "Wanna go in?"

"Sure. Why not?"

Once out of the alley we scraped bits of gravel and dirt from our knees and followed the man, reading the red-lettered banner flopping idly in a soft breeze.

June 15th to June 30th
BROTHER JOSEPH THOMAS WINDHEIMER
of WHEELWRIGHT, VIRGINIA!
8.30 PM: "A HOME IN HEAVEN—OR HELLFIRE?"
Music by the MIRACLE SISTERS!
Plus Special Prayers For The Sick, Healing, and
Calls To Christ Following The Service.
All Sinners Welcome!

"The Lord says, 'Suffer little children to come unto Me'," the bony grey man was saying, stepping aside to shepherd us through the doors, where the wild din of a hymn was in progress. He smiled encouragement as he placed us firmly in two folding chairs.

"Now, if you feel the call, just march yourselves right up there and tell Brother Windheimer." We sat rigidly apart, afraid to look at one another in case we lost control and burst out laughing.

The Miracle Sisters were three bored women who stared fixedly ahead during the hymn-sing. One was peeling polish from her fingernails, flicking the red flakes expertly to the ground. With the crowd nicely warmed up and grateful to flop back into their chairs, the Sisters came smartly to life.

Except for virginal white dresses, they could have been the Andrew Sisters, shorn of miracles and full of hut-sut-ralson. "*Jee*-zuz—sweet *Jee*-zuz, make me pure 'n clean—" dipping, turning sideways together, flinging a right, then a left arm, clapping hands right on cue—and loud, so that any harmony vibrated into one shattering sound of choreographed supplication.

Brother Windheimer clapped politely as they returned to

their chairs, and planted a hand on the table before him. A few sighs, a latecomer's "amen" left over from the song, shuffles. He waited for silence, swinging his smile around the room as though it were on the end of a rope. I glanced at Pinky uneasily, but he was alert and watchful.

"Yes—yes," Brother Windheimer began. Almost whispering, "We all know why we are heah. Evrah minute of this week—evrah day of this *week*" (now the voice was rising) "EVRAH WAKIN' MOMENT WE HAVE SINNED!" Gone the lazy smile. "In To-RON-no, one of mah fayvrit ciddies, the street raht outside this doah is *crawlin'* with sinners. . . ."

I was hazarding peeks at the people around me; what fun was it to sit here and get told off—like school? But they were grinning, nodding occasionally, wriggling in the excitement of their wickedness while the Brother lashed them with their iniquities. "Sins of the MIND, brethren! Jealousy, downright hatred, covetousness, lechery, mean-tongued rantin' where a kind word would turneth away wrath!" On and on, pausing only to gulp at the glass of water placed beside him until he had worked everyone up to a pitch of frenzy. Suddenly a woman jumped from her chair to run down the aisle, whining that she wanted to confess. Ears pricked up. The Brother, looking pleased, motioned her to kneel, and all hell broke loose. Moaning, singing without the guidance of the pianist's music, chairs pushed back in a pandemonium of scraping.

Gleefully, I realized that it was Mr. Meuller who led the Christian conga line now forming, the pale, wet-palmed grocer who dispensed our grab-bags with the gravity of a man selling jewellery. "Chlory, chlory I am saved!" he croaked, flopping his pin-striped arms and clumping awkwardly in his unaccustomed role of leader. It fascinated me, as contradictions in adults always did, but Pinky interrupted me with a hard jab of his elbow.

"Look over there—*no*, further back—"

I craned my neck, but could see nothing until the tail end

24

of the celebrating line had lurched past.

"Wouldja believe it?" whispered Pinky.

"Christ no—" I said, staring at what looked like a pile of dark clothes thrown on a chair near the back of the church.

"It's the old woman," hissed Pinky, "the one who lives acrosst from you—" With the piano thumping and the reverend's tambourine whacking against his leg we couldn't make out what Mrs. Upshaw was calling, but her mouth seemed to open and close in some kind of rhythmic chant. I grabbed Pinky's arm.

"Come on, I gotta hear this." We worked our way to the back until we found a vantage point just to the side and behind old Mrs. Upshaw. By now Brother Windheimer was calling for sinners to come to the front, and I was beginning to sense Pinky's edginess.

"Call out to the Lord!" hollered Windheimer, "Call out yoah trouble and lettim hear ya! You kids back there, it's nevah too early to tell it all to the Lord!"

"Jesus, let's get out of here—" Pinky's face was coated in sweat. The impending danger of having to say something in that crazy place drove all curiosity about the old lady away, and we leaped from the chairs to make a run for the doors when suddenly, cutting through the racket, we heard her voice—the dry, cracking whiplash I recognized. "FORGIVE HIM—FORGIVE HIM, LORD!"

"Amen," said the Brother pleasantly, doling out collection plates.

We flew from the place, charging the dusty streets in the cool dusk like animals set free. We imitated everyone we'd seen, all the accents, music and dancing, until we buckled with laughter, and gradually the stares of disapproval we'd been collecting like medals along the way silenced us.

"Where ja live?" I asked Pinky.

"133 Rushton," he said, still new enough to add the house number. "Come over tomorrow if you like."

"Okay."

"There're a lot of us."

"Ya? How many?"

"Ten kids and my Pa and Ma."

"I have two brothers," I told him.

"Do your folks know you go up there to watch?" I didn't understand why it should matter, but I said, yes, they knew, although I wasn't sure they liked it much.

"Will you be tellin' them about bein' inside, too?"

I expected I would, some night when things got dull around the table, or they weren't paying enough attention to me. "I'm the youngest," I added with some self-pity.

"I'm somewhere in the middle, lower half. Goddam ham in a sandwich," Pinky said cheerfully.

"Will you tell your folks about tonight?"

"I don't know. I don't think so. We're micks." He stated it flatly, without apology or superiority, as though it was one barrier that he had to climb before our friendship could continue.

This was a dark area of my education. What little I knew of Catholics and their "ways," as my grandmother would put it, hung precariously on a peg of old, inaccurate prejudices. I decided to come right to the point. "Will they give you hell?"

Pinky grinned, kicking a stone neatly into the sewer. "Not if we don't tell them."

I noticed the "we," and swelled up a little. "Then I won't either—okay?"

We ran and whooped exuberantly down my street, past the arching hoses, panting dogs and Mueller's silent, shuttered store.

3

All this, of course, happened before the August appearance of Shirley Upshaw. And, aside from a few verandah-framed glimpses of her, she remained a mystery. I was envied a bit for my front-row view of her arrival. But it was Pinky's newly acquired paper route that provided information, a reliable source because of his photographic memory. A few of us were hanging around the lamppost, waiting for someone to call us in, when we saw Pinky coming down the Upshaw driveway, his head bobbing along the top of the dark green hedge like an orange beach ball on the sea. We yelled for him to come on over. None of us walked on that driveway if we could help it, so livid was the old woman's temper. A ball accidentally kicked in that direction or bounced onto the lawn was rarely retrieved. By night, we knew, it would be scooped up in her curling yellow hands and taken inside, never to be seen again.

He jingled across the road, one pocket loaded with pennies from collecting. A thin *Evening Telegram* was rolled under one arm, picked up from a house whose occupants had gone away without telling him. Before he reached the curb we were pelting him with questions.

"What's the old bat like, up close?" Don White wanted to know.

"Nutty—nutty as a fruitcake. I had to wipe my feet for an hour before she'd let me in the hall." We looked at each other uncomfortably. If that was insanity, all our mothers would have to be committed too.

"You were inside, for God's sake, what's she like?"

"Beady black eyes, skin full of moles, with great white hairs hanging out of them—I dropped the change in that creepy place, she's so scary!"

"Ya?"

"She goes crazy! 'Money is *dirty*,' she says in that banshee voice of hers. That's when she called this girl to help me pick them up—'Get these up, Shirley, there's a good girl—'" (he'd given the old woman an Irish accent by now) "—and suddenly there's this kid dressed up all fancy like she's going to a party." He added this with the awe of a boy who gave all his paper money to his family and owned two pairs of pants—one for Mass, the other for everything else he did.

"Who's the girl? Didja find out who she is?"

"Sure," said Pinky, "I ast the old lady herself." He rattled the brown coppers with King George on them.

"Christ, you asked *her*?" murmured Don White, momentarily shattered by either Pinky's innocence or his courage.

"Kee-eeth. . ." It was my mother's voice calling my name through the trill of crickets.

Not now! "Be there in a minute!" I hollered, and the screen door slammed. "For Chrissake, hurry up, Pinky! Who *is* she?"

He furrowed his face, recalling the exact words. "She said, 'This is Shirley, my granddaughter, who has been left an orphan in this world. I am keeping her with me, caring for her. . .'" I waited, breathless. . . "'*forever!*'"

We stared at him in silence, appalled at the fate other people's kids had handed to them. Words conjured up pictures for us as surely as they did for adults. But our images were infinitely more dramatic, more frightening, never deflated or diluted by experience. *Orphan*. . .the word hung suspended in the air, draped round with Death displayed on a front door, gift-wrapped in a drooping black ribbon. I remembered the curved arch of the Oddfellow's through which trooped the silent string of children, adults stationed at each end like guards parading them to church.

"Little Orphan Shirley," sang Don White, making Daddy Warbucks circles with curved thumbs and forefingers around his eyes. A funny, idiot dance. "ARF, says Sandy, ARF. . . ."

I went up to my room earlier than usual that night, hearing the threat of the thunderstorm everyone wanted growling around outside. Through the open window I could hear people talking on their verandahs in lazy, wilted voices. Streetlights shot out, then disappeared, as a fitful wind moved through oak and maple. At the Upshaw house the lights were out, the house black.

Under my bed I had a shoebox, a bank for hunks of rock, blunted arrow heads found at the Humber, baseball cards. Digging around, I found a hard square of old bubble gum, pink as a dog's tongue. And my Orphan Annie decoder, used to put the dirtiest swear words and ugliest insults into numbered notes that only another club member could decipher. Within a minute, I'd twisted the inner ring to find the letters—SHIRLEY. Then—IS. Then—ALONE. No Doug tromping into her room with running shoes stinking like rotten turnip, which I decided was a plus for an only child. No Goodman records to borrow from George, who sometimes taught Doug to jitterbug, away from the rest of us, in his bedroom. I was beginning to realize that all homes did not unfold like a first-grade primer to reveal polite and perfect families in cheerful primary colours.

From the downstairs living room I heard the final trembling vibrato of Jeanette MacDonald's high note, applause rattling like alleys in a tin can, my parents' weekly murmur of delight when C. B. DeMille wished them goodnight from Hollywood. Nothing like that across the street. Only the slur of Mrs. Upshaw's slippers on the stairs, snatches of her whispered prayer through the girl's bedroom wall. *Forgive him.*

Ever since the night up at the Baptist church with Pinky, I'd wondered who the old woman meant. Her own dead husband, or the son my dad had mentioned at the dinner table and steadfastly refused to discuss after that night. "Mrs. Upshaw's business is her own, not ours," he'd said. I put the box away again, remembering Pinky's dramatic description of the kid picking up the pennies off the hall floor like the little match girl, while the grandmother slammed a door across her future: "I am keeping her with me forever. . . ."

I flattened out on the bed, curling my toes around the metal rung, my energy sifted to ashes by the long hot day, too heavy-eyed to enjoy the waves of sheet lightning that turned the room, for a moment, pale green.

"You have to stay forever, Shirley," I whispered sternly to the darkness, and I was glad. Pinky might see her once in a while and embroider the glimpses with self-importance, but I was here, just across the road. Somehow that meant she belonged to me. As long as the old woman held on to her, so could I: she could be, in my imagination, anything I wanted her to be. I slipped into a half-sleep with wind-whipped tournament flags blazing the length of our schoolyard field, my snorting white horse prancing past the suddenly trans- planted Upshaw house where a princess the colour of the moon smiled sadly. What seemed to be one sharp and dazzling reflection of the sun off a steel lance-tip caught and held my eye—

"God*dam* it!" Doug's faint hiss neatly sabered the dream. "George won my Park Place, my bloody railroads. . . ." I turned my back on him, hoping to recapture the dream, but nothing would come back. In the corner stood the present George had brought me from Sunnyside, given to him free by a friend working the concession—a rock-hard, yellow- feathered imitation canary. I'd tried it out that afternoon, launching it in trilling, swooping circles at the end of the

30

black bamboo cane, standing in the middle of the road. I remembered Shirley Upshaw's eyes on me, envious, contemptuous.

For a few seconds, lightning flickered, picking out the bird's sightless, sequinned eyes. Faintly I heard my father telling Doug to be quieter. Nothing now could prevent my eyes from closing, and I dropped into a leaden sleep.

4

"Quite a downpour, Mrs. Collins."

"Yes—kept me awake for hours."

My mother had just inspected the front porch I'd sloshed with suds and was leaning around the post exchanging negative-positive comments with our neighbour, whose radio poured out ads and organ music while she tugged at a bush bent into the wet garden soil.

"Ruined my hydrangeas—" declared Mrs. Collins, pale eyes flicking skyward for a second.

"Well, it's given us a cool day for a change." My mother winked in my direction, but Mrs. Collins tossed her last salvo just as we thought she'd finished.

"A crazy country. Bake yesterday, freeze today. It killed Mr. Collins. . . ."

My mother wasn't listening. "The verandah looks fine," she said, and told me the rest of the day was my own as she went into the house.

It was too early to call on anyone, so I stood weighing the possibilities for diversion when Shirley Upshaw came around to her front lawn, head bobbing with tight white rags that gave her a look of electric surprise.

Hoping for a better and more discreet look, I climbed our tree, buggy with neglect but full-leaved now and as cool as a fruit cellar. I settled myself down flat on a high limb, where I knew she could not see me, and was immediately rewarded with a full-length view of the girl. She was the perfect image of what an orphan should be: incredibly thin, with ankles and wrists like barley sticks, and slightly bowed legs that seemed too long for her body. She had a long neck and a very white face shaped like the oval stones I picked up on the lake side of Centre Island. Although I had no sisters with whom to compare her, I knew that ordinary girls did not dress like that for play. *White* sandals and ankle socks that would drip dew? A "good frock," a term I'd heard used somewhere? Pinky's sister, Mary, wouldn't be caught dead in that get-up unless something special was going on.

Shirley Upshaw continued to bounce a ball in some intricate game that accompanied the song she hummed to herself. She looked so thin, so clean and shiny, that I turned my own grubby palms upward for a second, examining the dirt already caked in the lines. Almost unconsciously, I wiped them one at a time down the sides of my pants, hugging the tree with my thighs to keep my balance. I began a private game, Supermanning her into Lois Lane, Shadowing her into the lovely Margo Lane—*Is that you, Shadow, up in the tree? I can't see you.* . . .

Her front door opened part way and half of Mrs. Upshaw's malevolent face showed under grey bobbed hair.

"Don't walk on the grass, Shirley. The green will get on your good shoes. And watch where you bounce the ball, I don't want the marigolds broken again. Move over to the sidewalk where I can see you, there's a good girl."

The door shut heavily and for a moment the girl just stood still, looking around her. Reluctantly, she moved off the grass as she'd been told, and I saw the sheer curtain at the window move, too—just a ripple, as though a bit of wind might have slipped unwelcome into the house. The humming had stopped.

Looking down at her, imprisoned by a strip of sidewalk and guarded by glaring marigolds, I felt a sudden compulsion to move out into the open. She would know that I had seen her, but somehow that did not matter. I swung easily down from branch to branch, rustling the leaves like cornstalks in a wind, suspended myself as an added touch of disdain for danger from the lowest branch, and dropped, knees bent, to the lawn. I saw her head turn sharply at the sounds, but I did not look at her. Instead, I scooped the ball out of my mitt and began an assault against the garage door. *Watch me! Carl Hubbell and Lefty Grove rolled into one. If the Maple Leafs had me* (whoosh, slam!) *they'd be in first place.* . . . My Dad had taken me to a couple of games at the Stadium a year or so back, and I knew how to look like a pitcher as well as throw. *Watch me, Shirley—hiding the pitch behind my back, nodding at the catcher's signal, letting the left hand droop insolently—see my ice cube eyes chilling the batter, slithering to second where a man waits, one leg slanted out and ready to take off? Watch what I do—*

A fast, breaking curve—plop, back in the glove. My knuckle ball, risky because I still wasn't that good at it—clunk, into the mitt. A sinker, timed to defy the batter's reflexes and make him swing air like a windmill—gotcha! Plunk, back in the mitt. Two men out—throw me another one! My arm was warm now and my eye absolutely deadly. I wound up slowly, the scourge of Malcolm Public School's '38 Pennant team, determined to split this guy in half with a fast ball he wouldn't even see. . . .

I let it fly between the knees and chest of the invisible batter-catcher-fielder. But it was too good, too fast, and I didn't recover in time to get the rebound—the ball deflected crazily off the tip of my glove. Plunk, plunk behind me as it bounced and rolled across the road.

I began a disgusted lope toward her hedge, where the ball had settled, then hesitated, because it looked as if the girl was going to get it for me. She had almost reached the cement steps when I heard a window being pushed up, grating and resisting all the way. A voice that scraped my spine stopped both of us cold.

34

"Shirley Upshaw! DON'T YOU DARE CROSS THAT ROAD!"

My eyes were rivetted to the windowsill where the old lady's fingers curled and clung like ancient vines, the rest of her swirling behind sheer curtains. The girl's eyes were wide, glittering with fear, and the two of us stood stock-still as though in a game of Statues. Was this the first time, then, that she had heard the gentle wheedling turned to terrifying command? Turning abruptly about-face, she ran up her sidewalk.

"And YOU, Keith Gillies!" The words sprayed me like lye, turning my name into a dirty word. "Keep your filthy ball and your filthy self away from us!"

I had never heard Mrs. Upshaw like this before, perhaps because her bile was usually spilled on us as a group, whenever our games got uncomfortably close to her property. Now I stood alone in the centre of the sunlit street, my heart hammering in anger and self-consciousness. No ray-gun, no roars of approval, no pennant.

Also, no girl and no ball. *Are you still watching from inside somewhere, Shirley Upshaw?*

The fragment of a possibility that the girl would see me helped me move to retrieve the ball under the seething stare of the old woman. Only her hands still showed, clutching, clutching. She might have the last word, but she damn well wasn't getting my ball. I bent for it with as much gangling insolence as I could muster, even pausing to mop it off with elaborate concern before I ambled back to my own side of the street. A fair performance of mock bravery, it was a beginning accomplished in spite of fear. I declared war on the dragon that day without even knowing it.

There was a nightmare that night, the first I'd had in a long time. In it, the Upshaw house stood before me deserted, all the windows gone and black, like the sockets of a monstrous skull. "There's no one in there," the voice of Lamont Cranston was saying, "the Shadow knows." My baseball was rolling across the road, and in a burst of excitement I picked it up and threw my fast ball through the gaping front door into the hall. Ignoring what must have been Mrs. Collins' knuckles cracking against her window, I went whistling up the Upshaw sidewalk, up the verandah stairs and through the door. Inside, I could hear humming. The walls were bare, all the furniture had been smothered and wound in shrouds of white cloth that vibrated as I watched, like the girl's curling rags. I saw the ball at the foot of the stairs and reached for it, when mottled yellow hands stretched out of a mist to snatch it from me. But it wasn't the ball the hands were after. The hands were throwing back the ball and keeping me!

5

"You look pale, Keith. Didn't you sleep?"

"Sure." I slid into my chair at the breakfast table and poured corn flakes.

"You sure made a lotta noise," Doug said. I threw him an accusing look.

"Who wouldn't, with those stinking running shoes so close? Mom, will you tell him to leave them outside?" They weren't all that bad, but they were real, and Doug was real.

"You have to be careful about perspiration. . .and, well, things like *that* at your age, Doug," my mother said, frowning down at the peach conserve simmering on the stove. "Things like that" covered a large virginal wilderness that begged for exploration—girls, hair growing where it hadn't before, new four-letter words chalked on the school fence. Now, to this rich lore were added smells. There was no end to the stuff we didn't know. My brother and I looked at each other over the china bowls, waiting, but my mother had retreated.

"I'll bet you two would like some of this on your toast."

"It sure smells better than Doug's shoes," I said, ducking his jab across the table.

"Come and look while I spoon some into a jar."

I stared down into the vast enamelled pot, rimmed in blue

and pocked here and there where the white surface had chipped. Down dipped the ladle, dripping the golden globs. Up came the rich mist of fresh peaches, glazed and bubbling in brown sugar, cinnamon and nutmeg.

She sat down with us, her strong hands folded around a big cup of tea. "I've already put ten jars down." They stood in a neat row on the windowsill. "I like the way they gleam where the sun hits them."

Doug stared at the toaster, looking bored, watching the wavy elements turning scarlet. My mother laughed. "I can't imagine what brought that on, unless it was the news I got today."

"What news?"

"You have to guess first." It was a baby game, but the excitement in her eyes told us it would please her.

"Is it about my birthday?" I demanded, with the faint hope that this year would yield something better than new socks.

"No. Your turn, Doug."

"We're having a picnic Labour Day?" Doug was no gambler. We'd had one on Labour Day since I could remember.

"No, but you're close—it has *something* to do with Labour Day."

"I give up," I said promptly.

"Durham Stott is coming to stay with us, just for a couple of weeks, on his way to Vancouver! You'd remember him, Doug—you called him Uncle Durry."

Doug grimaced. "Uncle Durry! Sounds like a kid's book!"

My mother ignored this and dug into her apron pocket to produce a faded brown photo, which she smoothed before handing it to my brother. "It doesn't flatter him much, he's really better looking than the picture. You'd have been around seven, I think, when he was last here, so of course Keith won't remember." She pushed a warm hand across my hair, leaving a scent of cloves and lemon juice. "He's written that he thinks a war is bound to come soon. Artists never know what to do when there's a war," she explained for my benefit, "because no one is thinking of pictures. . . ." Doug passed me the photo and I stared down at the strange beige face with a dripping bronze moustache, long waving brown hair and blunt dark eyes under thick eyebrows.

"That would have been taken before he went to France to live, I believe. He studied there for a while after being in England. You must remember him, Doug, wrestling with you and George, and getting up early to do exercises? People thought he was crazy, running around the block with the Halwick's dog chasing him."

"Yeah, I remember him," Doug said at last, rubbing a forefinger over his chin in absent pursuit of blackheads. "But he's not a real uncle, is he?"

My parents had several friends who endured a kind of family knighting process that dubbed them aunts and uncles the moment they clapped eyes on us.

"I suppose not. Neither is your Uncle Bert, your Uncle Frank—"

"Aunt Thea?"

"Yes, but not Aunt Pru. There may be some link there, but I'd rather not find it."

We smiled at this, because Pru was considered a bore. Thea was strange, but better liked. For one thing, she kept twelve stray dogs, all carefully trained *not* to bark at the sound of her doorbell. She walked them on three-pronged leashes, six at a time, after eleven o'clock at night and very early in the morning. She seemed to need little sleep, which my mother had once explained as being a sign of old age. Once a year, just before Christmas, we visited her to deliver a small gift, and those who went were the ones who hadn't gone last year. Thea had no Christmas tree, because she didn't believe there had ever been a Christ child. "My dogs," she pronounced grandly, popping fruit cake into a begging canine beside her, "are my religion."

"Is Uncle Durham like her?" I asked.

"In some ways. Much less eccentric."

"Does Dad know he's coming?"

My mother's eyes came calmly in my direction and fastened there for a brief moment. "Not really. . .well, he knows Durham was *thinking* about it, but today's letter . . . actually he's on the boat right now. Naturally, your Dad will know for sure tonight." She rose slowly from the table, gathering in the dirty dishes, harvesting our leavings.

Doug lingered with me at the table for a while longer. "It's George's turn this year."

"What for?" I was still looking at the beige man who was on the ocean now.

"To visit crazy old Thea. Did you know she bought a goat last month, to keep the grass down?"

"You're kidding!"

"I'm not—hey, Mom, she did, didn't she?"

"Yes, I'm afraid so. But don't call her 'crazy old,' Doug. You'll be old yourself someday and you won't want anyone calling you that."

Doug defended his description. "Well, she is. And I won't have a houseful of stinking animals around when I'm old. Just cars, maybe. A lot of cars."

"And what will you have, honey?" my mother asked, sticking labels on the cooled fruit jars jewelling the window-sill.

There were times when she got on my nerves, talking to me in that solicitous voice, forcing possibilities on me that I instinctively knew were beyond her control. "I dunno," I said impatiently. How could I know what I wanted, so far in the future? I heard Pinky calling from the front porch and fled the kitchen without saying good-bye.

"You're late," my father said. I had washed off the muck picked up during the run home, slicked down my hair with vaseline and changed my shirt. Even from upstairs I could tell that something was wrong. Our dinner table was like a weathervane. If there was chatter, dishes plinking, gossip, the wind was good. If there was silence, almost nothing *but* the sound of dishes, the wind was foul and pea-green.

I hesitated by my empty chair. "Sit down," he said firmly. "Nobody has a watch." I offered this thick-walled and impenetrable excuse before attacking the chop and mounds of potatoes on my plate.

"Nobody has a watch!" My father repeated this with a kind of sarcastic wonder.

"Well, it's *true*." I forked up the green beans like hay. Doug's shoe touched against my ankle, our under-the-table code for shut up.

"Too bad about that. Do you know, young man, that you are lucky to have the shoes on your feet? We used to cut up cardboard and stuff it into ours because we couldn't afford to have the shoes mended. Did you know that?" I'd heard it all before, but I shook my head, huddling around my dinner for warmth. George cleared his throat. My mother was sitting on the edge of her chair, rigid from the waist up like old Queen Mary, austere and thin-lipped. Indicating the full feast we were all enjoying with a sweeping hand, my father glared around the table.

"When George was a baby, we were on food vouchers—no luxuries like fruit." Five compotes of fresh peaches lay guilty before us on the tray. "Bacon fat for butter. And *we* were well off compared to the poor beggars who knocked on the back door, asking for what was left on the plates!" If this had not been a lecture, I would have liked hearing the stories that preceded my birth. In fact it was unusual for my father to tell these tales in anger, and I felt that something else drove him.

"Awful times, the Depression," he said, punishing his meat with a fork. "Mr. Halwick was selling apples on the street corner, did you know that, to keep food on the table?" I tucked this away in some corner of my mind to relate to my friends. *Drunken old Halwick sold apples.* "Men lined up at soup kitchens after waiting all day in front of Massey-Harris, hoping for a job! Women of the streets selling themselves for a nickel—" He stopped suddenly.

"Pass the bread, please, Edward," my mother said quietly. My father passed the plate, avoiding her eyes.

"How much were the apples?" Doug asked innocently.

"About three cents, five if you could get it," my mother replied for my father, who had subsided into a sad, tired silence.

We finished the meal without speaking. My father held his pork chop bones and picked them down to the last morsel, dipping a crust into the gravy until the plate was clean. The sliced peaches disappeared. One by one, Doug, George and I disappeared too, asking politely to be excused as though we were guests.

"Wouldn't you think they could afford five dollars a week?" I heard my father from my room. "Bloody millionaires! No days off for a year, at least, and I'm there 'til six Saturdays! Five dollars more—damn it, I *earn* my money! I'm worth at least thirty dollars a week!"

"Why didn't you rail like that at work instead of at the boys? George is already giving us seventy-five cents from his CCM pay! We're not starving." Something clanged on a hard surface. The bottom of a saucepan, I decided.

"Oh, no, we're certainly not! Not with the kind of meal *you* served up tonight! Was that to soften me up for Durham? Was it supposed to make me like the idea of another mouth to feed?"

"It's a stop-over. . . ."

I heard my father laugh, his Douglas-Fairbanks-on-the-wall laugh, full of scorn.

"Stop-over! If it's as long as the last one, and he eats as much as always, I'll be retired and ready for the pauper's house!"

"That's not fair!"

"That's the truth!"

I crept downstairs and went out without letting the door bang to sit on the front steps beside the nicotinia plant. The voices behind me rose and fell, finally stopped.

"Evening, Keith," said Mr. Halwick, walking unsteadily at the other end of the dog's rope. "Cooled off nicely, eh?"

"Sure has." The dog peed on our bush while the man's body wove slightly on firmly-planted feet.

"Wanna pat old Joe?"

"Sure." I obliged him by walking down the driveway and running my hand over the dog's rough curls. "Hi, Joe, you a good boy?"

"Fifteen years old," Halwick told me for the hundredth time, proudly. I knew what he'd say next: "When you don't have the comfort of children, Keith, you lavish your affection on man's best friend." The dog smelled of unwashed fur and dinner still moping around his old gums. I nodded and patted him again. "Well, we'll be going along now." He touched the rim of the hat he wasn't wearing with a jaunty forefinger and I saw his white undershirt moving away down the street, from tree to post.

"Keith, it's time for bed." I turned to see my mother at the screen door. Some residual annoyance left from the evening tightened her words, as if I were somehow part of her anger. "Put the garbage out first, will you?"

"Okay. Where's Dad?"

"Hosing the back lawn. And push the lids down tightly or the dogs will be at it—" I wanted to ask if it was over, if they'd made up, but that would be an admission that they'd fought.

I carried the cans stinking warmly of rot and mildew down to the curb, and was rewarded by the advancing blur of Shirley Upshaw's skinny legs as she dragged the garbage down the driveway. She stopped when she saw me, glanced swiftly back at the house, then continued without looking up.

"You have to ram the lid down tight," I called "or the dogs'll get it." She ignored me, but pushed her hands down hard on the top. I wanted, somehow, to make her talk. "Yours sure looks cleaner than ours."

"That's because I wash it."

"Wash what?"

"The can, after they've collected." She stood opposite me,

faceless in the heavy black night, intriguing me like some strange bird seen across a stream.

"Why do you have to do that?" I could guess, but I hoped to keep the conversation alive.

"Grandma says they breed dangerous germs." She had a high, clipped voice that gave the impression, as some old voices do, of rarely being used. Her sentences were sparse, unwelcoming, and ended like shut doors. I was hunting around for something else to ask when knuckles cracked on her window and she fled into the shadows of the driveway.

Humidity had mushroomed during the day so that the sheets on my bed and even the paint on the doorjamb felt faintly damp.

"You in bed, Keith?" My dad's voice, always more companionable from a distance, sounded cool, washed down, settled.

"Almost. . . ."

"If it's too hot you could try the back porch. Lovely out there. . . ."

"Okay." I'd pulled out my stack of comic books from under the bed, prepared to lose myself in the crashing primary colours and simpler crises of Detective Comics, whose cleft-chinned hero solved everything with outsized fists or lengthy conversations delivered through an unmoving slit of a mouth. *Slowly Sheena advances, eyes narrowed, nostrils flaring, confronting the Spectre, an eyeless skull garbed in green—*

"Well, good night, sleep tight," chimed my father, solid and predictable as a church bell. Never let the sun set on a quarrel.

" 'night." *No one knew that JIM CORRIGAN, hard-fisted detective, was in reality the earthbound Spectre!*

I knew. I was beginning to know a lot of things.

44

Something happened to all of us at summer's end. Our mothers were beginning to hate us. Grim-lipped, pale and overworked, they suffered through the awful heat, the rumours of war and the underfoot irritation of bored children. Because Durham was coming, my mother spent the last days of August waxing stairs to a dangerous brilliance and starching limp curtains to a standstill on scrubbed sills.

With our tempers heightened by heat, boredom and the inevitability of school, irritation sometimes flared into fights. We felt the return of school hovering in the air and so attendance at the schoolyard dropped—it no longer felt like a place to play. Instead, the day before Durham was to arrive, Dick, Pinky, Don and I headed for a spot near Lambton Mill where the Humber lay deep and still. Hastily pulling off our clothes, we leaped one after the other into the spinach-green water, threshing around, free and cool. But we were slap-happy, manic, and the merciless shove of heads beneath the surface began to cross the line between fun and cruelty.

When Pinky held Don down far too long, Dick lunged toward him, slamming a fist between his shoulderblades. "Let 'im go, you Irish bastard! You're drowning 'im!" As Don popped up, gasping for breath, and hauled his goose-bumped bones to the shore, Dick and Pinky began punching each other viciously.

"Fuckin' *plumber!*" Pinky screamed. He'd remembered the teacher's putdown, but barbed it in a way Powell had never intended. "Get used to standing in water, Jackson, because that's where you'll be. Only it'll be full of shit, like you!"

Don and I sat on the shore watching until the life ebbed out of the fight. While Dick's eyes followed, full of hate and hurt, Pinky kept swimming up and down as though none of us existed. But suddenly surfacing from a dive, he turned a sappy grin toward the shore. He'd strung two fistfuls of dripping green reeds over his head like hair and was wading toward the shore straight for Dick.

"Thank the sweet jesus you got here, Mr. Jackson! *Look* at this place, will yuh!" Pinky waved a panicky arm toward the river. "Sink's leakin' so bad, and my twenty kids scared and the mister out an' all."

We began to laugh helplessly, letting him manipulate us back into his good grace, and finally plunged in after him.

That night I walked into George's room to find him standing sadly in its centre, staring at the stack of records and books he was moving to a basement cupboard. It had been decided that Durham needed a room of his own, and since George was the oldest, out early in the morning for his summer job and often again at night, his need seemed the least.

His closet yawned like a toothless mouth, three metal hangers dangling empty, the picture of Lana Turner gone from the back of the door. The rug had been looped over our wire clothesline, beaten to death that afternoon by a corn broom. I was trying to remember what was missing from the walls: his class picture, the school colours, a photograph of him grotesquely padded and squatting with knuckles against the ground, almost hidden under the football helmet.

"It sure looks clean," I said helpfully. "I didn't remember you had wallpaper under all that stuff."

"Yeah, well. . ." he flopped his knobby, hard arms against his thighs in a gesture of futility. "I found some baseball cards under all this crap. You can have them, if you want. There's a Babe Ruth in there somewhere."

"But what will you put up when you get back in here?" I was feeling magnanimous. I didn't have to give up my room for anyone and could afford a little concern. He didn't answer.

I looked around me while he thumbed through some magazines. The oak dresser shone with oil, the mirror from a scrubbing of Bon Ami. A fresh linen runner lay waiting for the stranger's brush and comb. It seemed so anonymous, as if all the essence of George himself had been scrubbed away. George grinned at me, showing the blue front tooth that had been knocked hard in a game last year. "Don't look so miserable, Keeter. It isn't going to be forever, you know."

"Boys?" My father's voice from the foot of the stairs, exultant and harsh. "It's just come over the radio—" George and I looked at each other, mystified. "Chamberlain's declared war on Germany!"

"Are we all ready?"

She floated down the stairs in her good leaf-green suit with a white satin bow at the throat. A small, cup-like violet hat was held to her thick hair with a pearl hat pin. She looked like something blooming in the garden, and for a moment we were speechless. Then my mother briskly set about putting her plans into operation. Was the roast in the oven at three hundred and fifty degrees? Fine. It would be done just a short time after we got back. We were all expected to go except George, who was away for the day. "It will make Durham feel really welcomed if we're at the station when he gets here."

Maybe the week's upheavals in preparation for Durham's arrival annoyed me, or I was feeling suddenly stubborn. At any rate, just before we were to leave I stared wildly around me, bolted for the bathroom and began a careful imitation of retching. To make the whole thing sound believable, I filled the water glass at the sink and emptied it in hesitant little plops into the toilet after each rending effort. It was really effective—the r-r-RH-A-A-A! the spitting sound, the blurp. . . . By the time my mother had reached the door, slowed by her own highly-polished stairs, I was sitting on the bathtub edge, tie pulled realistically to one side and a weak smile on my face. I remembered to flush the toilet before she came in.

"Oh, Keith! What a shame! What did you eat this morning that I don't know about?"

"Nothing. I'm okay now."

"You don't *look* okay. Were you and Pinky at those green plums from Collins' tree again?" By now, Doug and my dad were standing behind her, jockeying for position in the doorway.

"I don't remember," I said weakly.

"I *told* you they aren't ripe." She turned in fond annoyance to my father. "We've got to be there in a half hour, but I hate to leave him."

"I'm all right now. It's just the streetcar. . . ." I left that thought dangling.

"No," my mother said firmly. "Can you imagine what would happen if you had to sway back and forth all the way downtown? You'll have to stay here. How do you feel now? I mean, I just don't want you getting worse without someone to help you." Right away I knew Doug would be selected to nursemaid me.

"I don't feel sick anymore. The plums are gone," I lied. "I'll be fine alone. I'll just lie on the bed until you get back. Doug doesn't have to stay." After a lot of humming and hawing they left.

The door shut, and silence settled gently over the house. I spent some time just wandering around, wondering why Doug would prefer a look at the train to this unique experience. No vacuum cleaner hounding dirt, no calls from room to room about dusters and polishers. I looked around the door of my parents' bedroom, a place I rarely entered now

48

that I was past the age of night horrors and the warm well between my mother and father when they took me into their bed. It was a serene, settled place; cream drapes over sheer curtains, blinds with tassels, a walnut highboy, faded grey wallpaper with white roses and garlands of crimson ribbon, a vanity studded with old bottles and a French ivory dresser set. By the bed stood what my father jokingly called his "man," a sturdy oak valet that held his one good navy suit as though it were being worn. Naked now, it stood like a wooden robot waiting for orders. I touched the miniature clock with gold-pronged feet that sat on the dresser, its silvery tick daintily snipping off time. I peered into the round ivory box with the hole in the middle that held the dark hairs taken from my mother's comb. Swirled into a ball, they reminded me of a small nest and I wondered why she saved them. On the double bed was a pale green pillow on which my grandmother had worked daffodils in crewel. I don't think my father liked it much. Sometimes he would tease my mother by saying "Oh, crewel fate!" and I'd hear them laughing through the door.

I went downstairs to our dining room where the table was already set for the evening meal with the heavy "good" silver. For all the display, nothing in the house was new and very little had been bought by my parents in the first place. Hand-me-downs, it seemed, held us together. The rugs were frayed and the tablecloth had minute mendings here and there as though my mother had played X and O's with thread. My parents had felt the depression ten years earlier as severely as anyone, though much of my father's retelling of it dealt only with other people's misfortunes. George's stories, filled with rich on-the-spot detail, were more interesting.

"One Christmas," George had told us, "there weren't *any* presents. Not one. No tree." This had been 1931, when my father could not get the most menial job and had finally gone on relief, the ultimate simmering shame.

"That summer they even turned off the water because

they couldn't pay the bill. Right out on the front lawn, in broad daylight! Mom sent me to fill the bathtub, pots and pans, anything that would hold water. . . ." It was a story that never ceased to excite me—adventure, privation, my mother's cool presence of mind. Under the eyes of curious neighbours, she had walked across the grass toward the hydro man, who was only doing his job according to George, and had smiled warmly as though his visit was not only expected, but welcome. "Ah!" she had said with satisfaction, pleased as punch, "that's *so* much better! Thank you. The tap has stopped dripping."

I was tired of house prowling and sentiment. As a guilty act of goodwill I emptied the basin of water beneath our icebox, then took a couple of cookies outside and climbed the tree to eat them. The leaves were dull green, a few already limp and curling. In the coolness I leaned back, crossing the pressed trouser legs and the gleaming shoes defiantly, letting them rub against the hard ridged branches. I was about thirteen feet up, completely hidden, and through the green spangle I began to shrink the world below. Houses were toys and the only car on the street, McLean's black Ford, could be moved with a push of my finger. If I wanted to, I could lift Mrs. Upshaw's cardboard roof and demolish her cellophane windows, then dump her down a sewer.

Who are you?

It's the dentist, old lady. I'm going to drill a hole through your lead head and hang you up in a tree.

The fantasy evaporated as I recognized Shirley Upshaw coming down Arlington, walking with her self-conscious head-down stride. She was wearing a navy coat, a white tam and white gloves that clutched a black book. A bible! So the old lady had her going to church on holidays as well as Sunday. The impulse to invade her prim, passive world came too swiftly to control. I cupped my hands around my mouth, took a deep breath and spoke in a hollow, disembodied voice. "Shirley Upshaw! This is God speaking. You don't have to go to church on Labour Day!" She stopped, as though struck by a stone. As she looked slowly toward the tree, her narrow face grew ugly with rage. I shrank and curled, waiting. But suddenly I heard her pumps clapping quickly on the pavement, then scuffing the driveway stones angrily. I remained there until I heard her side door slam, then slid down to the brown grass and ran inside.

Only minutes later, while I was still picking bark and leaves off my suit, I heard the sound of our front door opening.

"Hullo inside? Anyone here to greet the prodigal immigrant?"

In the hall I discovered a tall, barrel-chested man grinning down at me. He shoved a tweed cap back from his dripping forehead, dropped his suitcase heavily to the floor and before I could say a word bent quickly into a wrestling pose, looking like Lou Thesz in the Thursday paper. One arm pawed the air as he crouched and swayed, glowering. "All *right*, Douglas—let's see if you remember any holds!"

So it fell to me to stammer out my name to Durham Stott, who had somehow missed my family at the station. Maybe he'd mistaken me for my brother in a natural desire to return and find things unaltered, each of us frozen into the age he last remembered. I think he sensed my embarrassment, standing before him with so little to say, because he recovered promptly and reached to grab my hand.

"I apologize! It's *Keith*, of course! I'd know you anywhere." This made me laugh and that pleased him. "Tell you what I'll do to make it up to you. I'll paint you a picture while I'm here, one you can keep, or sell for a fortune when I'm famous!"

That was a splendid evening. There was more food than we usually had, my first drink of watered-down sherry, a feeling of warmth that encompassed my father, who rubbed his hands together and went to the cellar for two "nice warm beers" to enjoy while my mother made her apologetic way through piano versions of old English music hall songs. It didn't seem so bad after all, having Durham with us.

51

7

No matter how I hoped for a last minute delay, the first day of school began as it always had. I'd expected Durham to contribute something new to breakfast, but he slept in, exhausted from the long journey.

"Well, it will be exciting, won't it, having a new teacher?" This was my mother's day to buck everyone up with sweeping good cheer.

"Yeah." I stared gloomily at the factory on the Shredded Wheat box: *100% Whole Wheat—A Good Healthy Breakfast*. Two biscuits lay in my bowl like deflated pillows, sodden with hot water and drained, nothing like the fullblown golden promises Nabisco pictured on the package.

"And George in fifth form! It's hard to believe. It doesn't seem so long ago that I took him to kindergarten." She was sipping tea, still in her robe, staring out the kitchen window. "Well," she repeated with forced optimism, "maybe you'll have someone nice this year." Mentally, I flicked through the possibilities. Randall, the vice-principal. Miss Nicol, the little one with the wattle and a huge sister who taught the young grades. Miss Fellowman, lanky, red-haired, who approached slowly, smiling like a friend, then dumped all your books to the floor and spiked you with sarcasm while the class had to watch.

"These are the best years of your life, you know. Right now. You'll look back on them as—" I switched her off for a moment, letting one part of my mind skip stones off the Humber until I caught a word that made some reply necessary. On a still, clear, hot day like this, the river would lie like syrup beneath a veil of aimless heat bugs and the gathering wake of ducks. We could still swim—

"Isn't it time you were going? Don't be late the first day."

I dragged my wet feet from the warm water and looked at the kitchen clock.

"I'm meeting Pinky at the corner." With relief I saw that my mother checked her move to bend and kiss me.

"'Too big to kiss, to old to cry,'" she recited, "that's what your grandfather used to tell my brother."

"Bye," I called, halfway through the living room, and ran out the front door.

Shuffling along in lines of two, some of us squirming in heavy shoes that pinched after the free spread of summer, we waited for the first strains of Schubert's *Marche Militaire* to propel us through the gaping oak doors and into conformity.

Only the children of the very rich and the very poor had been to summer camp, so their faces shone with a democratic tan here and there in the line-ups, like occasional pennies in a row of dimes. Huddled in a bewildered mass beside the hen wings of Mrs. Pritchard were the kindergarten novices, who were getting a taste of what was in store as she constantly clapped her big red hands for silence. Had they had more wit and experience, a glance around would have shown them what to expect a couple of years later: Mr. Randall holding the brass bell like a club as he browbeat a laggard into line; the principal, making a rare appearance, stalking us with wintry disdain. Some of the school's small newcomers wilted into immediate and placid acceptance. The smart ones were crying.

Suddenly I spotted Shirley Upshaw. She wore something

starched out from her like a pincushion, a party dress that already had caused the girls behind and in front of her to huddle and whisper, giggling. I couldn't blame them. She looked terrible, ruffles blowing in the breeze, as out of place as a peacock among sparrows. Turning away abruptly, I caught Mr. Powell taking a last frantic tug on a cigarette before going to his post beside the line. I would miss him, I decided, hole in the *Globe and Mail* and all. Somebody's dog was barking sharply, darting and receding in excitement, as though he were herding cattle. He kept up the racket until most of us had disappeared into the red brick mouth. I turned, the last in line, to see the yard vacant and the dog now diverted by a bitch who offered her services with forthright abandon. Mr. Randall had seen them, too, and turned away hastily, flushed with anger, to direct his annoyance at me. "Shut the doors, Gillies!"—I did as I was told— "and report to the office at once!"

The two months' holiday had instilled a false sense of immunity. "But what did I do?"

"Sir! What-did-I-do, sir!"

"What did I do, sir?"

His gabled eyebrows slammed down hard over his nose and his eyes narrowed. "How dare you imitate me?"

There were some questions not meant to be answered, and this was one of them. Gone was the July-August thinking, to be replaced as fast as possible with the puzzling logic of September. "Sorry, sir. I was looking to see if there were any more children coming."

It was a bad beginning. Since our line had been told to report to Mr. Randall's room, I realized that I'd stood out in the worse possible way before classes had even begun.

But inside the room where Randall had bulldozed a long succession of senior fourths sat someone else, and we flopped into seats at random, shooting mystified looks at one another.

"Stand for opening exercises, please," commanded a smooth English accent.

"Bloody limey," whispered Pinky, grinning, but he was cut off by the harsh crackle of a newly-installed loudspeaker that gave the principal fresh, godly powers.

"This is your principal speaking," he began. "We are fortunate to be able to sing our national anthem in unison, and to say the morning prayer together as a school. . . ." His last word was lost in the fierce drum roll of a recorded "God Save The King." While we remained standing, Mr. Alder's voice returned.

"Before the prayer, I wish to announce the appointment of a new teacher, Mr. Peter Critchley-Williams, who will take Mr. Randall's senior fourth class in order to allow Mr. Randall to give all his time to the considerable work entailed in being our vice-principal. Let us pray. Our Father who are in heaven. . . ."

After a mournful amen, the loudspeaker died, leaving a heavy, suspenseful silence in the room. The new teacher heaved a sigh, rubbed his hands together, sat on the edge of the desk and surveyed us with gentle amusement.

"Well. . .my name is on the board. Critchley-Williams, with a hyphen, which I will expect you to pronounce, too, of course. Critchley-Hyphen-Williams. Since it is a bloody funny name, British as you've guessed by my accent, suppose we all laugh at it now and get it over with." A few uncertain titters met his suggestion; you could never be sure teachers meant things like that and we were sensibly cautious. "Not exactly hearty, but a beginning. Now," he slapped a hand down on his left leg, "there is something else we might as well get over with. This is wooden, which gives me an unusual walk." To our astonishment, he stood up and did a brisk, jerky turn around the classroom. "I could tell you that I lost my leg in some daring fashion but actually I fell off a ladder in Cambridge while repairing my parents' roof, crushed the thing, and that was that. Any questions?"

We looked from one to another, but no hands were raised.

"I might add that the ladder was badly broken, too, and had to be replaced by a human pyramid." This brought a loud guffaw from those who understood it, and the teacher grinned broadly.

"Ah, that's better! You *can* relax! Good. Now, down to brass tacks. I'll be teaching you history, literature, current events and soccer, if you're willing to stay after school twice a week. You will teach me how to say 'okay' rather than 'right-o,' 'truck' for 'lorry' and so on. I would also appreciate instruction on how to eat a hot dog, in exchange for which I will try to introduce you to Bubble-and-Squeak and treacle pie. In this way, we just might get through the year with as little unpleasantness as possible."

Current Events was something dear to the heart of our new teacher. After a quick distribution of texts and lined notebooks for his other subjects, he rushed back to the front of the room and pulled down the world map. A low groan rumbled through the seats—we felt we'd been tricked.

Up flew the sandy eyebrows. "We have to do something, you know. I don't intend to get at English or History today. And suppose Mr. Alder were to come in here and find me tapping away at my leg? I'd be sacked, wouldn't I, first day on the job."

Pinky's hand shot up. Critchley-Williams scanned the seat plan for a name to go with the arm. "Yes—Yorke?"

"Fired, sir."

"I beg your pardon?"

"It's not sacked, it's fired."

"Ah, of course. Thank you." He cleared his throat and stared at the map. Very quietly, he began to tell us what was happening in Germany, in France and in his own country. "In a way," he said, "you'll see that Current Events knits in all your other subjects, too. Geography, of course, because it can win and lose wars. Since my country has just declared war, you can see how its location and size are terribly important to us all. . . ."

A faint whiff of gunpowder intruded on the familiar room.

". . .you'll learn something of the importance of your language and its use by clipping items of interest from the papers and bringing them in for discussion. What the countries' leaders are saying and writing to one another is second in importance only to what they are doing, openly or in secret."

He opened a manilla envelope and took out some clippings of his own which were distributed from one aisle to the next. Poland was being bombed by Nazi Stukas, Londoners were colliding in the dark because all lights were covered. There was some fascination in this for us, but none of the troubled sadness we saw on the teacher's face.

Everything considered, the first day of school had managed to surprise us, and we taunted those who had drawn short straws—Miss Nicol, or worse, Miss Fellowman.

I trailed home in the heat to find my new uncle on the
verandah, sitting on my father's wicker chair and squeezing
paints from small tubes onto a palette. He peered over his
easel as I ran up the steps.

"Keith," he said with solemn emphasis. "There, you see,
I remembered. I'm painting my debt to you, as a matter
of fact."

"Can I look?"

"Of course. No comments, though. These things always
look like a mess of vegetables in the beginning." He was
sitting like a horseman, back straight, his left hand resting on
the thigh, his right hand making meticulously-controlled
strokes on the canvas. When he moved, the wicker creaked
under his weight. I followed the direction of his up-and-
down glances, wanting to make sense of the blur. "Do you
know what it is?" he asked without stopping.

"No."

He nodded in the direction of the Upshaw place and as
I looked over, Shirley came out to sit on her porch. For a
moment Durham remained still, narrowing his eyes and
pursing his lips in a way that displayed all his wrinkles.
"Mmmm. . .maybe I'll sketch her in quickly, before she
runs off somewhere."

"She doesn't *go* anywhere," I told him. "You can take all the time you need with the Upshaws." I took another look at the cooked spinach on his canvas. "Is *that* what you're painting?"

I think he misunderstood my question, interpreting it as criticism, for he seemed hurt. "It's for you, you know," he said coolly. "I chose it because it was the handiest subject."

Immediately I tried to reassure him that I liked his choice, desperately afraid that he would wipe away my picture in exasperation. His face cleared as the sagging cheeks ridged sideways into a big grin. "Don't take me too seriously. The picture is yours. Besides, I wasn't about to waste all that paint. Go get us a glass of milk and we'll talk for a while—get better acquainted, so to speak."

When I returned from the kitchen, he had begun the outline of Shirley, interconnected ovals and skeletal streaks which he explained would be filled in later. I perched on the railing beside him, relishing this inclusion in the adult world.

"I took your mother to the Ex today. Have you been?"

"Yep. I got some samples of Ketchup and Vi-Tone. And I bought a hat. Is Mom out?"

"Just up at the Stop and Shop on St. Clair. She wanted to get some groceries. I took her on the roller coaster."

"Ya? What did she do?"

"Yelled a little. But so did I." He had blocked in the girl's figure and the verandah pillars were emerging magically from the mess. He tipped back his milk and gulped it down without a pause. "And we saw the Germans closing down the Nazi exhibit. Police were there, seeing that no one got out of hand. They took down the banners, the swastika and all the folders. That was a bit of excitement I can tell you!"

"We just went on the Midway. And Doug took me to see the cars." I told him then about our new teacher and his talk about war.

"Bloody business," he said softly, "They never leave people alone, do they?"

I had no idea what he meant, or if he expected a reply. Until today, I had not heard anyone else talk much about war. Still, I liked to get out the books my father had kept on the First World War. Bound in brown leather, the three large volumes were too heavy for me to hold. I could lie on my stomach for hours, staring at the Serbs and Turks and Russians and French and English and Germans, some almost exotic in spikes and plumes. The captions and pictures kept me spellbound. STRATEGY AND TACTICS—cavalry bristled along a hilltop, peering through field glasses at puffs of grey smoke blooming instead of fruit in an orchard. THE DESPICABLE DISGRACE—that was about Edith Cavell's execution. She gazed at me, placid and steady-eyed in her white cap and apron. IT'S ALL OVER FOR THEM—prisoners of war lounged on a flat, fenced-in field sprouting pup tents and Boy-Scout fires built here and there. Some of them were swathed in bandages, or humped forward on crutches staring at the camera.

"Will you have to go?" I asked my uncle.

"Christ, not if I can help it!" He jabbed his brush into a luminous dot of creamy oil. "I don't think I can adjust to madness."

I was puzzled, for none of his comments dovetailed with the picture of survival and courage we had been given at school. "Does that mean you're afraid you wouldn't like it?"

"No—it means I'm afraid I *would*."

I was reduced to silence.

"You see, I was nineteen when the last war ended, Keeter. I knew fellows who lied about their ages just to get into it, boys fifteen and sixteen. The ones who lived to come back in one piece just didn't talk about it at first. Can you imagine Doug after an experience like that?"

I wrestled with that and lost. "I guess not. . . ."

"Near the end of it, you see, they were glad to get anything they could. My father was middle-aged, but off he went, happy as hell, tramping along behind the other old men and the kids. And, you know, he never really left the army.

His medals were hung on the wall and his old steel hat became an ashtray. And whenever something went wrong, his answers were the army's answers right 'til the day he died. 'Two months in the 20th Hussars would fix 'em,' he'd say, 'A week on bread and water in the lock-up would soon set them straight.' The poor old boy really believed it, too. Eventually my brother and I grew away from him. I left home very early, for the sake of peace, which he had *not* adjusted to." He sighed, and wiped a brush carefully on an old rag. Before him on the canvas was a half-finished verandah dripping leaves, soft pencil marks and a lot of empty space.

"Do you remember what the girl was wearing?" Durham asked, "because she's gone." His eyes were twinkling. "Blue," he replied for me.

"I don't notice things like that," I said.

He was jotting notes on a pad. "Well, *I* do. She may turn up in something different and I liked that colour. Not sky-blue—more cornflower, a touch of mauve in it. . . . Does Hughie Brown still live on the street?"

"Ya." Hughie was our street oddity, a huge, simple-minded man, cared for at home by his invisible mother and only allowed out with his dog. Hughie was retarded. When he went for a walk, he never used sidewalks if he could help it, preferring for his own reasons to amble down the centre of the road with his ugly English bulldog shuffling jaw-first behind him.

"Old Hughie," Durham said companionably. "A good, gentle soul is he. How about the Halwicks? They still around?"

"Yep."

"Still drinking?"

I nodded. Durham smiled and said Halwick could get drunk on wine gums. Then, for some reason, he nudged me and winked, pointing silently in the direction of Mrs. Collins' porch, which was only a couple of feet away from us. I listened and could hear her rocking chair moving in furtive creaks against the floorboards. Durham raised his voice. "And Mrs. Collins? Still tuned in to soap operas, is she? Land a-goshen, I'da thought she'da married again by now, mebbe that handsome lawyer-fella down the way. . . ." We heard purposeful feet marching across the porch and the door slammed hard. Durham rubbed his hands together, laughing fit to kill.

I hadn't expected to like him at all. I hadn't expected to like going back to school, either.

"Look," Durham said, "that's your mother coming down Arlington—go give her a hand with the parcels."

Relatives had come and gone at various times, usually staying only a day or two, but these visits were rare and caused little change beyond a bit of extra food and an atmosphere of joviality that usually worked to the benefit of any children involved. Someone would always send us for ice cream—nine scoops plopped into a white bowl which we carried with us, or perhaps two fifteen-cent bricks. Nobody yelled at us during the visits, and requests to stay up late brought consenting smiles, as though things were this way all the time.

Durham's visit was different. The big meal of Labour Day dwindled to regular proportions almost at once, and the week-long ordeal of housecleaning became meaningless the moment he set foot in the door. Cases, boxes, a yellow straw suitcase with leather straps and his portfolio of paintings cluttered up the hall until my mother prodded him politely to take them upstairs. It took him only two days to turn George's room into a swamp-bottomed art gallery, while my oldest brother was struggling for neatness in the living room and developing lower-back pains. Durham rarely ate breakfast with us since he ran around the block a couple of times first. Apparently he fixed his own later.

Both my brothers stayed at the high school cafeteria for lunch. Because I was the only one home at noon, I think I noticed the change in my mother before anyone else. On my second day at school I came in to find her playing our piano, which was unusual. I knew she could play, but thought she'd dropped it, as any other sensible person would given the choice. One of my earliest memories of her was the erratic plink of her duster dancing up the piano keys and down again—all in haste and only accidentally musical. Now she was *playing*, while I quietly fixed a peanut butter sandwich in case she heard me in the kitchen and stopped.

At first, hearing the icebox door close, she became red and flustered—"Good lord, is it *that* time already?" and promptly jumped up, leaving the resonance hanging in the air.

But Durham interrupted her, pointing out that I was quite capable of doing some things for myself now. Then he would spread the slices of bread, cut in lop-sided chunks, with a little butter and some jam and shove them, smiling, in my direction. "Bet you're the only kid in your room who gets a concert at lunch, eh Keeter?"

Conversations roamed much more freely at the supper table, too. It took a little getting used to, hearing all the taboos like religion and politics being openly discussed. Durham had more sophisticated and catholic views on both subjects than either of my parents, and for a while, because he was a guest, they accepted what he said with neutral murmurs. It took a little more time for me to discover that my mother generally agreed with Durham, while my father generally did not. Durham seemed to find all religions a source of amusement, though he was not unkind in discussing them, nor even patronizing. He liked the music of Catholic and Anglican churches, he found Jehovah's Witnesses brave and child-like, admired the Jewish concept of family and had some sympathy for the original courage of Protestant faiths—but he left no doubt that most of it was poppycock. My father saved that phrase for Catholics alone. It was only because Pinky was too young to know better that he was allowed to be my friend.

Politics was so tied in with the war that any discussion of

that bred a battle of its own. "People are fools!" Durham would cry, "ready to pick up a gun and shoot it off without thinking twice!" Since my father had served a full four years in 1914 and agreed with fighting again if it was necessary, he quite naturally fell into the group that Durham scorned. This didn't make our dinners very peaceful, though I found them more interesting. Only once did Durham mention his mistress in France, which would have been a subject worth exploring, but my father turned fierce eyes on him and my mother choked on her tea. He did not mention her at the table again, though he must have worried about her.

It was obvious that Durham felt very much at home, partly because he shared many memories with my mother, who had apparently known him long before her marriage.

"Remember the day Bruce and Peggy went with us to Cobourg on the *Noronic*, and—"

"Peggy was the fat girl who could do bird calls!" my mother remembered triumphantly. "She got sick on—"

"Ham sandwiches, the ones we didn't eat," Durham put in.

"—and threw up over the side of the boat!"

"—on a *calm* night, too!"

They would laugh uproariously at the memory, while my father looked from one to the other. That made my mother stop and try to explain who and what and where. "Peggy Bracken, dear. You didn't know her—we went to school together."

George appeared to accept Durham with his usual easy grace, but Doug spoke little, especially after an evening when Durham forgot his age and the years that had passed and insisted on a wrestling match like they used to have. Doug gave in after a lot of jocular pressure to be a good sport. Circling the living room rug, he looked stricken and trapped, his thin jutting wrists flapping awkwardly from temporary lack of coordination. Being heavier and more muscular, Durham floored him in seconds with a whoop of victory. After that night, Doug disappeared into our room after supper to stretch out on the bed and stare at the ceiling.

One night a week after Durham arrived I followed Doug up and flopped stomach-down on my bed.

"I've got hair under my arms, see?" He was standing before our dresser with his shirt off, staring happily at his armpits as though they had brought him a gift. I heard the front door close after Durham, out for his constitutional to wear off the full meal.

"Well, at last," I heard my father grumbling, "he doesn't go out much, does he?"

"What is that supposed to mean? He goes out every night."

"Some life! Sometimes he's just getting up when I leave for work, and he's here when I get home."

I looked over at Doug to see if he was eavesdropping too, but he was folding his arms before the mirror, tucking his hands under at the top to make the muscles look larger.

"He's hardly had time to get settled, Eddy. He's been to the *Star Weekly*, and he told me there was a chance of some illustrating for the *Journal*. It's just the nature of his work. And he livens up the place a little." This remark angered my father, because the pages of the evening paper were being turned with rapid, unread rustlings.

"Oh, I'll bet George finds it lively, sleeping on that damned chesterfield with his legs dangling over the end! And Doug scarcely leaves his room except for meals."

Doug looked over at me, letting his upper arms go slack again. He seemed pleased at finding his name among the list of saints.

". . . and speaking of meals, has Durham contributed anything, *any*thing at all for his keep since he arrived?" There was a long, strained silence. I put down Flash Gordon to listen more closely.

"What a suggestion! I wouldn't accept money from a guest, especially one who has no job."

"Too bad he can't get something for those topics he introduces at the table every night, while he's shovelling in *my* earnings!"

"That's terribly unfair. He's an interesting man, and the

things we talk about are infinitely better than the price of shoes, or what we're having for dessert. And I think it's good for the children to hear another viewpoint of war, too."

This made my father snort, ready to bite Durham's Achilles heel. "The war! We'd be over*run* if the country was made up of Durhams! Can't squeeze courage out of a paint tube, I suppose."

I began to look for the repeat pattern on our one papered wall. Arguments before this had been about things that were minor and could be solved, like the amount of bluing or starch in my father's shirts, or whether or not they had enough money to pay for a show on Saturday night. Under this assault, I felt confused and a bit frightened, because the questions had only ugly answers and there was a sense of choosing up sides. Durham made my mother laugh, and me, too, but my father saw something selfish in him that escaped me entirely.

Lifting the small unframed canvas Durham had finished for me, I held it under my bedlight. It really looked like the Upshaw house. Only the figure of Shirley appeared out of focus, when I would have liked to have seen her face. As it was, I had to be satisfied with the impression Durham had caught; a vaporous trail of pale hair, a featureless oval bending over a book, a bit of blue fabric.

"Why doesn't Dad like him?" I asked Doug, still hearing the voices below, muffled as though they were speaking through wool.

"I dunno." Doug always prefaced what he knew with that statement. "I guess because he eats too much, and he hasn't got a job."

"Why isn't painting working?" I wanted to know, but Doug shrugged and opened up *Tom Swift and His Underwater Machine*, so I was left to figure it out for myself. The painting I held was infinitely more unique to me than my father's job selling silverware on Eaton's main floor. Though a trip downtown was a rare occasion for us, I had gone with my mother last spring because I needed shoes, and it was then that I had seen my father at work for the first time. We had just bought ice cream waffles in the underground passage connecting Eaton's Annex to the main building when my mother asked me if I'd like to visit my dad. She paid a dime for our lunch and we made our way to the first floor.

"Here we are," she said, after what seemed a ten-mile walk in my hard new shoes. We stood for a moment looking around for my father, but neither of us could see him. I stared into glass cases shimmering with silverware imbedded in purple, crimson and deep blue velvet, awed by the carving sets with staghorn handles that looked like ancient weaponry.

"Ah! There he is!" my mother declared, but she did not call out to him or wave. Something forbad that, something in the place itself and in the eyes of my father as well. He had a customer, so we stood to one side while he made muted suggestions, gently displaying a pair of silver-handled scissors across his palm. I remembered clearly the odd new tone of voice he used, unctuous and eager as he bent slightly forward. Though we were just a foot or so away, not once did he acknowledge us, nor did his eyes stray to us. Money was stuck into a brass tube and blown up to the ceiling where high wire rigging sped it to some unseen place and the proper change was made.

"Perhaps you would like a gift paper?" my father enquired as they waited. He bustled to a spot out of sight, returning with plain grey paper which he began to pleat and fit to the small box in deft gestures. I was watching the dangling cage returning along the myriad ceiling wires, fascinated by the choreography above me.

When he finally turned to us, his mannerisms remained the same: he spoke in the polite voice, his eyes cautious and darting away from ours as though someone might catch him being himself. His hands below the frayed shirt cuffs fussed with other items he had brought out and I realized that he was pretending we were customers, too. I felt immense relief when we left for home. When I asked my mother later why he acted so differently at work, she explained that the job was simply too important to risk losing, that it could be jeopardized then by as innocent a thing as relatives visiting during working hours.

I turned Shirley's picture upside-down to see what she looked like hanging from an upended floor with steps flying away above her into a green sky. The front door opened downstairs: Durham had returned from his walk.

"Leave it open, will you, Durham?" I heard my father call pleasantly. "Let a little breeze in." And as though neither one had argued, my mother and father joined in to ask how he had enjoyed his walk, and would he like a cup of tea with them.

Doug looked over the blue cover of his book and grinned at me. "Well, it's over for tonight," he said simply. "You can borrow this after, if you like."

"Is it any good?" I liked the series, even if I got the books after Doug had mucked up the pages with spilled cocoa and dog-ears the size of a napkin.

"S'okay." At the moment, this was Doug's highest praise. "I don't think the guy goes to school," he added, "or else they solve everything on weekends."

Downstairs, I heard the end of the Jack Benny show, which my father had turned down during their argument and now put up too high in an effort to prove his good nature. I decided I could risk a trip to the kitchen.

"Want anything when I come back?" I asked Doug, returning a favour for getting the book someday.

"Doughnuts and milk," he said without looking up.

"Aren't you going to hear Charlie McCarthy?"

"Too much homework." He turned the page. I clattered down the stairs humming to "Je-LLO, everybody, Je-LLO."

As it turned out, he wouldn't have heard the program anyway, because when I passed the living room I found my father and mother and Durham sitting stiffly around the radio. When I started to speak they shushed me in unison.

A flat, dry voice advanced through the cloth speaker, curiously toneless and neutral. Mackenzie King was telling us that Canada was now at war with Germany.

"Well, there it is," my father said briskly, straightening up in his chair.

"Good old Mac," whispered Durham.

My mother had scarcely moved. Turning her head in my direction, she looked right through me with wide, unblinking eyes. "George," was all she said.

"Now, Mother," my father smiled, "don't go crossing bridges before we get to them. He won't be eighteen 'til February and we'll beat the hell out of them by then!"

I felt suddenly irritable, watching this cluster of misery. Weren't they excited? Who was surprised anyhow? Everyone had expected it, Critchley-Williams had said so last Friday.

"Any doughnuts left?" I asked.

My mother just nodded, so I collected two each and a couple of cups of milk and made the stairs as fast as I could under the circumstances to tell Doug the good news.

The excitement of war was temporarily forgotten on Monday morning when we learned that John Bench had died. He was to be buried very quickly from his house on Bracondale Avenue, just around the block from us. My dad explained that the type of polio he'd contracted was very deadly, that "he hadn't had a chance." At lunch hour Pinky and I went around to watch the hearse arrive. The bereaved family, cloaked in black and navy blue, were weeping softly together on the verandah. In front of the surrounding houses, neighbours formed knots of sadness, showing their sympathy from a distance. There was an awkward moment when the men who were putting the coffin in the hearse exchanged directions to move it this way, or that, as though John were a piece of furniture on moving day.

"Was he in the house all *night*?" I whispered to Pinky. We had stationed ourselves across the street.

"Two nights," Pinky corrected me, "with a candle at the top and bottom and probably someone sittin' up with him." He bit into a reed of sweet grass and spat the end neatly. "I've seen a lot of that stuff."

"I'd sure hate to die," I admitted. I hadn't given it much thought before that day. Children lived forever and that was that. "Now they're going to bury him," I said, years of dead birds in matchboxes returning to haunt me.

"So what? He's probably in purgatory right now."

"Where?"

Pinky sighed with the strained patience of the knowing: "*Pur*gatory. It's kinda like a laundry where your soul gets bleached clean, ready for heaven—" but he stopped short, possibly recalling the long laundering required for a protestant. The cars drew away with their headlights lost in the radiant sunlight. Old Mario, who sharpened scissors, was coming down the street toward them dragging his wheeled flint and bonging the bell. He saw the motorcade and moved to the gutter where he swept off his black cap, pressed it to his chest and crossed himself as the hearse passed by. As we rose to leave, the wet grass making an itch through our pants, a small white truck pulled up on the Bench's driveway and a man and woman got out, carrying flat boxes. Printed on the side were the words CARLEY'S—CATERERS TO THE DISCERNING. Pinky broke off another shoot to chew and said blithely, "That's for the wake."

But I was getting a little sick of his lofty attitude, so I hit him cruelly with some of my own knowledge. "Dogs *pee* on the grass, you know, and it's full of germs!" I was rewarded by a look of naked horror, and he spat repeatedly on our way home.

Our school managed to make a party of the war announcement that afternoon. The intercom sent the principal's voice jarring off the walls. "This is indeed a momentous morning for us all," he boomed, barely covering the happiness in his voice. "And to commemorate the event, the afternoon lessons will be postponed so that every child at Malcolm Public School can take part in a patriotic ceremony."

After lunch, the whole school was marched out to the south yard, all of us delighted to be free of classes for any reason. A small platform propped against the brick wall of the school held three chairs, one bull horn and a podium. Flanking this were two big cardboard cartons, guarded by the Nicol sisters.

Mr. Powell ambled up and down the lines, a pack of Turret cigarettes jammed into his breast pocket, frisking us with his eyes. When we had quieted down, he strode over to the Nicol sisters and ordered the opening of the boxes. Not a breeze stirred. The grey cement simmered and reflected back the bulbous sun, baking the shoe soles. Up and down marched the teachers, giving out miniature Union Jacks and paper hats with the same flag on the side that made us look like a field full of patriotic ice cream vendors. We shuffled restlessly. Through the open window of the kindergarten rattled the national anthem, and we drew our broiling shoes and sweaty arms into a semblance of attention. Mr. Randall mounted the platform, picked up the bull horn which amplified his chalk-on-blackboard voice and announced the sequence of events: God Save The King, a word from Mr. Alder, our principal, the singing of a new song under the direction of Miss Berry—

"A *new* song?" Pinky complained to our teacher. "What if we don't know it?" Like most of us, Pinky hated to sing, especially in public, and had evaded induction into his parish choir by purposely singing off-key for a full two bars, which in itself showed considerable musical skill.

"Of course you won't know it, you nit," Critchley-Williams whispered back. "Nobody does. Just waggle your jaw and look impressed."

At last Mr. Alder came striding to the platform. His "word" expanded in the sultry heat to almost an hour; the young children were beginning to crumple their hats and stick their flags into their mouths, up their noses and into each other. Rambling on, he seemed intent on recounting every crisis from the dawn of the Empire to 1914.

Interest swept us awake when his speeched ended and Miss Berry's name was announced. She would, the principal declared, teach us "There'll Always Be An England," and he rapped unnecessarily for attention as she bustled to the front of the platform, watermelon breasts heaving under the poppy-flowered silk blouse.

"I'll sing it through once, to give you an idea of the tune," she said, (another big breath—Pinky nudged me slyly) "and then we'll try it together a couple of times." The piano tuned up and away her voice flew across the dry field, each note falling on its predecessor in relentless order, as unshaded as marching feet: "Red, white and blue, what does it mean to you?"

Pinky poked me in the back. "Look by the fence." It was Hughie Brown, rocking from side to side as Miss Berry's rendition reached him without benefit of a bullhorn.

"Now all together!" cried Miss Berry. Hastily correcting wrong turns with vocal slips and slides that were always a half-beat late, we tried to weave our way through the unknown maze of notes.

Whether it was the music or the lure of coloured flags and bobbing hats, I'm not sure. But some compulsion drew Hughie away from his ordained course down the street and through the gate toward us. He skirted the sidewalk with caution until he could cut past it to the large cement rectangle and the platform. Behind him, the bulldog dragged his broad feet and massive head and sat down the moment Hughie halted. Miss Berry's voice faltered briefly when she saw them, but rallied vigorously as she decided to ignore the interruption.

A few children managed to keep singing, but for most of us the growing gift of distractions was beginning to prove too tempting. Hughie had stationed his shapeless bulk just beneath Miss Berry, where he started to imitate her energetic conducting and donated a soft falsetto to the singing. Some of the kindergarten children laughed outright as she became increasingly agitated and her pale freckled skin darkened.

Wanting to laugh and not being allowed to finally proved too much of a strain for some children. Ross Willard's nose began to bleed and he ran into the school dripping scarlet all over his paper hat. Moments later a little girl wet herself and waddled bow-legged around the drooping yellow panties, weeping in humiliation. But these were minor side shows.

73

Much more interesting was Miss Berry's heaving discomfort and the principal's voice trudging stolidly on—"The EM-pire too—what does it MEAN to you?"—as though he was royally trained to ignore the fool.

Critchley-Williams dipped his head beside my ear and asked: "Who *is* the fellow, d'you know, Gillies?"

"He lives on my street, sir. His name's Hughie Brown, and he's kinda simple. You know, a little soft in the head."

"Is his dog vicious?"

"Benjamin? No."

When the song was over, Miss Berry retreated in relief to her chair.

"Before we disperse," Mr. Alder gloomed into the bull horn, "I have taken the liberty of asking a recent citizen of the British Isles to deliver a short speech. Mr. Critchley-Williams is, after all, English, and may convey to us the significance and gravity of this occasion better than anyone else." This was said with a lightly accusative edge to his voice, as though our teacher's advantage and our ignorance were both sources of annoyance to him.

Critchley-Williams swung his stiff wooden leg up the steps to the platform with the grace of a pole vaulter, and stood for a moment smiling down at us. He began to talk about the littleness of his land, threatened against its will from without. "When the wolf comes roaring at your doorstep," he said quietly, "you do not take time to pet it, simply because it is an ancient relative to the dog. We will defend ourselves, and we thank you warmly for your support."

He slipped on a pair of glasses and examined the program in his hand. "I see by this that we are to end the program today with the singing of O Canada." He turned for affirmation from the principal, who cooled the afternoon with his lemon-twist smile. "With Mr. Alder's permission, I would like to suggest that we do this in a symbolic way. We have a visitor with us who owns a beautiful bulldog, an honoured British symbol of the courage and tenacity we may all need

74

in the days ahead. I am going to ask Mr. Hugh Brown to join me on the platform with Benjamin."

Before anyone had the time to understand exactly what he was suggesting, Critchley-Williams had leaned over to the smiling Hughie just as though he were as normal as the rest of us and said something inaudible to him. Hughie's grin broadened. To our amazement, he bent down and lifted the surprised and slathering Benjamin on to the platform, where the dog stood in bandy-legged splendour, looking exactly like the calendar beside the sink in my grandmother's house. Only the flag across his broad back and the background battleships were missing.

"Would you come, too, Mr. Brown?" my teacher asked. It had to be repeated before Hughie caught on. I looked around me to see what effect this extraordinary departure had caused. The children were struck dumb. On Mr. Alder's face was the look of a man wanting to run somewhere, but pinned to the spot by convention.

"Might we have a note on the pipe, Miss Berry?" The music teacher's eyes flew imploringly to the principal; but he was staring straight ahead, avoiding decision, avoiding implication. She picked up her pipe and blew.

So the war began and our summer ended that day under the fulvous sun of September. Innocent, avid and beflagged, we flung our Canadian anthem into the balmy air as though our singing alone might win the conflict.

10

Since Canada had officially entered the war, even the fun of our Saturday matinees was flattened by lengthy, urgent newsreels. Sharing a box of Happy Jack Caramel Corn, we hissed Mackenzie King when he appeared in his dark suit and stiff, round collar, eagle-wing eyebrows above flinty little eyes. He had interrupted the films we'd paid to see: *Jimmy the Gent* with James Cagney and *Tarzan and The Diamond Smuggler*. Then the cartoon and the fourteenth episode of Wild Bill Hickock. (Last week he had plunged off a cliff rather than be captured by Mexican bandits, our last view of him being an explosion of rocks and sand and horse-hoofs clawing the air as they dove for the rapids below.)

The Prime Minister didn't stand a chance with that competition. Hitler proved more interesting, grey and erect, jutting the defiant salute. We booed him luxuriously. Then a posturing Mussolini drew derisive laughter as he wooed a crowd below his balcony, fez jammed on a pumpkin head.

None of it registered fully. We scanned the smiling faces of "boys across Canada" jamming induction centres. An air of jollity and bravado filled the screen, helped along by the hearty overvoice that assured us "these boys will be *men* after weeks of healthy training turns them into fighters for freedom!"

Gagging down the caramel corn, idling the time away until the feature began, we were content to let Canada Carries On and the swift-moving Movietone News jerk before our eyes until Hickock emerged from the rapids below, grim-jawed, unhurt and shooting from the hip—action we could understand.

My father swore he would enlist. No one was with him, so we could never really know if he actually tried. I certainly couldn't equate his elegant mannerisms over the silverware counter with armies in any form. But my mother showed no surprise, only anger that he would even think of such a thing, regaling him with his responsibilities at home and, as a last resort, his age. She had begun to argue more openly with him since Durham had arrived, deserting the premise that a woman should never oppose her husband before the children. Wisely, Durham took no sides, but left the room or buried himself in a book.

As children we were too young to be sobered for long by events so far away. The routine at school, despite its surface nod to patriotism, remained essentially the same. Fresh flags in the glum brown hallways hung as limply as the dusty emblems they had replaced. Few of us understood the importance of the battles fought with arrows and red chalk lines criss-crossing the blackboard.

I got thoroughly sick of the war, in fact. It was discussed too often at home and had become a subject at school, so I deserted it whenever I could. We could still play baseball; we reveled in the warlike collisions of football played on cement without a pad or helmet in sight. And when I wasn't playing, there was always Shirley Upshaw to watch.

She was never late. While I grubbed around looking for a shoe, she'd be leaving for school, neatly dressed and carrying a plaid schoolbag. Down the driveway she came from the side door with her mechanical little walk—always alone because no one called for her, no one walked with her. Precisely at the break in the hedge she would turn to wave at the hand fluttering like a duster through the front door.

Pinky's sister, Mary, was in Shirley's class and had told us that she'd tried to get to know the new girl. Mary was just slightly younger than Pinky, and it wasn't too difficult to imagine her gangbuster's approach flooring anyone. The attempt, she told us, had petered out, not from rejection but from lack of response. "She answers questions in *school* without any trouble," Mary declared hotly, swishing back her fat carrot curls, "but just try getting her to talk any other time!"

"Maybe she's shy," I suggested, recalling the girl pinned against the school fence like a butterfly, watching everyone else play. Recess must have been a compulsory horror to her.

"Shy my foot! A snotty snob's more like it," Mary retorted, "too fine for the likes of us!" This comment complicated my thinking because I'd developed a minor crush on Mary, too. She was the kind of girl boys liked better than other girls did—pretty, with fine, vellum-white skin and a stocky body that smelled of talc and warm apples up close. She ruddied when we made her mad, her eyes pale green and glittery. Like her brother, she had the inborn cocksureness of a natural leader, but in her case it was coupled with a stinging tongue.

We were on our way home, spilling off the sidewalks and barely avoiding the smouldering bonfires that festered here and there along the gutters. A full cool breeze rustled the dry, flaring leaves. Up ahead, about a half-block away, Shirley had bent to pat Hughie's dog. Hughie watched happily from the centre of the road as Ben's blunt nose pressed against the girl's knee.

"Christ, would yuh look at that?" Don White was incredulous. "I wouldn't touch that bastard if you paid me! Once they lock their *jaws*—"

Mary glared in disgust. "Don't be a jerkimer, herkimer! Can't you *see* how tame he is?"

"Ya, but look at the *face* and those bloody crooked teeth."

"So? Don't you know they're *bred* to look like that, dummy?"

Shirley had straightened again, leaving the dog reluctantly. Hughie must have decided that she was going in his direction, and started down the road parallel to the girl, still grinning and nodding. The dog elected to stay on the sidewalk, shuffling slowly behind Shirley. At her house, she bent once more to pat him. When she left him, he raised his leg to wet the hedge thoroughly, then sent a spray of earth and stones flying as he scratched inaccurately to cover his work. It was a dog's compliment, the damp calling card that marked a new stopping place in his territory.

"Pretty scary, eh, Don?" jeered Mary, never one to let a lapse on his part go by unnoticed. "Even the *new* girl isn't afraid of him, pattin' your dragon like it was a kitten!" Don shrank from it, turning the subject blandly to our chances in the football game next week with Regal Road. But I took Mary's insult to Don as a backhanded compliment to Shirley. Obviously, patting the dog had won grudging approval, and the pecking order being what it was, I knew Shirley's position had become more secure.

In a show of affection and gratitude, I shoved Mary off the sidewalk.

The price Shirley had to pay for her impulsive gesture toward the dog became evident the next day. Mrs. Upshaw was at the school gate to meet her at noon hour and again at four in the afternoon, putting an end to whatever chance Shirley might have had to make friends. I happened to be there when it first happened. Shirley's face registered surprise, disbelief, then simply subdued shame as she moved through the clumps of sniggering children with the grandmother slowing her footsteps.

"Kinder*gart*en ba-bee!" someone hollered, "gotta be grandmawed home!"

Pinky and I went up to the Dive on St. Clair that night to watch George in action. Though we weren't allowed inside, we could see older kids shove nickels palm-first in the jukebox as the floor jumped with feet jitterbugging to Miller, Ellington and Barnett. Incredibly old-looking girls with pancake makeup, blood-red lipstick and bobby socks jolted in a frenzy of complicated steps we could not follow.

When the music stopped the girls hung themselves slackly around the wall, giggling together and trying to look nonchalant. That's when I saw George cruising the perimeter, pushing back the oily forelock, a predatory Clark Gable grin on his face.

"Lookit! He's going to *dance!*" We pressed our noses against the screen, waffling them neatly, trying to see through the haze of cigarette smoke and blue lights. The violin opening of Artie Shaw's "Frenesi" began and George's arm went around a blonde as they slipped away from the wall.

"A lot of mush," declared Pinky, forking out a nickel for a malted milk chocolate bar frozen on a square of ice. "Want half?" He broke it and I gave him my last two cents. "Wanna go now?"

"Yeah," pretending indifference. *Be home before dark*, my mother had warned, and already indigo was spreading from the east to the slit of the rose left along the western sky.

"Come on," said Pinky.

When I left him near the corner to turn along my street, I glimpsed the rump of Hughie's dog making his night rounds. Clouds had cut the colour out of the sky, though the wind that brought them still remained high, with only the scrackle of gum papers sliding along the pavement and the fitful scratching of leaves hinting at the weather to come. Near her hedge, I saw Mrs. Upshaw attacking a mess the dog had deposited, scooping it in a shovel and throwing it in the gutter. Then she picked up a corn broom and swept furiously at bits of earth he had ploughed backwards, muttering savagely to herself. I crossed the road quickly, hugging the shadows. Her ugly, ominous figure conjured up visions of Grimm's gothic horrors, the gulping fear I experienced when Dracula's night people emerged from damp new graves. I softened my step. Would I turn to stone if she looked right at me? Behind her the house loomed, seeming lightless, as though all the lamps were off. I wondered if Shirley was afraid of the dark.

11

I was sent home sick a few days later. Critchley-Williams had substituted a spelling bee for the usual half-hour of grammar. We waded through rhinoceros, panzer, propaganda, deceit, not easily, but correctly. When I drew "said," those on the opposite team moaned at the simple word. A mental block fell squarely on my brain, scrambling the order of the letters like a child's alphabet puzzle in my mind. I stood gap-mouthed, unable to decide anything, and the teacher announced that my ten seconds were up and went to the opposition, who rattled it off correctly in a second flat. Later in my seat I felt suddenly dizzy, as though a draft had blown me sideways. The history lesson floated past me and by now the girl in the seat across from mine was staring at me uneasily.

"You sick?" she asked, sliding slightly away in case I pitched up in her direction.

"Ya, I think so." Immediately she whip-cracked an arm importantly for the teacher's attention and the complex business of getting me out of the school began. A note from Critchley-Williams for the nurse: "Gillies has had a weak spell and seems feverish." I trudged down to the Health Room where a woman starched from head to toe regarded me with trained scepticism and took my temperature. She

82

seemed to doubt even the thermometer, and shook it vigorously before sticking it in my mouth for a second time.

"A hundred and one." Turning away from me, she wrote on another piece of paper, folded it carefully three times and told me to go to the office.

"The nurse said to bring this here," I told the secretary.

Balancing her hair like a mauve toque, Miss Vickers pounced. "We don't say 'this here.' We just say 'this.'"

"I meant this *down* here. . . ." I braced my shaking legs against the floor. "The nurse said to bring this note down here."

"Yes." She was satisfied. "Are you sick?"

"Guess so."

"Don't you know?"

I shrugged through the shivering, my legs trembling and seeming thin and much longer, like Alice in Wonderland after she'd taken a slug of the lengthening liquid.

"Sit down there on the bench, and I'll take this to Mr. Alder." There was kindness in her tone now, which for some reason made me feel sicker. I slumped down on the carved oak bench and looked at the pictures hanging on the panelled walls around me. Queen Elizabeth, black fringed bangs below a jewelled coronet; King George in a naval uniform iced with braid, his long, sheer Windsor eyes staring steadily across the room at me. My stomach jolted. *Oh, please, lady, hurry up or I'll throw up all over your floor.*

In a few moments, Miss Vickers minced cheerfully toward me after closing the inner door with extreme care, as though someone were napping within. "Here, Keith. Take this up to the teacher and you may go home."

After convincing Critchley-Williams that I didn't require aid, and that my house was just a couple of blocks way, I left. The cool air felt good on my face. I could not hurry, so I savoured the sights and sounds. A woman in a print apron was snapping a rug from her porch stairs, sieving dust into a mellow shaft of sunlight that splintered through the bare poplar branches. The fever had heated my eyeballs, blurring the autumn colours but sharply defining any single thing I looked at. Before Wilma Gee's house the baker's horse stood stiff-legged, head down, and I thought about the street gossips who claimed the deliverymen lingered much longer than was necessary within Wilma's place. The horses, in fact, had worked those prolonged visits into the stops and starts of their memorized route. The moment the driver drew up, the horse fell alseep. "What horse," Durham had asked wickedly, "is going to look a gift house in the mouth?"—which was nothing compared to the obscene comments made by kids on the block.

I got to my house, prepared from past experience for the seductive rites illness brought: aspirin washed down with hot chocolate, pillows shaken and smoothed, Aunt Thea's eiderdown worked in dog profiles tucked gently around. Oh, it was great, the care, the consolation, the family forming one solid and solicitious mound of attention! Letting myself in the front door, I heard my mother playing the piano softly, romantically. I felt happily sorry for myself, but I was home now, in no hurry to bring her immediately from the music. As I often did, I walked down the narrow hall to the living room door to watch her without calling out.

She was seated on the round stool, her back toward me, and Durham was beside her, standing, one arm wound about her shoulders. He began to rub the muscles of her neck while she played, rubbing softly, rhythmically, easing them gently beneath his blunt hands.

"Mmm, that feels good. . . ."

"Why the hell didn't you keep it up, Georgia?"

"I *am* keeping it up, silly."

"You know what I mean," he said impatiently, but his hands remained on her neck, massaging. "By now, I might be sending you roses up on the stage of Massey Hall. You'd be—let me see—in something velvet, plushy. Dark green, I think, with the small cap sleeves they're wearing now—not Empire styling, though—too much bust." They both

84

laughed. "—a dress that flowed to the floor. I'd send six dozen yellow roses—"

"—and I'd pick one off and toss it to you—"

"—after the umpteenth curtain call of course!" He stopped massaging.

"Of course," my mother repeated softly. Durham's hand went to her chin and tipped her face up, and he bent to kiss her. I stood dumbly staring at the sight. My ears sang, that terrible and monotonous whistle that accompanies fever. A peanut vendor in my head and an unreal movie going on before my eyes. I had never seen my mother and father actually kiss. They exchanged passionless pecks on the cheek when my father came home at night, but nothing that remotely resembled the lingering, mutual urgency I was witnessing now.

A fear of being seen suddenly paralyzed me. Everything about me seemed noisy: my held breath, my hot face, the blink of my eyes—

I backed off swiftly to sit down on the first stair, where I knew they could not see me, and waited for some inspiration that would save us all. I hallucinated what I wanted to hear: *That's quite enough Durham!. . .I'm sorry. . . . That's not good enough, being sorry. I love Ed, the children, especially Keith. . . .I know. I'm beyond contempt. . . .(C-r-rack! her hand across his face) Leave instantly!. . . .I will. . . .* My senses were heightened, my body hunched into an instrument of total listening.

"Would you leave with me if I asked you to?"

No sound. Then, "You know better than that." But not said in the way I had planned for her. A small collection of noises—the creak of the piano stool, feet moving an inch or two on the floor. I knew they were kissing again.

"I'll make some coffee," my mother said in a strange, husky voice.

"Damn it all, I don't *want* coffee! Can't you see that nothing has changed for me?"

"That's true, exactly true. Nothing *has* changed for you. You see me as if I were still single and about to plan an evening with you after work. Your life is your own to live as you please, as it always was. And when you walk in and out of that door, it is because that's precisely what *you* want to do."

"It could be like that for both of us, if you wanted it badly enough."

"You aren't thinking, Durham!"

"And you aren't feeling. You put your feeling for me away in a box somewhere, like a damned brooch. You don't admit what every action you make tells me." He blew an angry bitter sigh at her stubbornness. "All *right* then, just answer one question: do you love him?"

"Naturally there is a bond after nineteen years, for God's sake. There are qualities I admire and respect. . . ."

"But do you love him the way you love me?"

I drew myself into a knot, knees against my chest, praying for the word that would banish all my anxiety and dismiss the sombre Sunday-school hints I never understood about wife-coveting and lust.

"He is kind and a hard worker and—" she stopped abruptly in mid-sentence. "No," she said finally and firmly, "no, I will never love anyone the way I have loved you."

"Then leave with me, when I go to Vancouver. Don't answer me now, just think about it carefully. Think about the rest of your life. For once, think about yourself. I can make you happy, Georgia."

Happy? Wasn't she happy now? *Georgia, Georgia.* I worked the word over, kneading it in my mind like plasticine. My head throbbed, burned, though my hands were numb and cold. I did the only thing I could think of. I got down on my hands and knees and crept the length of the hall, back to the front door. Begging God to keep me quiet, I turned the doorknob in stealthy slow motion. Once outside, hit shrilly by the fragrant October air, I poked around in my jacket for the note that would explain my condition. Across the road, Mrs. Upshaw's hand showed against the curtain, and I knew she was watching me. *Go straight to hell, you old bitch! What do you know about anything, anyway?* I pushed my thumb against the doorbell, spinning with fever. It was a frantic pretence that I was really coming home for the first time, that nothing had happened.

My mother opened the door, her kind mouth dropping open in surprise.

"Darling! What's the matter?"

"I'm sick—" but I could say no more. I pushed the note at her, ink smeared and paper creased from my sweaty hand. She read it right there, right away. Tears began streaming down my face, and sobs came that sounded like they were being scraped out of someone else's throat, those big noisy gravelly things I hated in other people. In a gesture as old as my life, she reached to touch my forehead, drawing me in the door still speechless and weeping. Durham came up behind her.

"Hey, sport, what's happened? Keep that up and we'll have to ask you to wipe your face on the mat before you come in!" *Oh, no—you're not going to make me laugh at your dumb jokes, and I'm no bloody sport, either.*

I was plied with aspirin, and Durham made cocoa. My mother plumped and smoothed my pillows and dug out Thea's embroidered dogs; the thick quilt was tucked around me. And I got some small measure of revenge from watching Durham running around after a hot water bottle for my feet and a cold cloth for my head, while I lay, warmed by indulgent self-pity, in my bed.

For a few days I slept on and off as my body gave itself up to limp serenity. The school doctor came once, a large figure in blue serge with a heavy gold watch chain across it. My pulse was taken and he leaned close, plugged in to my heartbeat with a stethoscope so cold it made me jump. "Say, 'ah'," produced a vicious gagging on my part, and I was then lectured on the fact that choking during a throat examination was all in the mind.

He left without saying he would check back, and my mother did not ask him to come again. She brewed beef tea, supporting my head with her strong hand so that I could sip it. She ran hot tap water over the bed pan before I had to use it. When I urinated in a tall pottery bottle I had not seen before, she made a joke about not using it for flowers again. Since the cough worsened at night, Durham suggested that I be placed in his room, where care could be given without disturbing Doug. Young and sick, I lapped the attention up, ignoring the violet fatigue around my mother's eyes, not caring that Durham's legs would hang over the edge of my short bed. Let them hang, and let him have to drag his painting things down the stairs. But Durham, of them all, was the most imperturbable.

He insisted on saving my mother steps by catering to the petulant whims I developed as I grew stronger—orange juice, a piece of toast, the new Captain Marvel comic Pinky had dropped off, a hot cup of Vi-Tone. I did not want him, but there he'd be, grinning around the door.

"What on earth is *that?*" he demanded one afternoon. "Looks terrible!" I had removed a soggy mustard poultice and opened my pyjama top to air myself. He handed me an eggnog, staring at the crimson map blotched across the thin ridges of my collarbone. "For your cough, I expect," he answered for me. When I started to drink the nog, he rested a hand lightly on my arm. "If I were you, sport, I'd take this first, then drink that eggnog to kill the taste." He produced a teaspoon and a cereal bowl containing some noxious liquid with floating particles drifting like pond insects across the surface.

"What is it?"

He stuck a forefinger to his temple, mocking the straw man in the Wizard of Oz, and recited: "A little boiled water, juice of a sliced onion soaked overnight, a touch of lemon and brown sugar." He grimaced. "Sometimes I think she's trying to kill you!"

If he had to be here, I would use the opportunity to get

even with him. Feigning tiredness, I rolled over. "I don't want it."

"One spoonful, just to please your mother. She's trying to get you well, you know. Hell, you should be grateful I talked her out of the turpentine!" In sudden panic I recalled the fate of John Bench and the fact that one of the Nicol sisters often took on the job of tutoring any child with a lengthy illness at home. I swallowed it reluctantly. Durham sat down carefully at the end of the bed.

"You're looking much better, do you know that? Wouldn't surprise me if you could get up soon." I would not reply, but concentrated on ploughing the fuzz on the eggnog with a spoon. *I saw you kissing her, making her kiss you, I'll bet!*

"Pinky's been around a few times, and Don White, too." He cleared his throat. "Yep, I'll bet you'll be right as rain in a day or so!"

So you can get the room back, George's room.

I watched his eyes lingering on the dresser-load of tubes and small bottles of oil and turps, his belongings. Working at a protracted, false yawn to get rid of him, I said wearily, unforgivably, "I like this big bed," wriggling my toes to show the long distance between them and the foot railing. "It makes me sleepy, though."

"Oh, I won't stay long. But you just woke up, remember? I thought I could help pass the time, relieve the boredom a little." I was about to tell him I didn't feel like it when he tossed in the clincher. "Besides, it gives your mom a rest. She's napping on the chesterfield at the moment." I subsided against the pillow, studying Aunt Thea's stitched spaniel, his wavy brown ears outlined in beige thread. "Well, then," he said heartily, "what'll we talk about—or me, at least, since you're tired. Thea? You've met her I know, the old scallywag. Went to see her myself the other day and she claims she's going to Dog Heaven." He laughed easily, and alone.

"She's not a relative, either," I said.

"No, she's not," he agreed, "though she seems like one to

me." I fidgeted, uncomfortable with myself in this new and cruel role. Durham started to hunt for the tobacco for his dead pipe, then remembering my cough, put it back in his pocket. "A pipe always reminds me of Cody," he said casually, moving to the padded armchair near the window. "He used to have one poking from the side of his mouth, like Popeye. Couldn't smoke it in the house."

"Why not?" He had caught me with the only subject that could make me forget.

"Hasn't anyone ever told you about Cody?" he asked, as though it was a parental lapse that should be quickly put right. "Not anything?"

"Not much. I know he's Mrs. Upshaw's son."

"Was," Durham put in. "Of course, I was boarding down the street at the time and going to art college. Thea footed the bill, being a lover of the better things in life." He grinned at his own joke. "I discovered she had a passion for Constable's works and promptly did a couple of things burgeoning with splendid cloud effects. I think I painted one of the Montgomery farm out by Islington— quite accurate, jack pines, a collie by the snake-rail fence—but I changed the flat blue sky to roiling banks of storm clouds—cumulus, they're called—and she went into raptures of praise. 'You simply *must* have formal training! Do you realize you paint like *Constable*?' Anyway, I wrote my father that I would be staying in Canada for some time and rented a small room over at the Halwick's place. The world practically *ended* at St. Clair Avenue then. Oh, there were a few houses, the odd little store northward, but I could go sketching in the country in a half hour's walk."

"Did you know Cody then?"

Durham sighed and scratched at his beard. "It was an odd friendship. I don't think anyone ever really knew Cody. He was working for his Pa in a tailoring shop somewhere around Bloor; a cutter, I believe. Young as he was, he was really good with his hands, made frames for me sometimes, and an easel, but always outside in their garage. That's where he had to smoke his pipe, too. Mrs. Upshaw had black hair then, but I can't see that she's changed much beyond that."

I felt dimly frustrated. Durham's ramblings didn't add much to my information on the Upshaws. I had the feeling with him, as I had had before with my parents, that he was not telling me everything. A vision of Durham bending over my mother's face flashed across my eyes again, and I felt ruthless.

"Is that the time you and Mom knew each other, too?" I asked bluntly.

He returned my look steadily. "Yes, as a matter of fact. This house was her father's—I suppose you know that. Your dad bought it when they were married and your Grandma Bidwell stayed on with them for a time after your grandfather died. But before that I used to take your mother out occasionally. Remind me to bring in my photo album one day—you'll get a kick out of some of the pictures I took at the time." His chuckle was rich and tinged with sadness, as though someone had just shown him an old pair of plus-fours he'd worn when he was young and good-looking. He talked to me in a way that few others did, certainly more at ease than my father.

"I took odd jobs to supplement Thea's donations, but your mother was working a full six-day week as a clerk, nine hours a day, no overtime, for *under* the minimum pay." My puzzlement showed, and he slowed down, explaining more fully. "I'm sorry, I forget you're only ten sometimes."

"Eleven."

"Yes, eleven. Well, the minimum pay was supposed to be $12.50 a week. But jobs were so scarce that any complaint would just get you fired: there was always someone out of work, waiting to jump right in and work for even less than your mom was getting. At any rate, I got restless again. I didn't like art college much—so little new happening, and even nude models get dull after a few sittings. So I packed up and left for the States, then Mexico for a while, then back to England, after a few months in Europe."

"But didn't George and Doug remember you?"

"That was my last trip back here, to see if there were any opportunities around. I only stayed for a month." He regarded me closely. "I'm tiring you out, I think. Why don't you try to sleep a while and I'll bring your medicine up at four?"

Typically, he forgot the empty eggnog glass, which would cloud and harden on the table beside me. But he tip-toed back with the overblown delicacy of an elephant balancing on a ball and picked it up. I could hear him later downstairs at the sink, washing it out for her, as he had visited me, for her.

I lay back, exhausted and trying to hate him, turning his charm into threats against me. Plans of suicide to be accomplished by standing naked before the open window fox-trotted through my head: how horrible they would feel, discovering my body with an explanatory note! Then I remembered how horrible *I* would feel, and dropped the plan. But I sure wouldn't be suckered into a conversation again. As long as he stayed I would be polite, cool, no matter how many orange halves he carted up or "Keeters" and "Sports" he tossed my way. I would begin, I planned, by refusing medicine from him, a nice practical touch that had unexpected and pleasant side effects.

The big hand gently shaking me awake at four: "Time for the syrup, Keeter. Just one swallow and you can go back to sleep."

I let myself go limp.

"Keeter?" more sharply. "Come on, now. I haven't got all day."

I rolled over, letting him know he'd disturbed me. "Don't want it. . . ."

After a day or two of this treatment, his lack of success was followed by the appearance of my mother, a result I quickly learned to put to good advantage.

"Durham tells me you won't take your medicine from him. What's that all about?"

92

"I like you better," I said, adding with heavy emphasis, "and Dad."

"That's silly. Your father can only come up at night. Durham's just trying to help, but you're making it difficult for him."

I let my head flop weakly in her direction. "If Dad works in the daytime, why doesn't Durham?"

"He does." She walked briskly across the room and picked up an illustration, a dark-haired woman in a serape and sombrero, black spit curls stuck below her ears. "This is for the *Canadian Home Journal*, the front cover. Not everybody has a picture on the front. He took it from an original sketch he made in Mexico."

I made a mild mouth of distaste, but she was not put off. "And there's something for the *Star Weekly* novel around here somewhere—under all that mess, I suppose," she said cheerfully.

Spider Man sprung. "He sure *is* messy," I said. "George was neater than *that*. I'll bet Durham didn't even notice all that cleaning up you did before he came." I could tell this remark hit a nerve, because she began to absently arrange the dresser, lining up the bottles and bending to inspect a place where the finish had been whitened by a drop of thinner. "Take your medicine," she ordered in a level, preoccupied voice. I did it promptly. Then she sat down by me, worrying my face with her eyes. "I have a feeling you're ready to get up, young man, at least for part of the day. Suppose we bring you down for supper tonight? Your dad called today to tell me he's registered with the ARP as an air warden. He'll have a steel helmet, a bucket of sand. . . ."

"Ya?"

"You can hear all about it from him tonight. I think he has to learn to identify aircraft, too: he says they show silhouettes on a screen for just a split second, and he has to know whether it's friendly or an enemy!"

"He's real brave, isn't he? I bet if they let him, he'd go to the front line." I had not the remotest notion where or what the front line was, but since it had been bandied about in newscasts I felt it lent impact. I was feeling stronger by the minute. "A lot braver than Uncle Durham," I blurted, determined to push my cause to its limit. "*He* says they'd have to drag him—" but I halted, terrified by my own nastiness in the way that making ugly faces at myself in a mirror had frightened me when I was much smaller. There came into my mother's expression a look of wary and austere love, but she did not reply. I withdrew under the embroidered dogs, wishing that I could unburden myself honestly, asking the questions I felt deserved answers. Why was it that she could not see my anguish, as I saw hers?

12

I was well and back at school within a week. The world not only did not stop, it didn't even seem to hesitate. Some of the math at school had taken on the flavour of a foreign language, and I was asked no questions for a few days while I frantically copied notes from Pinky's scribblers. A little paler and slightly skinnier, I returned as though nothing but an illness had occurred. I found more small black swastikas spidering our class map of Europe, and headlines pinned up now blared Canada's preparations for all-out war: GUARDS SURROUND HYDRO PLANTS, one said, and OUR AR-MORIES PROTECTED ON 24-HOUR SHIFTS. Things were moving so fast that even the stunner contributed by Daisy Dobbs about the sinking of the *Athenia* had been buried under a new barrage of *Globe*, *Tely* and *Star* reports. I carried in one myself, PETAWAWA PREPARES, just to show them all I was still around. But shrouded by the layers of daily habit was the fear I could never have put into words. It came to me in surprising places. In the school basement bathroom, reeking of urine and damprot and coal fumes: *They are home together! They are there alone!* Slumping against my desk while Miss Foster's honed monotone whined the facts of wind velocity and air currents in Geog-raphy: *She said he had to go downtown today, but what if he comes home early?*

What if fretted at my mind, and I would tear home in a cold sweat the moment the bell rang, afraid I might find them together, even more worried that they would *not* be. I would imagine a note stuck to my noon sandwiches that explained their future plans without me. The simple act of leaving the house in the morning became a nightmare of reluctance—if I was there, if anybody was there with them, surely nothing could happen. When I sat with the family, I was always watching them for signs that might sway events one way or the other.

My mother: "You seem awfully quiet tonight, Eddy," handing him a cup of tea, stirring in the milk first. "Was it a bad day at work?" He would grunt, shifting in his chair. Knowing his mood better than anyone, my mother would leave him alone, but I shrivelled. *She will hate you, she will go.* At other times, when my father's sales had been good, he'd beam over the dinner: "Best soup you've made yet!" And idiotically I'd leap in to echo the praise. Whenever I could I'd find occasions to bolster his image.

"Doesn't he look good walking up the street? He's so straight."

"The war years did that, I think, all those heavy packs would pull anyone's shoulders into line." And my mother would tousle my hair and turn to the dishes.

"Yes, but Mr. Halwick was in that war, too, and look at him." She misunderstood, and talked solemnly of the way *some* people have of handling their problems.

Ironically it was Durham who seemed to sense that something was wrong. I once overheard him mentioning that I looked peaked. Maybe I was still weak from the bronchitis?

"Oh, both Doug and George acted like that around twelve," my mother had responded artlessly. "We'll just have to wait it out." But I would catch Durham's glance of speculative sympathy across the supper table, allying himself to me, and it would anger me more. I did not want support from the author of my problems. I didn't smile back at him. I didn't pause to watch him paint, and if he was in a

96

room with my mother or listening to her play the piano, I made it my duty to plunk myself down where I could observe them.

That's what I was doing one evening when my father was out on his street rounds, checking houses for black-out curtains and scanning the starry skies of Toronto from the rooftop of the local firehouse for Stukas or Junkers. Durham and my mother were in the living room. Earlier, Durham had mentioned how pretty she looked in a new coral dress, and my dad agreed that it *did* become her, but his thoughts were already on the possibility that tonight the enemy might drone up the St. Lawrence to our waterfront. He set his lips against her cheek and left. The moment the door closed I joined my mother on the chesterfield, where she had settled herself to read *Jamaica Inn*. Across the room, Durham occupied the chair by the radio, listening to the Voice of Firestone while he read his mail.

"No homework, darling?" my mother asked, placing a finger on the line she did not want to lose.

"I did it."

"*All* of it, so soon?" There was no real concern in her question, just the habitual query. Already her eyes were back on the page.

"I'll finish the grammar when George comes down." I shuffled the comics in my hands, trying to decide between *The Phantom of The Fog*, *G-8 and His Battle Aces* or a Black Bat detective mystery, copped from Don White's superb collection of literature.

"Got a moment to hear Monique's letter?" Durham asked, turning the radio down. I flicked a quick glance at my mother to get her reaction. No small hesitation or demurring pause; no annoyance or jealous pout. Because *I* was there, I was sure. I plunged my nose closer to my comic.

"You can listen too, Keeter, if you'd like to."

It won't do you any good. It won't change things. "Okay," I said frostily. One thing I would not do was leave the room.

Durham's eyes ran across a few lines, mumbling, pausing.

"Ah, here's what I thought might interest you—she writes mostly in English, but there's the odd French phrase here and there: 'We feel alone, very much so, though who can we blame but ourselves, considering our dishonoured pact with Czechoslovakia? If we had remained by their side, would it have come to this? Jean-Luc—' Durham paused to tell us quickly that he was one of the group of friends he knew in Paris '—was in Bremen just days before the declaration of war, and he saw a sign hung about the shoulders of a German soldier saying: Do Not Buy Jewish Merchandise. It is incomprehensible. *Te souviens-tu des promenades*—do you remember the walks we all took, linking arms in the evenings while you tried to teach us Lullaby of Broadway? And the picnic on the Rhine, with the little bridges and German canoeists waving to us from the other bank— carefully, so they would not spill? The little bridges have been taken down, and the large permanent ones are guarded and mined. Yet, in Paris an ennui prevails that somehow frightens me more than the barrage balloons and the sound of armoured trucks moving before dawn. Monsieur Bouget remembers—aloud and often—the Somme and Passchendaele, and mourns us lost before the battle has even begun!'"

Durham paused here to stuff and light his pipe. The tiny eddying flame bounced above the bowl, lighting momentarily a dark sorrow about his eyes. "There's not much more," he said quietly, raising his eyebrows toward my mother. "Do you—"

"Yes, finish it, Durham."

"'It is a form of fatalism without health in it, *n'est-ce-pas*? People buy their bread, sit beside the war memorials as though that alone would save them in some way. My trip to London made the difference so marked—would that be the right word? Marked? I was to buy wools for our winter collection, but I was so struck by the sense of being prepared, of anger, of working around the clock to get ready for the worst. You were here when labour got us our forty-hour week—1937 wasn't it, the year Edward came here with Mrs. Simpson? How we adhere to that forty hours! Lounging about the cafés, the army men leaning smoking against the lampposts. All that is lacking is joy—it is leisure out of place.

'I am sorry that this is such a sad letter for you, but the times make a gay one impossible. You asked me in your last letter if I intend to stay, and I find I cannot answer. The Seine is sluggish this year, and so am I! I may consider a post in Switzerland, but just saying it makes me feel cowardly. I *do* know that I will not cross to Canada or the United States, as you suggested. The ocean floor prowls with U-Boats now —it says something for the state of languor in Paris that I feel safer here than anywhere else. So, the future is unknowable: Jean-Luc and I talk about it, but it is like sifting air through a sieve. Please write. . . .'" He trailed off, carefully folding the thin pink paper and replacing it in the envelope.

"Wouldn't you know," he smiled, "that she would perfume the thing, even under those circumstances?"

My mother smiled, too. She rose without speaking to make tea. The signature theme of the program thumped warmly through the room as Durham turned the radio up again—*and now each flower is sweeter, dear; I know it's just because at last you're here.*

I ploughed back into Black Bat, where reality could be shut off the minute you opened the pages. Until the tea was brought in, Durham simply sat, reflective, saying nothing as he poofed round clouds of smoke which hung about his hair like Indian signals above a hill. But sorrow never appeared to remain with Durham long. The tea tray with its hot Aynsley pot and pinked English biscuits arranged like buff invitations on a plate lifted his gloom. He sat upright, placing the pipe to one side, and rubbed his hands heartily, creasing again with smiles. I could not help noticing that— quite unconsciously, while chatting lightly to my mother—

he had put the ashtray holding his smouldering pipe over the pink, perfumed envelope, and grey ashes fell on it like careless punctuation.

PART TWO

There was a time when I could fly. I swear it.
Perhaps, if I think hard for a moment,
I can even tell you the year.

Alden Nowlan
"I, Icarus"

13

For a few terrible weeks, fears that Durham intended to take my mother from me consumed my days. What I considered to be a genuine threat was hidden, mulled over and endured until I began to wonder if I would go crazy like Aunt Thea, or Hughie Brown, or the old man who let pigeons poop all over his shoulders while he sprinkled breadcrumbs. Or Mrs. Upshaw—the maddest of them all.

Because there was no one in whom I could confide, I worried that I would soon be among that group—and worse, I could see reasons *why* my mother might prefer Durham to my father.

My father was a product of his time, brave because he'd fought in a war, and had once, without hesitation, pulled his own decayed tooth with pliers when there was no money for the dentist. But he was a treadmill man, physically able to walk miles to work when he had no ticket money, enduring a job that required him to accept insult and low pay because the spectre of workless depression haunted him. At work he was a yes-man. At home he ruled kindly, but with a weary lack of interest. Though he spoke rarely, he usually parrotted something he'd heard or read in the paper, lacking the spontaneity and originality he might once have had. I think he looked to my mother to brighten days that were as predictable as the lined sheets in his order book. Her flashes of humour and the inventiveness that turned everyday events into a half-hour's diversion would bring an expression of complacent gratitude into his tired evening eyes.

With alarm, I'd sometimes lie awake knowing how plodding a man my father seemed beside Durham's fiery and expansive presence. For a change, my mother was being entertained by someone whose conversations leaped with assurance and wit, by tales of Mexico, Paris and the West Coast, as seductive as travel posters. Daily, I could see how he pushed back the walls of our lives. In defence, I tried to shore up my hatred by purposely picturing him kissing my mother, the slick smiling cad of Saturday movies who was all the more dangerous because he was charming.

In that confused state, I felt that everything they said to each other was touched with hidden meaning. Bits of sexual information lapped up at recess by the far back fence flew together like iron shavings in my mind at any gesture Durham made toward my mother. That in itself would have been enough to send me around the bend: what made it infinitely worse was the realization that deep down beneath my shabby pile of hatred, I liked Durham better than I liked my father.

So September passed in a downward spiral for me. Unable to concentrate by day, I was rapidly becoming a sneaky, sullen spy at home.

None of this confusion interfered with the excitement of my birthday coming on October sixth. I was too practical for that. Through the maze of self-pity and suspense sat the fact of "twelve," waiting ahead of me. I wanted gifts with the part of my mind that had to do with movies, ads, dreams. Conditioned by my family, I would be satisfied with whatever came. ("You understand, don't you, honey, that we just can't afford to get a bike? But there'll be *some*thing.") I went through the schoolday with my father's hesitant morning hug around my shoulders, the kiss of my mother lingering on my cheek, knowing that it was the evening that brought the real birthday.

The dinner table was set "nicely" and the meal itself was a kind of negative present: no cabbage or cauliflower or squash. My mother leaned forward, shiny with nostalgia. "You won't believe this, Keith, but you were born in a snowstorm!" I'd heard this before, but I attempted my annual look of astonishment. "You were the only one to be born in a hospital, you know—George and Doug were born at home—and your father had to dig out the doctor's car. Remember that Model T he had, Ed?" My father nodded, mock anguish crumpling his face. "And there I was, holding my stomach with one hand and wanting to help them shove the car." Durham leaned back in his chair, smiling. Doug and George kept eating, smiling, too.

"—and when we got to the hospital, you came almost at once. I never *saw* a child so eager to get born! I saw you before they even got you wrapped up—I heard you first, actually. *Singing*! I swear to this day, noises like music."

"Even after they'd whacked him on the backside?" Durham put in.

Everyone chuckled, coming together briefly and warmly, my brothers sending me grins of commiseration because they'd been through this memory agony themselves.

We finished our stew, full-stomached, but waiting for the cake ceremony. No matter how distended you were, the cake was the commemoration. It was chocolate, the flat moist layers satiny with a boiled icing. Twelve candles shivered in the darkened room. "Happy birthday to you—happy birthday to you. . . ." repeated as it was each year, solemn-cheerful, wax dripping and cooling, faces glowing in the light.

Then the communal present, bought by my parents with something chipped in from George's CCM job and whatever Doug had saved from mowing lawns.

"Wait!" my mother said suddenly. "You have to blow out the candles first. Make a wish. . . ." Make a wish. Most years I found my mind vacant. Who could think with all those faces expectant and urging, with the gift sitting there? "Don't tell anyone," my mother warned. I stared at the candle tips. *Oh please—please*. My mind, unused to requests of the spirit and the soul, floundered. Nothing would come except a pleading to the icy altar of the cake—*please, please*—I inhaled and blew my breath in a sweeping circle that extinguished the flames.

"Open it," Doug demanded, getting a little impatient by now with the heavy emotional atmosphere.

I rooted in the masses of tissue, discovering first the key, then the roller skates lying on their sides with the new tan leather supports sticking stiffly upwards.

"They're not Doug's old ones, you know," my father announced proudly, giving my brother a small loving punch on the shoulder. I could not believe what I saw, the wheels smooth and rustless, whirring at a touch on ballbearings.

"Can I try them now?"

"Before your cake?"

"I'll eat it later. Can I *try* them?"

There was some discussion between my parents about the late hour, the bout of bronchitis, the autumn weather. But Durham leaned back in his chair, hooking giant thumbs around his suspenders, and said how really mild it was, for the time of year. "No snowstorm," he winked at me, and I leapt for my windbreaker.

While I jiggled eagerly on the front porch steps, my father adjusted the strap length and skate length, and clamped my oxfords firmly into place with the key, which my mother had strung on twine to wear around my neck. Propped between George and Durham, I made it to the sidewalk. "Tuck your scarf in!" my mother called from the doorway, but I was busy trying to stand up.

"Let me go now!"

"Are you sure?"

They launched me, dropping the support of firm arms like poles away from a puppet. For fifteen minutes my arms

106

flailed and legs skittered sideways. Under the streetlights I tottered uncertainly, the swift oiled wheels always a roll ahead of my reflexes, until at last I felt control, a coming together of feet and head. A light rain cooled the excitement burning on my face. Encouraged by the five-headed audience silhouetted against the living room window, I ploughed along seven cement squares without getting caught in the ruts between. These lunges always ended in a teetering halt, but I knew I could do much better on the road. I sat on the curb to catch my breath and to assess the stretch of asphalt gleaming darkly under the leafless trees.

This is what real athletes do, I told myself. I'd seen Bobby Jones squat to find the deceptive rolls and dips before he'd putt, stalking the green as if it were a serpent asleep beneath his cleats. I slid my eyes along the road, mapping the sewer grates, the yawning crack outside Mrs. Collins' place. The rain had thinned and vapourized into an ombre fog that rose from the damp earth to finger tree trunks. Old Ben, Hughie's bulldog, was snuffling at poles and dead gardens. There were no cars. No one was out. It was quiet enough to hear water gurgling in the sewers.

My eye was caught and held by a light flicking on upstairs in the Upshaw's, a burning rectangle that revealed flowered wallpaper and dotted white curtains. And Shirley, standing in her window, looking down at me. In my imagination I must have consigned her to some foul corner of the cellar on a fairy-tale bed of cinders and old newspapers, because I felt distinct surprise that she had a bedroom and looked from windows like a normal human being. I stared back, transfixed by the smooth flat nightie, the loose long hair, the light behind her. I would give her something to watch.

Slowly I rose, gaining control, and began a series of elaborate long strides, moving my elbows and crouching like the people I had watched over at the Strathcona rollerskating rink. I had just accomplished my first uneasy turn, feet planted wide and awkwardly, and had glanced up to see if this feat had been recorded, when a shadow loomed behind the girl. Before she had time to turn around the blind was plunged sharply to the sill. The light went out. Struggling to keep my balance, I was torn between humiliation for the girl and hot pleasure that she had been watching *me*. *Rapunzel, Rapunzel, let down your long hair.*

I kept practising a moment longer, trying the turns, hearing my father calling through the damp night to come in now, it was too cool. I glanced up at Shirley's window once more before clambering up the sidewalk, and what I saw raised goosebumps.

Slowly, inch by inch, her window blind began to lift, as though the girl were guarding against it slipping from her fingers. Her bedroom light was not on now, but I could see her white gown against the pane in the muddy glow of the streetlamp, a moth pressed to the windowpane. She smiled down at me and waved quickly before carefully lowering her blind again. TWELVE, I'M TWELVE! slammed into my brain. For the first time in weeks Durham and my mother receded in my mind to be replaced by the furtive wave of the girl's hand. On the strength of that, I skated into my manhood convinced I could handle anything.

14

Shirley Upshaw had initiated a conspiracy that was to last as long as the evenings had one ray of light left in them. The blind would slide up in the darkened room (I could imagine the conversation inside her house: "Is your light out, Shirley? Yes, Grandma. Blind down? You don't want peepers! Yes. Go to sleep then, there's a good girl") and my performance began. What was not permitted for her to do I'd do, her surrogate athlete: run, climb, skate, play ball, always with an eye to the curtained gallery. It was my way of using up both our stores of energy in an attempt to make her unreasonably early bedtime more bearable. If I was unable to storm the castle walls, nothing could prevent me from parading my knight's colours on the road the girl could not cross.

The result of this was a growing dislike of me on the part of the old woman. I was careful not to look up too often, and I'm positive Shirley's ear was alerted for the tread of a foot on her stair, so Mrs. Upshaw did not put two and two together. Though she was used to my playing outside, this was not the indifferent Keith of old. As I tore wildly up and down the street I became more and more a focus for the hatred she seemed to have for all boys. She stormed out onto the porch once, threatening trouble if I did not stop. I ignored that, of course. At other times, I'd spot her head parting the curtains. But what really brought her into the open were the evenings when my friends turned up for a game, and our yells shattered the October evenings.

Then any pretext was enough to draw her out on the porch, huddling in a man's heavy sweater, glaring and hostile. We were disturbing the driveway stones; we ran on her lawn; the racket was terrible; our language was disgraceful (an accurate charge brought on by Don White's narrow vocabulary of washroom expletives). And I was the ring leader. Finally, she took action.

I'd just come home from school, wet and hungry. "Can I have a hermit?"

My mother nodded. "And milk, if you wish."

The "if you wish" wasn't a good sign. My father showed displeasure with his body—glances that bit, too straight a back, jawbones working. With my mother, it was words—formal, cool, snipped off with scissors. I sat down, rubbing my bare toes together because they itched and ached a little from the house's sudden warmth. After pouring a cup of tea, she sat opposite me with the remote look of a stranger sharing a restaurant table.

"I had a call from Mrs. Upshaw today." She spaced the words levelly. "She has had to call the police, I believe, because of the noise and fooling around at night. I don't like you to bother her that way."

I bit into the cookie. "She's just mad 'cause they couldn't find us. The cop wasn't mad. I think *he* thinks she's batty, ready for nine ninety-nine Queen—"

"She says the language is shocking."

I made an elaborate face of tried patience, brushing off the ridiculous charge. "That's just Don. He talks like that all the time." I had known Don from kindergarten and could swear that the first word I ever saw him print, baby lips clamped in a perfectionist's concentration, was fuck.

"I've never heard Don talk like that," my mother declared. "Does he call Mrs. Upshaw. . .names?"

110

"Nope. He's not *that* dumb. She stands there listening and watching all the time, so she hears things. So would anyone else, if they did that. Don always talks like that. So does his old—his father."

My mother persisted, not to be put off by these revelations about someone else's upbringing. "She says you run over her property."

"Oh ya? That's a lie!" I lied. We ran on everyone's property at one time or another. If Mrs. Upshaw got it more, it was because she made so much fuss. "She just wants to find something wrong!" I detected a guarded glimmer of agreement in my mother's eyes as she appraised me, like a prosecutor being unwillingly won over by the witness for the defence.

"Well," she sighed, "from now on I'd like you to try a bit more consideration for the old woman. Telling her to dry up is hardly the way to win her over."

"I don't want to win her over," I mumbled, remembering her assault against me when I had retrieved my ball, the clinging ugly hands, the baleful looks at the schoolyard gate where she waited for the girl. That comment got me a lecture about age and privations, a list of generalities on goodness. Swilling the mush of the cookie around my mouth, I panned it with my tongue for an undiscovered raisin or a fragment of walnut, not really listening. I found my mother unreasonable when she expected me to be polite to adults who were rude to me.

"Keith, are you listening?"

"Sure! I'm sorry. . . ."

"I didn't *ask* you if you were sorry." Her eyebrows drove a winged wrinkle across her forehead. She had very young skin, permanently rouged by hours of ironing and cooking, and carrying things up and down. "I was saying that Mrs. Upshaw has had her share of troubles, and more than her share of grief. I suspect the business of Cody would be enough to make anyone bitter."

"What was it about Cody?" As though she had touched

111

on something that should have remained private, her eyes clouded over. She poured another cup of tea. "Why did he go?" I persisted. "I wish somebody would *tell* me something!"

"Well," she said simply. "Well, you are twelve, aren't you?"

I sensed her hesitation, and prodded her back to the point before she became mired in the miracle of my growth. "Was he Shirley's father?"

She had the expression of a diver, poised on the top board, trying to determine the safety of the plunge. "All right," she said quite firmly. "All right, I'll tell you how we got to know them.

"Your Grandpa and Grandma Bidwell came out here from England when I was around your age, I think, and my brothers and Aunt Betty were young, too. We started out on Madison Avenue, but my father had his heart set on living further north, up on the escarpment above Davenport. He found a piece of land for sale here—" she waved a hand east and west, indicating our street "—and this is it."

"Yeah?" Durham had told me a little of this, but I knew better than to stop her when she got going.

"He built this house with some other English friends helping, and with more resentment from the Canadians already here than you can imagine. We were limeys to them. We toted our things up from Madison on an open cart pulled by two horses—a hard business getting up that hill!"

"What about across the road?" I interrupted. She seemed bogged down with memories. "The Upshaw house?"

"It was already there, but vacant. No hedge, lawn like a hayfield—well, of course, most of the land here *had* been orchards or hayfields not too long before. Your grandfather got busy on our lot, making a little transplanted Somerset out the back, with gardens and a tomato patch."

Casually, she drifted over her meeting with Durham, as though it were of no particular consequence. "I dated several men—Durham was going to art school and lived with

112

the Halwick's. That's probably what started him drinking—
Mr. Halwick, I mean!" She blurted it suddenly, laughing. "I
met your dad at a church picnic. Don't laugh, but the first
thing I noticed was his straight back, the way he walked, as
though he knew just where he was going. I liked that." She
grinned at the memory.

"But when did the Upshaws move in?"

"Oh! That's what started all of this, wasn't it? After
Grandpa Bidwell died—I had married your dad the year
before—he left us the house, and shortly after that the
Upshaws arrived in a big Robertson's moving van. They
were older than us and kept to themselves. We just assumed
that the young man was their son, though we never were
introduced. I'd guess him to be around sixteen—Durham
knew him better. You know Durham—he just ran across
the road while the boy was putting in the new hedge and
gabbed! I think he made some frames for him because once,
when we asked Durham down for dinner, the boy came to
the door to check on some measurements. When I asked
him to step in, he stood just inside the door, dressed in a
white shirt and tie—imagine! at that age!—and flannel
pants. Most embarrassed lad I've ever met. I convinced him
to come in for coffee, but I think he only did it because he
had no idea how to say no. There he sat, on the edge of a
chair, your father and I trying to make converation,
Grandma Bidwell shouting questions at him because she
was deaf. He got the information from Durham and left."

I heard George come in, yell "Hi! I'm going up to Kres-
ge's for some reinforcements, okay?" and leave again. My
mother looked at the clock.

"Can you listen while I cut the beans?" she asked. "We're
having cold ham and I've got baked potatoes in the
oven. . . ."

"Let me cut some beans," I offered, not out of thoughtfulness. I'd do anything to hear what I really wanted to know.

"Okay." She got out the wood chopping board and two
sharp knives and we guillotined away. "By the way," she

113

glanced up at me, "what are reinforcements? It sounds like an army word."

"Little white circles you glue around the holes in loose-leaf paper."

"Oh." She was slicing the beans in a thin slant, a sign of time to spare. "About Cody," she went on. "It didn't take long for us to notice how strangely he was treated. Nothing nasty, just—not natural. He didn't play with other boys on the street. None of you boys were born then, but I had seen enough of my own brothers to know how protected Cody was. We gradually realized that he didn't play with others because he wasn't allowed to. Not even Mrs. Upshaw's husband could divert her from that boy. Mr. Upshaw seemed like an elegant hired man or boarder, never rough-housing or playing catch like your Dad did with you boys later. He came out in the morning and touched his grey fedora to the face in the window, and disappeared into the house after work every night."

"Shirley waves," I put in.

"That's what Cody did, too, on his way to school. I'll never forget that first Hallowe'en, when Mrs. Upshaw went around with him—"

"But he was sixteen!"

"He was a child to her. She must have lived in fear from the moment he was born." I told my mother about the old lady waiting for Shirley at the school gate every day. "I'm not a bit surprised," she said sadly. "God knows what she thinks will happen to a girl if she felt that way about Cody."

"But Dad said Cody went away. . . ."

My mother ran some cold water into an enamel saucepan and placed it between us. "Put them in there," she said quietly. "Cody did go away, very soon after his father died. It was so unexpected, all of it. Mr. Upshaw went for his usual evening stroll for the paper—your Dad always said he looked like he was marching without a band, arms swinging, looking straight ahead. He just keeled over by the hedge and died, as though he'd been shot. Cody left two days after the funeral, just packed a bag and went."

"Did you see him?"

"No. As a matter of fact, Mrs. Halwick did."

"And he never came back?"

"Well—"

"You said he didn't, that first night we were talking about Shirley."

"Well," she repeated, some apology in her tone, "that wasn't quite true. He *did* come back a year or so later. It was really quite terrible. Things come out in bits and pieces. Apparently, during the year away, Cody had got himself involved with the Appleton girl who lived up on Greensides, a scruffy young thing with a slattern for a mother and a father who just took off and came home whenever he felt like it.

"Cody came to the house with the girl—she looked like a child dressed in her mother's clothes. It was summer, very hot, and most people were on their porches—not Mrs. Upshaw, of course. Cody drove up in an old car, drunker than Mr. Halwick ever was, even on Friday night, and pulled the girl out after him. He started to bellow at the house, awful things, demanding that his mother open up. He swore a lot. The girl was leaning against their car smoking a cigarette, hair frizzy and peroxided, like Jean Harlow's. Finally his mother did open the front door and he ran in, putting up all the blinds, turning on all the lights! He yelled out for the girl to come in, but she had spotted Hughie coming down the road. She went tottering over to him in those silly spiked heels. 'Come on in for a drink!' Cody said, but they couldn't get Hughie to walk up the sidewalk, so instead they tramped across the hedge and the garden—all three of them, right into the hall."

Here, my mother paused, as though some invisible Victorian thread was making so much revelation difficult. She cleared her throat, put the last of the slivered beans into the pan, mopped at the table.

115

"Anyway—before he left, Cody stood on the top step, one arm around the girl's shoulders. She was so little that the weight almost pulled her down. He yelled 'We're not married,' so proudly it made me ill at my stomach. 'And we're going to have a baby, too. How about that?' Those of us who'd come outside went back in. The last thing that boy needed right then was an audience. He should have had someone to listen to him much, much earlier."

I was trying to picture that house with the doors flung wide, lit up like a pumpkin, and Cody barrelling around the rooms.

"I expect Shirley was the baby, Keith," my mother said softly, but something stopped her there. Perhaps she felt that she had told me too much without excusing the disclosure on moral grounds. I could tell by her reddening face that there had to be a warning for me in there somewhere, a verbal guard rail hastily erected against the edge of a tempting precipice. I began to squirm in my chair, wishing now that we could be interrupted by someone.

"It can happen all too easily, if we aren't careful," my mother began. "I suppose by now you know that babies don't grow on trees?" Was I supposed to answer this incredible question? I nodded dumbly. I had little or no real information on the making of babies. The stories I'd heard whispered behind garages had nothing to do with trees, but I wasn't about to tell my mother that. I was glad she'd told me about her own life, and the Upshaw's problems, shedding a shaft of light on the other puzzle of Shirley. But somehow I resented having it end this way, my images of sex as hotly purifying and somehow beautiful now measured by the sleazy mess Cody Upshaw had gotten himself into.

Rising quickly, I mumbled something about hearing Pinky outside and left my mother struggling with a sentence about emotions.

15

If this account had been given to me a year or two before, I'd have made a beeline for the first kid in our gang and spread the word. Being the bearer of news—good, bad or *really* awful—was a mark of distinction that buried Sunday-school conscience and melted lines of loyalty. The urge still beckoned, the sirens of gap-mouthed astonishment, of "No kidding!" of another step up the ladder of popularity singing sweetly in my mind.

I awoke the following morning too sleepy to remember, drowsily focusing on the Sunnyside canary, still propped against the wall, vaguely aware of clouds shredded like bits of kleenex over a vivid blue sky. Then my mother's revelations flooded back and my eyes shot open. I lay for a moment more, hearing the slow morning voices below. Sitting up on the windowsill was the picture of the Upshaw house Durham had painted for me. It was still summer in the painting. Humping myself up on an elbow, I looked down over the road. Blood red berries stung the bare hedge now, the one that had held her grandfather like barbed wire when he collapsed. The vines clung stubbornly, no green dark arrows curling round the pillars. The wicker swing was covered over in a piece of heavy canvas.

In my picture the small figure read a book. For the first

time, I wondered how innocent she really was. Had she known, sitting there while Durham dabbed away, what I knew now? I was sure, then, that I would not tell my friends. I knew because of her hand waving to me that something special and secret was there, apart from her past and more important than any ambition to be special among my peers.

I went downstairs, ate, hunted around for my shoes and took a spoonful of Maltlevol lately inflicted on me because I'd had the nerve to get sick.

"It's full of iron," my mother insisted.

"Just don't stand too close to a magnet," said Durham, sitting in his bathrobe eating three shredded wheat daubed with melting butter.

"Do you have to go downtown today, too?" I asked him.

"Later. Things are looking up!" He grinned and sucked at hot coffee.

"Oh!" My mother suddenly remembered something. "Your Aunt Pru is coming today."

"In *that* case, I'll go look at the galleries as well," Durham said briskly. "All I need is that case of woe breathing turkish delight all over me."

"You're thinking of her perfume," my mother said, pulling my windbreaker collar up. "It isn't turkish delight."

"All I remember is the scent of roses and lemon when she stuffs in a box of that candy—damn it all, it *is* turkish delight, that wobbly stuff covered in powder. Sounds like Pru herself." He winked at me.

"That's enough, Durham," my mother said with mock sharpness. She turned back to me. "Just remember your manners, Keith. Don't, for heaven's sake, tear through the house when you get home."

"Okay."

"She feels badly if you don't say hello, so say something to her before you disappear."

"Okay."

"Even if you only stay for a few minutes. It pleases her."

"*Okay!*"

118

I felt relieved and happy swinging along the street that morning, knowing that Durham would be away from my mother for the day while she was getting ready for Aunt Pru. We saw most of our relatives only once a year, at the July family picnic at Centre Island. Because they were infrequent, these get-togethers took on an atmosphere of rollicking abandon. As each branch of the family shuffled off the *Bluebell* there were whoops of pleasure, arms flung around one another, hands pumping as if for water. The women opened baskets and shopping bags and old shoe-boxes to spread their jam-jars of potato salad and pickles and cold meat; the men organized a baseball game beside the lagoon with paper plates for bases. Despite the general poverty, there was always one sweating, expansive uncle who could dig up enough nickels for ice cream cones all round.

At dusk rambling memories were relived: the men discussed business matters in flat, patient voices as they sat on benches, rubbing at shoulder muscles now better suited to hunching over desks than swinging bats. By the last boat home, all the relatives had gorged themselves on the family news, storing it up against the uncertainties ahead.

By comparison, I knew Aunt Pru's visit would follow its formalized course: a tea tray, something special to eat, hours in which she would unburden her own thoughts while gathering in crumbs of information to feed bit by bit to Uncle Gerald, waiting stiff and bored at home.

I ploughed through a pile of leaves someone had raked neatly into a mound for later burning, grinding them to pepper. For a moment I stopped to get a good look at old Ben as I patted him. Like the dog on my grandmother's God Bless England calendar, he was brindle brown with a jet black nose, although his was stuck with flecks of earth and mucous. The first bell rang so I left him to run through the gates, narrowly missing Mrs. Upshaw who scuttled past, making a wide circle around the dog and around me, too. This time her glance of hatred didn't bother me as much.

There was new power in knowing more about her, and even more in knowing that a part of the wall she'd built around Shirley was crumbling.

Near the back fence our afternoon recess was spiced with the smell of somebody's chili sauce sifting through bonfire smoke. Coming toward us, the insolent swish of Mary Yorke's pleated skirt, topped by an inch-thick cream wool sweater, the same kind Pinky wore on cold days. The bitter wind had made her face bright pink.

"Guess *what*, you guys?"

"Here comes all the news that's fit to print," Don yelled back, edging himself nevertheless carefully behind the oak.

"Shut your face, smart alec," she growled at the foot sticking out, "or I'll cauliflower your *ears!*" Mary was getting tough these days, more belligerent. I wasn't so sure I liked her this way. "Okay, *guess* whose birthday it is today?" She clamped her red lips, daring us to guess correctly.

"Not mine." I said.

"Come on, get it over with," Pinky said, "then get back with the girls where you belong."

"I'd say there's more *boys* here who belong over there than me." She glared directly at the oak tree and stuck out her tongue. "It's Shirley Upshaw's, that's whose. In class, Miss Jones asked who would turn twelve in October, and little-miss-browner stuck up her hand. 'It's today,' she says. 'I'm eleven.' Didn't even hear about being *twelve*, though—" (rueful pause: Mary was rotten but she was honest) "—that's about the only thing she ever got wrong."

Pinky sighed. "So bloody what?"

"Anyway, Miss Jones is kinda nice, and she asks if Shirley's going to have a party and that's when it happened. Someone called out 'No, she *always* dresses that way!'"

Don guffawed, overdoing it because he was really afraid of Mary. Pinky snorted. "What happened then?"

"Did she cry?" demanded Don, like most frightened people only too eager to discover cowardice in someone else.

"No, but I could hardly stop laughing, the whole class was

laughing, so if she said anything *we* couldn't hear it. And then the bell rang—"

Suddenly, over by the school where the girls were, I saw a knot of skirts whirling madly, saddle shoes plunging and scraping. "ONE! TWO!" Clamped harshly across someone's knee, grasped by the wrists—my god, panties showing!— was the unmistakable finery of Shirley's clothing, everything matching, the gloating polished shoes, the fine coat and upturned plaid shirt. "THREE! FOUR! FIVE!" I watched in horror. Someone took her grey tam and tossed it in the air like a trophy. "*TWELVE! YOU SAID TWELVE!*" screamed one girl. Birthday paddy-wacks. Everyone got them. "Saw your panties—they've got *lace* on them—"

They let her go and she stood for a second in the centre of the ring, tugging down her clothes, feeling her hair, messy as hay, for the tam. One girl broke the circle and shoved the tam like a vaudeville pie, hard, right in Shirley's face. By then Mr. Randall was on his way, his vaulting giraffe steps narrowing the distance. But he was too late. Skinny legs apart, breathing like a bull before its tormentor, Shirley brought her arm close to her body and swung it with all her force, back-handing the girl's cheek in a mighty crack that must have left knuckle marks.

I'd have hit her, too! If you'd only dress different! If you'd just talk to the other kids—they probably thought you were defending your clothes, your dumb tam!

The group fanned back, now shoved aside by Mr. Randall, keeper of the peace. He marched the girl and Shirley into the school, the hit one sobbing, the birthday girl deadly white, the teacher saying loud enough for us to hear: "That *girls* would fight! Wait 'til Mr. Alder hears about this!"

Mary told us after school that Shirley had had to stand in the corner for the rest of the afternoon, as an example to the other girls in the room. I wondered what would happen when she arrived home, hoping that she'd be smart enough to lie about the torn white stockings blotched with mud and the dirty tam with a hole where the tassel used to be.

16

The moment I opened the front door I could smell Aunt Pru. Her English lavender floated like summer in the hallway where O'Cedar wax continually battled the winter fact of wet rubbers and damp newsprint. Her purple coat had been neatly placed on a hanger, buttoned to keep its shape. Around the neck curled the fur piece tipped with a shrunken fox head that always repelled and fascinated me: tiny perked ears, clear amber eyes, miniature needle teeth set into its V-shaped skull. Beside my rubbers on the newspaper stood her furred black velvet boots with the small protruding buttons that were done up with a little ivory hook she carried with her.

"Lydia would have wanted it that way. I *truly* believe that." I stopped before the wall mirror to slick back my hair, readying myself for the inevitable inspection. "But to put in your *will* that you want a cheap coffin and no fuss—you remember Lydia's plain way of talking—and there it was, written in her hand: 'I don't want people paying a fortune to plant me!' *Plant* me, imagine. Like a geranium, not a human being at all. Her coffin looked like a carton from the Stop-and-Shop store." An indignant sigh, audible clear through the door. "Gerald says she favoured my father in that way, blunt, said right out loud what he was thinking. Unbecoming to a woman, I think, even if she was my sister. I just hope that I don't die until this stupid war is over! People get so upset about the young dying that they have nothing left for natural death any more—" A book slid from under my arm and thumped to the floor. "Who's that in the hall?"

I opened the glass door then, smiling rigidly, trying to look as if I had just come in. "Hi, Aunt Pru."

"Hel-LO, Aunt Pru," she corrected. "Well, Keith, you haven't grown much since I was last here." I immediately felt shorter and pencil-thin.

"Keith had bronchitis a while back," my mother explained. "He has a little catching up to do. Sit down for a while, honey, and have some cake." I obeyed because I knew I would not be expected to talk much with my mouth full. My aunt leaned stiffly toward the tray, too, pleasure-cruising her way through the sea of tarts and cookies.

"Take a page from your Uncle Durham's book," she advised, selecting one of everything. "He always liked his food. Who was it who told me he wanted something to eat the moment the ether had worn off, after they took out his tonsils?" I manoeuvred a sticky butter tart, conscious of her eyes on me, remembering not to lick my fingers. Pru's plump body burgeoned above little ringed hands and wrists and her tiny feet dangled daintily an inch from the floor. A rose brooch outlined in pearls pinned some old remembrance to her breast. With her pouting mouth and pekinese eyes, I wondered unkindly if she'd yap excitedly if I held out a piece of tart toward her.

"And what have you decided to be when you grow up?" she demanded brightly. I had not been listening so my mother prodded gently, "Keith?" nodding in Pru's direction.

"Oh!" I swallowed hastily. "Uh. . .a baseball player I guess, or a dentist."

Her eyebrows raised slightly in polite distaste. "I don't know much about ball players, of course, though I recall my father saw games on the field behind Hanlan's Hotel. All I know is that they don't appear to do much the rest of the year. And I've always been afraid of dentists. Those terrible drills—so hot! Of course, one of the great advantages of aging is that you needn't see them anymore. Gerald hates his false teeth, claims they never did fit properly." She bit heartily into a brownie to show her toothy advantage over her husband, and I sat morosely counting the minutes. I was not sure just how long I should stay, since Pru was deserting me as a point of interest and had returned to the past—the subject dearest to her heart—managing this with jerky speed, like a film in reverse.

"Remember the lovely cruises, Georgia, on the *Chicora?* But no, you'd be too young then—"

"Still in England, Aunt Pru. . . ."

"Yes, of course," she said coolly. Pru's family went back to the 1800's in Canada, which gave her the chance to reverse the snobbery attributed to British immigrants by flaunting her solid colonialism in their faces. "My mother bought family tickets—goodness, you could sail clear across the lake and back for about fifty-five cents. What good times! We'd buy a basket of peaches for a quarter at the dock and that was our dessert. Such fun, then! Gerald, so young and full of pep; dear Lydia—" Her lower lip began to quiver, but she pulled the fat little pouches on her face into line, like straggling and inept newcomers to a regiment. With a mighty sigh, she left the maudlin mood, and waved a hand toward our front window.

"I saw the girl going into the Upshaws as I came. Skinny little thing—but then she was in an orphanage, wasn't she?"

"Yes, I believe so." My mother turned to me. "Keith, if you'd like milk, why not get it now?" Probably she was indicating an escape route, but the mention of Shirley was too intriguing. I hurried back with my glass, hoping they'd go on, but my reappearance must have shed new light on me, for Pru's eyes narrowed to inspect me.

"Does Keith always squint like that?" she asked abruptly. "The left eye?"

My mother turned to me in bewilderment. "Squint? I hadn't noticed."

"The *left* eye," Pru repeated strongly. Now they were both squinting themselves to get a better look. I opened my eyes as wide as I was able, wishing now I'd stayed in the kitchen.

"Durham squints, I've noticed," my mother said with some exasperation, diverting my aunt with a cookie. "But then artists have to diminish things, don't they, to get perspective—"

"Macaroons, how nice," Pru crooned. "I'd have thought Keith might want to be an artist, too, now that Durham is here. Children tend to have crushes on professions, when they like the person. Of course, I am no fan of his style— they teach such odd things in art college these days." Her pursed little mouth disappeared as she looked meaningfully at my mother.

"You mean the nude figures?" my mother asked, with a small, light smile. "Oh, Keith, I've shown Aunt Pru the painting Durham did for you—the one in your room." I said nothing, not happy to have anyone invading my privacy, especially the ego-shattering Pru.

"I *like* that one," Pru admitted, surprising me. "An excellent likeness of the Upshaw place. Though I must say I felt it in bad taste, including the *child*." She sat very straight, firmly corsetted. "*That* whole episode would be better forgotten, much less committed to canvas! Scarcely a present for a young boy."

"Poor Mrs. Upshaw," she continued, "losing her husband so suddenly, seeing her son become a criminal, then stuck with the job of raising the result of that *disas*trous union." She tongued her false teeth back against the roof of her mouth with a faint click. My face had begun to burn. "The wages of sin," she said darkly. "As the twig is bent, so grows the tree." Her damp, sad, warning eyes settled on me. "As we sow, so shall we reap—"

"That's not fair, Aunt Pru," my mother broke in. "Who

would blame Cody for running away in the first place? You call her *poor* Mrs. Upshaw. Well, Mrs. Upshaw nearly drove him crazy, binding him hand and foot, never letting him grow up. Of course Cody would take real affection wherever he could find it! It must have been very flattering to. . .to just *feel* something and act on it. Cody failed in the real world because Mrs. Upshaw had kept him a baby all his life!"

"Oh, certainly," Pru said testily, "blame everything on the parents—I believe it's the modern thing to do, isn't it?"

"I *do* blame them," my mother exclaimed heatedly. I was nonplussed by the suddenness of this exchange. It had been so unusual for my mother to disagree with anyone but my father, and that was less vehement than this. But she had changed since Durham came. He said what he thought, he was his own man, and this was what my mother loved and had begun to copy, discovering a measure of freedom in honesty. She faced Pru shining with anger.

"It's unthinkable to blame either Cody or Claire, to pile shame on them! They were simply too young, Aunt Pru, and that's a fact, not a sin. Mrs. Upshaw kept Cody a child, she neutered him, just as she's doing to Shirley. *Her* idea of a boy—*her* idea of a girl!" She stopped to take a deep breath, while Pru stared in shocked disbelief. My mother smoothed her voice, trying again for reason. "Supposing he had not *had* to leave—"

"He did *not*," Pru interrupted stubbornly. "He chose—"

"—suppose he had found it possible to stay, to face his parents honestly, to learn from having some freedom how to use it properly! None of this fearful business would have happened, I'm sure of it! His having to run away was the saddest part of the whole tragic affair. Loving Claire and having the baby still didn't solve his old problems. They just added new ones. They were like three children living together!"

Aunt Pru was so incensed she had stopped eating. I felt as though they had both forgotten I was there.

126

"Georgia, how can you talk such nonsense, such immoral drivel? And you a baptized member of the Christian church!" My mother made a supreme effort to control herself, stuffing her anger down her bosom like a handkerchief.

"I am sure," she went on quietly, "that Cody carried every problem he ever had with his mother right along with him, clear up until the day—"

"—he was *hung*." Pru said it for her, thudding out the last word with a heavy satisfaction that showed me the taut rope, the limp body swaying. Thick silence crept like fog in the room. Late, low sun slanted across the teapot, outlining the gold around the rose design. I felt ill, my own throat stuck with butter-tart syrup. My mother turned to me, knowing it was the first I had heard of this, her eyes rich with sympathy, showing me against her will the corpse beneath the blanket. "It's true, dear. He killed the Appleton girl after a quarrel up in the Dufferin tavern—"

"Over another man," Pru interjected, "as if anyone was surprised."

Obviously, the afternoon had not gone as planned. My mother began to collect the plates. Nothing was left on the server. "Well," she said, "I'm glad that Cody knew *one* warm and affectionate person before he had to die, even if the ending was so tragic. And I like to think he loved his baby, in some way." Aunt Pru viewed her as coldly as her molasses eyes would allow.

"What helter-skelter morality, and in front of your own son! That they could bring a child into this world, not bothering to marry! That you could *defend* them!"

"I didn't say I could *do* it—easily, at any rate. I'm not like Cody, Aunt Pru, and nothing in my upbringing has prepared me for running away. But I've been tempted more than once to take a road without a map, just for the heck of it!" I felt a helpless shiver of fear as she spoke, because I knew that she was thinking of Durham and Vancouver.

Aunt Pru had turned pale violet. She fussed with her skirt, brushing away invisible crumbs, the argument, the afternoon, barely able to contain the indignation she'd feed like a dessert to waiting Uncle Gerald.

"Will you stay for supper?" Sometimes I wondered if my mother's good manners became weapons. "I have a nice shepherd's pie in the oven. . . ." She was bowing back from the unpleasant dance as politely as possible.

"No. No, thank you. Gerald would sit and starve and I'd never hear the end of it." Aunt Pru stood up, stolid, quivering, and laid a suede cheek against my skinny, squint-eyed face. After thanking my mother for the lovely afternoon, she bent with difficulty to put on her boots, tossed the dead fox around her shoulders and left. We watched her short, careful steps until she disappeared from sight. She didn't turn to wave.

"I'm sorry you had to hear all that," my mother said.

"That's okay."

"You had to know about Cody sometime, although Pru's version is pretty one-sided."

"Do you think she'll come again? She looked kinda mad. . . ."

"Yes, she did. But then Pru gets angry easily—I guess we'll just have to wait and see, won't we? If I were you, I wouldn't worry too much about it."

Not about that. Never about that.

I skated for a while after dinner, perfecting a smooth figure-eight in the gnawing cold. No one saw the improvement: Shirley's blind was pulled down, the street deserted. In a sense, Shirley's blighted birthday and the afternoon's chilling revelations had their uses, as a horror movie provides some diversion from problems left back at home. Over the uneven dread I felt about Durham and my mother swept a wish to salvage something. So I printed *Happy Birthday* on a piece of paper, wrapped it around the cane of the singing canary and crept up the driveway to place it by her side door.

17

By the time six or seven weeks of grade eight had rolled by, we had realized that it was no ordinary year. For one thing, friendships had hardened into cliques, and we knew that we could rest, at last, at the top of the heap. No longer at the mercy of teachers whose tricks and tactics we knew so well, we proceeded to put what we had learned to work bullying younger students, who now eyed us with envy and fear.

After so many false forays, this new status brought the real dawn of sex. During September, we had noticed that girls we'd barely tolerated the year before had grown breasts and hips, like a bonus crop, during the warm summer months. With eyebrows newly darkened under HB pencil and Lily-of-the-Valley oiling their earlobes, they clustered in scented groups, trying to flirt. Very soon, we'd learned to get around this by staging mock fights with them, disguising our carefully placed shoves under a blanket of distracting noise.

This was a sexuality that could be measured in decibels, something that most adults never seemed to catch on to because they mistakenly linked sex with their own secret, rustling silences. Still, some of our rampant energy spilled over into the classrooms and hallways, causing a panicky reliance on the strap to put down the signs of defiance.

Pinky was caught and strapped twice in one week, with more added at home by his outraged father for having caused trouble—a loser's game of double or nothing that outraged his sense of justice only for a day.

"All I did was yell 'Hey, STUFF!' at Betty Pibschel," he fumed, sticking puffy palms forward for the usual post-mortem. "Should burn his bloody school down—"

"On Hallowe'en!" interrupted Don White, reddening now at the imaginary fire. "We gotta do something bigger this year." Unaccountably, Pinky nixed the idea, looking perplexed. We'd forgotten that he wouldn't understand shelling out, or any of the other North American intricacies of Hallowe'en. The joys of being able to threaten somebody and come away with candy were quickly explained. His eyes gleamed and narrowed.

"When is it?" he asked.

"Next Tuesday. We'd better make it good, because none of us will be going out next year." The sophistication of high school trembled in the air, with its solemnity of last names, girls called *Miss*, tea dances, and a thousand books to carry home each day on one adult, out-jutting hip. First formers did not shell out.

"Well, let's think of something," Pinky said, making for the furthest corner of the schoolyard.

"How about sticking up Meuller's with licorice guns?" Just last week someone had broken both his windows and scrawled *Nazi* on his door so he was fair game for anything. This was immediately vetoed as too tame.

"We could take off a few gates—"

"—or spy on Wilma Gee's through the back window."

"How about taking all of Mrs. Collins' wash off the line and spreading it over the Upshaw's lawn?" This seemed like a good idea since there was always something hanging on her line, any season of the year: galleon sheets taking the wind, ready to blow her house to Spain; bed pillows like marsh-mallows strung to toast in the sun, and in winter, bloomers and housedresses frozen rigid, like clothes for paper dolls.

Pinky just lounged back against the slat fence looking disgusted. "Baby junk," he said contemptuously. "What we want is something useful. . . ."

"*Useful?*"

"Something that will help us, something really hard to make it more fun, but not so rotten that we'll get hauled off by the cops." Considering the tender state of his hands and the fact that he was the one who had to make weekly confessions, I could see his point.

"Like?" Don demanded, scratching his crotch nervously, darting glances around to see if we were being overheard.

Pinky spoke softly, with spaces between each word so the import would sink into lesser minds. "*Like*—getting the balls back from the old lady." For a moment, neither Don nor I said a word, though we knew exactly what Pinky was suggesting. Go *inside* that spooky house where the old witch lived and take back the balls.

"You gotta be crazy!" Don whispered.

Pinky hitched his trousers like a Celtic Bogart. "Yeah?"

"Well jesus, how'd we know where the bloody things are? All over the goddam house probably!"

"You'll know because *I* know where they are," Pinky said. "I carried out some garbage for the old bag once, when I was collecting. I could see through the back window, right into the kitchen, and that's where they are, piled in a great jeesly carton, and right on top, our football."

"*My* football, you mean."

"Yeah, well, what I'm tellin' you is that they're *all* in one box, dummy. Now, there's a milkbox leads clear into the kitchen. Supposin' one of us keeps her busy at the front of the house—shellin' out—"

"And suppose another acts as lookout," I jumped in, "so I can get into the kitchen and pass the balls out to the lookout! If we time the whole thing, plan it out right, we can take off with the balls and she won't even know!"

Don shuddered, slack-mouthed. "What if she finds out who we are, though?"

"Masks, you screwball, Hallowe'en masks!" crowed Pinky.

"Genius!" I whacked Pinky on the back. "It's genius!"

"Whad I tell yuh?" he grinned.

"Ya, but you don't want cops, you said," protested Don, "and that's stealing." At this, Pinky exploded quietly, like a bomb going off underground.

"*Who* the hell stole them in the first place I'd like to know? It's like—" he rooted around for a handy hero to make his point "—like Robin Hood, the English bastard who gave back to the poor. *We're* the poor, okay?"

"And if you're too damned scared to go through with it," I added, "you'd better say so right now!"

"You kidding?" Don's voice strutted, "I'll be the lookout."

In his relentless circling of the yard, we saw Randall turning our way, his lean, mechanical strides keeping time to the bell clapper tapping in his hand.

"What are you boys up to?" He stopped, and the clapper stopped, too. He had strapped Pinky the last time—witnessed by Miss Nicol and the principal—and he was strapping him again now with leathery brown eyes.

All of Pinky's imagination must have been poured into the Hallowe'en plans, because he seemed suddenly tongue-tied, staring dumbly in the vicinity of Randall's belly button.

"Testing each other on the early Canadian explorers, sir," I said quickly.

"Cartier, Champlain—" Pinky recovered, confidently back on familiar territory.

"—and Pizzaro!" Don blurted. Pinky looked incredulous, while I scrabbled around in my head to put the proper place to the name. But it was recess, and we were literally saved by the bell. Miss Nicol jangled the first warning which snapped Mr. Randall into an automatic response. Up went his arm, down crashed his bell, and at once the air hung with aborted laughter and stifled squeals. As far as we could see, the restless bodies had become statues, waiting with breath suspended for the second bell to release them.

Above the silent yard a gull, coming inland ahead of rough weather, dipped and cried. Randall stood like a planted post, only his eyes roving over the field to catch an offender. I have often wondered what would have happened if the second bell had not rung out. Would we all still be there?

Properly, perfectly, October thirty-first dawned. No sun burned through a sky mildewed with grey clouds. By noon, a ghost wind had gathered to shrill around the school, fingering windows and spinning dry leaves into rasping funnels across the deserted yard. Through recess and walks home we repeated our plans again and again, trying to beat down fear with slick organization. I would enter the Upshaw house through the milkbox. Don was to be lookout and receiver of the balls, a responsibility so easy he couldn't screw it up. We would supply him with a pillowcase to hold the balls as I passed them out. Originally Pinky wanted to be the one to go up to the front door, but we discarded that as too risky, even if he was masked, because his accent was well known to Mrs. Upshaw. Instead, we shamelessly commandeered the newest boy on the block, using his eagerness to be accepted as bait. He was believable, too: who else would be innocent or dumb enough to try to get a shell-out at the Upshaw place?

When I came down around eight o'clock that night, my mother surveyed my shabby tramp's outfit. "What are you supposed to be, anyway?" she asked, dropping a piece of homemade fudge into my shopping bag.

"Nothing, I guess. I don't know—nobody tries to *be* anything. You just go out and get stuff."

"While the getting's good?" my dad called through the hall door.

"Yeah."

He put down his paper to look at me, his glasses low on his nose. "Going as Charlie Chaplin?"

"Guess that's as good as anything," I agreed.

"This will be your last year for this, I suppose. Oh, by the way, did your mother tell you I've moved to a new department?" He took off his glasses and assumed a grave, deciding look, giving the impression that the whole move had been his own idea. "Men's ready-to-wear," he said proudly, reaching to brush off my old tramp's jacket as though he were still at work.

"That's great."

"Well, I liked silverware better," he admitted, settling back into the chesterfield. "You meet a better class of people, people with some taste. But it's too quiet now, because of the war."

I spent the next few minutes going back and forth to the bathroom. By the time Don and Pinky called nervousness had dried my mouth and bladder.

Because we wanted to carry out our raid as late as possible, reducing the number of witnesses and amount of light, we first toured a few streets for shell-outs, picking up several apples, one marshmallow-broom each and a lot of putty-coloured candy kisses. The new boy came with us, his voice piping pleasure behind a chalk-white clown's mask, and we pointed out neighbourhood idiosyncrasies as we trudged along, boasting and blustering to show our advantage over him. Flattered by all the attention, he hung on every stupid word we uttered, and I quickly tired of his annoying habit of nodding agreement before a sentence was finished. But we needed him tonight, and Pinky had told me he had hands like flypaper—"and we could sure use a good outfielder."

"We'd better head back now," Pinky ordered. A black wool toque pulled down over his ears hid the copper hair that would give him away even on this inky night. Don, Pinky and I had applied cork to the lower part of our faces, something Pinky's father had told him about. "The IRA do it," he told us, as if everybody should know what that meant. Covering our upper faces were black bandit masks held on painfully by looped elastics around our ears. They gave us a slightly jug-eared look, so no one, not our own mothers, we believed, would know who we were now. The

134

clown worried us at first—he stuck out like a traffic light. But while we were shelling-out we had counted at least ten other costumes exactly the same.

After an hour, the streets were empty. Porch lights went out, one by one, with only a couple of houses still displaying swollen orange pumpkins in a window to announce a few candies still left. Small children had disappeared entirely, lugged home by an adult arm to count the goodies. As we made our way back, a sheeted ghost floated whitely around a corner toting an Exhibition bag with MINARD'S LINI-MENT, KING OF PAIN printed on it. The wind was fitful, billowing out the new boy's clown legs, eerily creaking Wilma's gate back and forth, swaying skeletal tree limbs. Above us, the black sky glowered with clouds moving too swiftly to drop rain. We walked silently, covertly, too tense for small talk. To me, the familiar street, the landmarks so taken for granted, were suddenly sinister. All the houses looked haunted. At last we stood before the Upshaw place.

"Well?" said Pinky, propping his gloved hands on his hips, "all ready, are we?" I nodded, but felt as though someone had run rope through my arms and legs. Don couldn't stop spitting. "And *remember*," Pinky's accent was thickening again, "if anything goes wrong, we just follow Plan Two."

For the life of me, I couldn't recall Plan One. The new boy giggled hollowly behind the cardboard.

"Let's go then!"

Errol Flynn would have howled at our clumsiness, but it was the memory of his daring that kept me going up the driveway in what must have been the noisiest creeping anyone had ever done. I could hear Don behind me, sud-denly all conscience, whispering legal warnings—"Christ, it's breaking and entering! D'yuh know we could go to *reform* school for this?"

Creeping gravel-dinted past the curtained side door where Shirley came out each morning, where I'd put the singing canary on her birthday, around the enclosed porch, on to stiff dead grass now, safer, quieter. "It's *stealing*, too," Don was husking away. I found the white square, showing dimly through the darkness. God, it was black! "—stealing could get us two years—"

"Open the bloody milk box!" I hissed. "Were you counting?"

"I forgot—" We didn't want to risk a whistle, so Don, and Pinky out front, were supposed to count to a hundred before sending the clown up to the door.

"You *stupid* bastard—" I began, when I heard the new boy's fist banging loudly on the front door. "Hoist me up—wait a minute, there's an empty bottle." Feeling past it gingerly, I tested the inside door. It gave lightly against my fingertips. I thrust the bottle at Don. "Drop that and we're dead! We'll put it back after. Now get the goddam pillowcase ready and *stay right here!*" I skinnied my shoulders, snaking through the opening, petrified. When my head emerged inside, I found myself over a counter by the sink in a dark, turnipy, empty kitchen. I hesitated, listened, hearing my own heart banging away at the V below my throat. Pinky had guessed Mrs. Upshaw would stay at the front of the house on Hallowe'en, watching out for trouble, and he was right. I could detect the slipper-scuffling sound of the old woman, muttering, worrying behind the curtains in the living room.

I squinted into the shadows. Right where he'd said it would be—a square cardboard carton packed with balls of all sizes, like some toy clearance display downtown. I folded myself carefully onto the counter top, praying I wouldn't tip an unseen jug or tray, and let myself down gently to the floor. (More insistent pounding on the front door, "Shell-out! Shell-out!") The box, with Don's football perched on top like a brown egg, sat between the kitchen and what would be the dining room beyond the oak archway. I tiptoed to it, found I could lift it. ("Shell-out," and the flat click of a lock sliding, a chain clinking at the front door.) Beating down a panicky urge to run, to hurry, to get out, I carried the box to the counter, opened the milk box and began pushing the

136

balls through one by one into Don's gloved hands. He dropped the first one, softly cursing, but had the sense to hold the pillowcase closer to the opening, and the rest were easy. ("I don't shell-out—I'm too old for that now. Are you new here?" The old woman's voice, greasy with forced good-will.)

I tossed through the last ball—*keep her there, you stupid bugger! Tell her where you live!*—and replaced the box, quivering with fear. Outside, I heard Pinky's second diversion, planned to give me more time if I needed it. Disguising his accent, he was running up and down the lawn shrieking nonsense, drawing her attention and finally her rage. I heard her voice further off, out on the porch flinging threats at him.

By the one lamp burning in the living room beyond, I could see well enough to know that the downstairs rooms were vacant: if Shirley had been out, which I doubted, she would be back and in bed now. Something pulled me further toward the living room, the knowledge that I had time, that I would never be here again, that Shirley walked where I was walking and sat sometimes maybe over there—I poked my head cautiously for a better look. In my haste I saw the room in brief, sharp detail: miniature glass, ivory antimacassar, the bulging plaster face of Victoria with her coronet and a bun beneath it. Plum-papered walls, overweight furniture with menacing claw feet. Pictures everywhere, dozens of them, concealing table tops, cluttering the bay window, propped on the mantel, strung on plate shelves rimming the stucco ceiling.

But one picture on a wall facing me stuck out in this dark, baroque museum-room—and it filled me with horror. Under glass and framed in plain black were neatly arranged clippings from the Toronto papers; a big photo of a man handcuffed between two policemen, dipping his head down to hide from the popping flash bulbs, the Albert Street arch of City Hall above him. Around this, smaller photos and headlines, vivid through the amber lamp-light:

137

MURDER SUSPECT ARRESTED AT NOON
Brawl Over Girlfriend Ends In Murder!

COURT CRAMMED FOR UPSHAW TRIAL

JURY UNANIMOUS—UPSHAW TO HANG
Prosecutor Praises Verdict

1 A.M.—THE MORBID DEATH-WATCH

I turned away from that awful gallery of failure, running as fast as I could into the kitchen. Almost diving through the milkbox, I bruised a knee badly in my haste and scraped my stomach getting to the ground.

Before me was Don, jumping silently, gleefully, shaking the lumpy pillowcase in a triumphant mime of joy.

In the accounting that followed, there remained only one ball whose owner we could not identify. I knew it was Shirley's, the rubber one she had bounced out front months ago. Since nobody else cared, I kept it.

"Holy father, didja see her?" Pinky demanded, his face as concerned as burnt-cork creases would allow.

"No."

"Christ, are you *sure*?"

"Well, what the hell do you think? Wouldn't I know, you jerk?" We were all beginning to talk like Don White. I finally convinced them, and we broke up, full of self-congratulations, declaring it the best Hallowe'en we'd ever had. But going up the stairs of my porch I felt enormous outrage, knowing now that Shirley was confronted every day of her life with the catalogued and public history of her parents' tragedy.

"Well, then, how did it go?" My father, slippers on and a mug of tepid beer in his hand, was full of vicarious good cheer.

"Going to share that with us?" grinned Durham. "My God, but you look strange in that outfit!"

"I'm Charlie Chaplin," I said.

138

I'd eaten all the good stuff, marshmallow brooms and peanuts and the one chocolate bar handed out somewhere on Bracondale. But I turned the bag upside down on a spread newspaper, preparing to share the remains, and Shirley's ball rolled on to the rug.

"Can't eat that," Durham protested, peeling paper from a molasses candy. "What rotter gave that out?"

"Found it," I said, which seemed to satisfy everyone.

"Hallowe'en," my mother mused, 'it's always so much fun."

18

"Now then, White, would you read the next stanza, please?"

Don moaned lightly, pulling gangling, uncoordinated arms and legs upright from the ochre seat with a sigh of resignation. "The Ancient Mariner" was about as far removed from his life as a punt is from a square-rigger.

"Be-yawned the shadow of the shi-pie watched the wadder snakes:
They move-din tracks of shinin' whi-tand when they reared the oafish light
Fel-loff in hoary flakes."

"Thanks. You may sit down." Critchley-Williams shoved his thick glasses back up the thin bridge of this nose with a forefinger. "It isn't *meant* to be rushed, you know. By the way, the word is *elfish*, not oafish, there being in fact a world of difference between the two. Anyone besides Coleridge know what that difference is? Yes? Ann Kirkpatrick?" Up popped Ann in her middy blouse and navy skirt, flopping heavy braids. Her bright, tinny voice stuttered through the definitions.

"Nicely done, Ann. Yesterday, you may recall, we talked of the poet's use of the word elfish instead of the more familiar elfin." He scrawled the two words swiftly on the

140

blackboard. As he wrote, his suit jacket lifted to reveal wide suspenders like a bridge spanning across his back. "I believe the bell rang before I got finished, so let's try to discover together why Coleridge chose the unusual description." Out in the hall Miss Nicol was berating someone for stopping to drink at the fountain before entering class: *You can do that at recess! Five hundred lines and no recess for two days!*

"Both words pertain to elves, but I find *elfish* the stronger, clearer description. We are made to *see* the light, aren't we, prancing like elves themselves!" He smiled around at our numb faces, then sat down on an empty desk near the window. "Poets, you see, paint for us. They colour a picture with words that may seem to be a difficult puzzle at first. But when we finally understand the shades of meaning, we can see and taste, feel, hear and think as we never have before. . . ." He paused to dream out the window, tapping the piece of chalk absently against his teeth. Without his teaching face, his bony, freckled profile softened to the wise, rural look of a man used to gazing out from hilltops.

Until we came to know him, all of us took these lapses to be traps, and for good reason. Other teachers had used the device of soft voice and unexpected silence to find out who was paying attention. Suddenly there'd be the rifle crack of a ruler, the triumphantly slammed book, then a pointed finger and the demand for an answer. Critchley-Williams' silences, on the other hand, were inevitably followed by a soliloquy on something he loved: an anecdote from his past; a bit of poetry he'd pasture on, hoping, I suppose, that we'd join him. Most of us were grateful for the breathing space that took us with him on a side trip away from the worn road of prescribed curriculum.

"—frequently hear that poetry is sissy stuff, a lot of unrelated words written by crazy people for other crazy people—"

As I watched him, I began to ease into that peculiar state of reverie that fuses reality with visions of the mind. My eyes

141

widened and lost perspective: there seemed to be two Critchley-Williamses, amber imprints against the backdrop of the cloud-filled window.

"—need to get used to the idea of love, which poetry can open us to as no other art form can. Have you ever noticed how easy it is to yell 'I hate you,' when you're angry? But I'll bet none of you would yell 'I love you,' even if you were paid to do it. Well, poets do these things for us. . . ."

Shirley slipped before my eyes, free of her house and her shuddery past and of the old woman who leaned on her like a human cane. Her arms were stretched wide, she was laughing with impatience for me to throw her the ball. And as it flew without effort from my hands, the stripes blurred in a kaleidoscope of colour, noiselessly marbling the space between us, to be caught easily in her hands. *Now you!* And in the daydream, I followed the ball and flung myself like down against her, my face in her blowing cream hair, my hands on her firm clean arms; through the warm skin I felt muscle, surprisingly strong, and the long hard bones above her wrist. *You are real! As real as I am.*

"Gillies?" I had not heard the noon bell. While I remained propped on an elbow. Critchley-Williams regarded me quizzically. The last pupil was shuffling from the room. For a moment I only stared back at the teacher, an equal because somehow I had understood what he had been saying. Then my youth settled back on me like a caul, making me jerk upright and forcing blood to my face in a furious blush.

"Well," sighed Critchley-Williams, searching his desk drawers for his brown bag of lunch, "at least I know that I have one pupil with some sensitivity. Perhaps you'll be a poet, Gillies. . . ."

With textbook photos of rose-lipped men in what I thought were white blouses floating at me, his suggestion struck me as almost frightening.

"I don't exactly know. . .I'd rather be a pilot, or maybe a dentist—"

His thick eyebrows bristled upwards and he smiled, finding the lunch bag and peering happily into it as though there might be a prize at the bottom, like crackerjack. "Really? I can understand wanting to fly, but a dentist? Difficult profession, mucking about in all that filth and foulness." He glanced up to see if I'd realized that he was kidding me. "Just don't lose that nice mixture of heart and head, will you? Be a poetic dentist, Gillies. Believe me, it'll be a welcome change. . . ."

He talked to me as we went down the echoing hallway, musing on the importance of matching personalities with jobs, until he reached the stairs leading to the men's lunchroom. "I should think, for instance, that a person choosing dentistry would be wise to have a happy personal life— he'd see enough misery in his work. *And* he'd need a hobby, preferably a sport, to offset all that standing around. Well, all that's ahead of you, Gillies. Lucky man."

And he was off down the stairs with his stiff wooden leg rapping out a swift, syncopated rhythm. Going much too fast, because he liked to prove himself as physically adept as anyone with two legs. But on that noon hour, demolishing my bologna sandwiches, all that remained with me was the reality of Shirley Upshaw, and the fact that Critchley-Williams had, in an ordinary, friendly way, called me "man."

I'd called on Pinky early the following Saturday so we'd have time to get our candy at Stein's Variety and be near the front of the long afternoon lineup that formed at the Christie theatre. There was no side entrance to his house. Two dinted garbage cans and a badly-tilting baby carriage were parked by the front porch. I'd been inside before, but rarely past the hall, so I could only guess at the cause of the unending clamour. Doors were continually slamming behind one of the ten children, all of whom looked so much alike that they resembled a series of time exposures when they were together in a group. Pans clattered in the hidden kitchen, and smoke from frying kippers mingled with steam from something soaking in the sink. Someone always seemed to be running hard up and down the stairs, yelling in a harsh twang at someone else out of sight.

I hammered on the front door, prepared for a long wait in the cold rain because the sound would have to penetrate the commotion within. A young Yorke wailed angrily in the distance, and Mrs. Yorke's high, plaintive voice, growing nearer, keened, "Maureen, give Daniel a cookie and tell him not *yet*!" The door jerked open and Pinky's mother took a quick step backwards.

"Oh! Keith, isn't it?" I nodded, wondering why she didn't know after all this time. "Step inside, then, on the paper there. . . ." It was hard to associate her with all those big, rosy children, for she was no taller than I and had no visible fat or colour. A slight woman whose hands flew to her hair, or chin, or to the tiny permanent earrings in nervous inventory, she had about her the fading beige anonymity of a tintype found in an attic. "You'll be after Eric?" And without waiting, she turned to the stairs and bawled "ERIC!" just once. A sound of splintering china came from the kitchen. "That child. . ." muttered Mrs. Yorke, and promptly disappeared behind the door where an argument had begun in hissing whispers.

"Be down in a minute," hollered Pinky, and a door slammed shut behind him.

I shuffled from one foot to the other, trying to stay on the paper. At the head of the stairs, a doleful Christ was strung languidly on a black cross. The gilt had chipped off his halo. Around the living room door came Mary Yorke, gnawing on an apple.

"That's Jesus," she declared juicily, adding with her usual condescension, "*you* people don't have him in your houses, do you?" I narrowed my eyes in the direction of what had become her family's exclusive saviour.

"Well, not exactly like that," I replied, hoping to give the impression that her slumped and gaudy version was hopelessly behind the times. "My Aunt Thea has a picture of

Jesus with sheep all over the place." I didn't bother to add that Thea would hang up anything with animals in it.

"My Pa says the British like pictures of royalty." She punctuated the sentence with another sharp snap at the apple.

I'd seen Mr. Yorke once, straddling a kitchen chair, his chest so wide it made his checked shirt look like a table cloth, a mass of black curls over his head, his throat, the back of his mammoth hands, even spewing out of his ears as though it grew inside his head, too, and had begun to escape. Pinky had told me that when he got drunk, not regularly but fearfully, they all lit for their rooms to wait out the storm except his wife, who let him bang his fists and bluster out his self-pity and homesickness while she said her beads in a dark corner of the dining room.

"Your people are British," Mary persisted.

"I'm Canadian," I insisted, wishing she'd get the hell out of there and glancing impatiently up the stairs to show her I had come for other reasons.

"Did you see them when they came over last spring? The King and the Queen?"

"Yeah. Outside the hospital on Christie. He didn't look real."

"What about her?"

"She looked okay. She was waving right my way. . . ."

"I mean, what was she wearin'?"

"*I* don't know! One of those big hats and something furry. You sure are interested for someone who doesn't care about royalty."

"We weren't allowed to go," she said, looking me square in the eye. "My Pa says they're going to get the shit beat out of them—the British. The Germans are sure to win, he says."

"Yeah? Tell Pinky to get a move on, will you?"

She ignored me and concentrated on picking peel from her front teeth. A look of sly watchfulness crept into her eyes. "Oh, and by the way, speakin' of *queens*, guess who's been put on to Senior Fourth, bein' so damned smart an' all?" She leaned against the door, smug now with message-carrying.

I shrugged. "Search me—"

"Shirley Upshaw is who. Little Miss Perfect. Not that it'll change things much, with that daft granny of hers to live with. Both of them are goin' to waste away and die in that house, you know. They'll find their skeletons bleached all white and propped up in bed covered in cobwebs, like the horror movies. D'yuh know she can't even go off her porch now? Wasn't allowed to shell out, a great jeesly girl like that?" She was staring at me steadily, her white teeth smashing into the apple's red skin.

"It's not her fault," I said as smoothly as I could. "Call Pinky, will you?" She bellowed his name just as her mother had, the same strident tone, the tilt up at the end, and turned back, complacently nibbling the core.

"Do you like her better than me?" she asked flatly. Upstairs, I heard a toilet flush.

"Who?"

"*You* know who."

I stared down at my buckled overshoes, which were dripping water on the newspapers. "How should I know?" I was caught offguard. Christ, what if somebody overheard her talking like this? "I haven't thought about it. I don't know—"

"May-ree—" A shout from the kitchen. "Put Sean on the pot—"

A toddler blubbered through the hall dressed in a flannel shirt and socks, no shoes or underpants. "Poo-poo," he wailed, "Sean poo-poo—"

Mary's eyes rolled up in disgust as she took the child's hand. "Come on then, and don't you do it before we get there or Mary'll knock your brains out—"

"Anybody know what class she's going into?" I said to her back as she started up the stairs. But she was angry, and wouldn't turn around.

"That's for you to find out, isn't it?"

19

For once I was almost impatient to get back to school, and throughout the weekend the thought that Shirley might be in my class helped me to forget the fears about Durham and my mother that I carried like stones in a pocket. But after a couple of routine days back in the classroom, I was beginning to think that Mary's information was just the usual wrong rumor.

We had just finished our morning period of Current Events when Critchley-Williams spoke to me.

"Gillies, would you distribute these for me, please? Class, this is not a test, so don't work yourselves into a frenzy. In fact it's not any part of your senior fourth curriculum—" A corporate sigh of relief rippled across the room "—just a small map of Toronto on which you will mark major roads—highways, you call them—tram and bus routes—" The telephone by the door jangled and he swung toward it with a tic of annoyance around his mouth. "Hullo, hullo? Critchley-Williams here? Yes. Yes. No, that's quite fine—" He continued as if he'd not been interrupted, sailing along on his splintered sentence. "—as a special individual project you may work on both here and at home."

A few hands waved in the air. "Can we use colours?"

"All the colours of a char-à-banc. Anyone remember what that is?"

"Bloody frog word," Pinky whispered to me, but rose smoothly: "Yes sir. An English excursion bus painted in bright colours."

"Good lad. Yes, May?"

"Do we have to fill in the colours all in one direction? That's what Miss Fellowman makes us do." He allowed himself a smile and bit his lip. "Well," he said mildly, "some people *think* all in one direction, don't they? Do it in whatever way is best for you. Try to make it neat enough to be legible. . . ."

I was rounding the desk nearest the door when there was a faint rap. May jumped to answer it, monitor-of-the-month, smelling of naptha as she brushed past me.

"Ah, the new pupil?" smiled Critchley-Williams. And as I put the leftover maps on his desk, he came in with Shirley Upshaw, introduced her quietly and assigned her a seat two aisles away from me.

"Perhaps you'd give Shirley a map, too, Gillies."

I heard Don White snicker as I walked over to her desk, my face red as fire, damning my nonchalance. For a moment, she and I shared the concentration of the whole class's attention. But she was used to it. She didn't blush or look up at me, but sat primly staring at the inkpot. Gladly I deserted her to sink back into my seat, relieved to become just another observer of the new curiosity.

One part of me wanted to rise above the rest of the class, to be so visible and heroic that I'd be the only one worth her attention. But stronger loyalties bonded me to the group, and I had to remain firmly allied with them until, somehow, it would be natural for me to let her know how glad I was that she was there. What I wanted to happen so much, a normal everyday closeness, was going to take a lot of adjustment on my part.

"Spelling bee!" sang out Critchley-Williams, pinging the words out as though he was tossing us candies or coins. He wanted volunteers to captain, and simultaneously Pinky and I shot up sweatered arms.

"Pick your teams, then. Yorke has first choice this time."

"Ann Kirkpatrick," called Pinky, smirking with satisfaction at having cornered the browner. I glanced over to Shirley Upshaw. In the few days she had been in our class I had noticed that it was her trick to remove herself from us by posture, by controlling her expression. None of Ann's self-importance or Don White's mugging. She sat upright, the looping curls framing a still, porcelain face, an elusive china doll with clear dead eyes who waited in festive shop windows to be bought.

I wasn't ready yet to risk the obvious. "Robert Tunney," I said, knowing that he always knew which came first, the *i* or the *e*.

"Betty Pibschel." Pinky's shrewd combining of brain and emotion. Though it was true he had a consuming crush on her and had been strapped for showing it in the schoolyard, he still wouldn't have picked her if she'd lose him the game.

I hesitated, scanning the rows. One more, then I'd get her. "May McKay," I said. Not as good a speller as Ann Kirkpatrick, but monitors didn't rattle easily. May flicked me a congratulatory smile and rustled confidently to my side of the room.

"Two more each," Critchley-Williams said pleasantly. I was watching Shirley boldly now, hoping she'd look my way. I would choose her next, not last, in case she interpreted it as pity. Then, if Pinky didn't get him, I'd land Wally Morgan. Despite the white shirt and tie and sucking up to teachers, he could spell—

"Shirley Upshaw," said Pinky.

"Miss Pretty-pants," hissed May, "good riddance!" But I was staring dumbfounded as Shirley slid with surprised dismay out of her seat and moved towards Pinky's team, standing slightly apart from the others. *Dirty traitor!* I wanted to split his orange Irish head, cave in his grinning teeth. I finished my choices in a wash of indifference, glaring hatred at Pinky across the room.

"Righto," said Critchley-Williams. "Let's go over the rules."

While the teacher was stressing the necessity for friendly fairness in competition, I contemplated jamming the bloody spelling bee down Pinky's sly and thieving throat. His motives bothered me less than the fact that he'd removed my chance to choose her, to let her know that I wanted to have her.

"Then let's begin with you, Gillies. *Aggravate*." I took it slowly, grouping the syllables with care.

"Now, Yorke? *Symbolize*." Pinky rattled it off, grinning down at the fearful, worshipping face of Don White. Two rounds went by without mistakes, until May McKay left an *r* out of *blurring*, and Ann Kirkpatrick corrected it. We were one less. Then, in rapid succession, Pinky lost Betty Pibschel with *torpor* and another member who mistook *irrigate* for *irritate*. Overconfident, Robert Tunney tripped over *prism*, and I watched Shirley Upshaw, her lips twitching in self-consciousness, spell it properly. By now, both teams were keyed up and careless, and after another round, Pinky and Shirley had only me for opposition. The three of us got through *perusal, deceive* and *enigma*.

"Yorke," said Critchley-Williams, "try *parliamentary*."

I saw Pinky's face go slightly lax, his eyes widen and glass over. *Where's your goddam photographic memory now?* Shirley glanced up swiftly, then away.

"Time's nearly up," said the teacher. "Are you passing?"

Pinky opted for bravado. "P-A-R," a moment's hesitation, "L-A-M-E-N-T-A-R-Y." Ann groaned. Everyone was watching Critchley-Williams.

"Sorry, Yorke. Gillies?" I remembered Pinky's halt, his flat *lam*. Nerves and an Irish brogue had made him omit what I'd heard said with punctilious respect for detail over our dining room table: "When Chamberlain goes before the par-lee-ament." And with that planted in my head, I shot

150

Pinky down. Now, across the sea of faces I saw Shirley Upshaw outlined against the blackboard, miserably alone, staring back at me.

"We've only got two minutes 'til the bell." Critchley-Williams dove into his box of folded scraps. "One word each, as fast as you can—Gillies, yours is *Hallowe'en*."

In the passage of a second or two I imagined with irrational terror that someone had told, that the word had been planted by some vengeful god to diminish me in her eyes. I might have seen the word a thousand times, but now I struggled to remember its shape. Is there an apostrophe? Where is the apostrophe?

I floundered stupidly into it, forgetting the capital, dropping in the apostrophe with blind abandon: "H-A-L-L-O-W-apostrophe-E-E-N."

"Sorry—Shirley?" What went through her head as all faces swung her way, pinning her with eyes that held a mixture of disdain and curiosity, I don't know. Critchley-Williams had to lean forward to catch the whispered words— I barely heard her. Somehow, she got through it, capital, apostrophe, everything. Pinky's retired team roared delight and the girls of the class, suddenly claiming her win as a triumph of their sex, clapped for her. She sat down, red in the face, distraught with exposure, like an exhausted rabbit finally free of the hounds.

During afternoon recess I waited through the good-natured insults of my friends, edging with them closer to the girls, looking for my chance. Things had loosened up nicely since Randall had been away, stricken with a cold we fervently prayed would develop into fatal pneumonia. Since Powell was on yard duty in his place, and was inexplicably striking up a conversation with Miss Fellowman, we obliterated the boundaries between girls and boys. Pinky had wrestled Betty Pibschel against the fence, whipped off her hat and taunted her into chasing him.

I began to jog slowly down one side of the board fence past

Shirley Upshaw, who was standing awkwardly with Ann Kirkpatrick, also lonely because she bore the stigma of brilliance and could never make ordinary conversation. Ann never got less than ninety on tests, and she stuttered.

"H-Hi, Keith. H-how-c-c-c-ould you miss th-that word?" Ann's apologetic, hoping eyes did not match the tactless academic tone.

"May McKay was looking for you," I told her blandly. "She's down there, by the stairs."

"P-probably wants m-m-my notebook. . . ." She marched off with her peculiar measured walk.

"I didn't want her to stay," I said to Shirley. "I'm glad you won today." The words sounded hollow and false. My heart was thudding and I could not stay still. Turning from side to side, my head felt like one of those sideshow dummies that move mechanically and repeat a recorded patter.

"It wasn't a hard word," I bumbled on, "just tricky. . . ." With immense effort, I stopped my head in mid-swing and looked right at her. It surprised me that her eyes did not shift or drop as they did in class, but appraised me almost coolly. Precaution, mistrust, I couldn't tell what else lay within that look. The natural curve of her lips was drawn straight in bitterness or forbearance.

"Well, anyway—" I dug into my pocket and held the striped ball toward her "—I found this in the gutter a while ago under the snow. I thought it was yours."

She stared at it with a small rise of her eyebrows. "In the gutter?"

"Yeah. Guess the snow'd covered it."

"Thank you."

"Not much good to you in the winter, I guess, but at least you've got it back."

One corner of her mouth tilted upward, the first time I'd seen her smile since she'd patted Hughie's old bull dog. "Not much good to me in the summer, either. But thanks, anyway."

Heady with even this small success, I ploughed on. "Do

you ever go to the show, on Saturdays, I mean? Or could I maybe walk you home?"

Her face went flat and tight with anger. "Are you saying that to tease me?"

"No."

"Then why are you asking? Don't you know?" I stared miserably down the field where Pinky had a half-nelson on Betty Pibschel.

"I guess I forgot. That's all. I forgot. She isn't at the school gate anymore and I thought maybe, you being in Senior Fourth—I don't know. . . ."

Her voice dropped. "She's afraid of the ice, of falling. She's old."

The first bell rang.

"We could still walk together, as far as Greensides. She wouldn't know. We can talk at recess." I felt intelligent, glowing, infallible.

"But she hates boys. She hates you. I don't know why. She even hates the canary you gave me—"

Recklessly, hearing the second bell, I persisted, "I don't care. If she breaks it, I can get you another one for a dime at Sunnyside. She can't go on hating canaries forever." She didn't laugh, but I understood. It took practice. It took time.

"Quickly quickly *quickly!*" snapped Miss Fellowman.

"Get a move on there," called Powell, his webby, wind-reddened eyes roving without interest over the slow ones.

"I'm going to ask again," I said to Shirley, but surrounded now with the others, her face became blank, remote. It didn't matter. Even with that, I recognized that we'd both detected the thread of hope.

Ironically, all this high excitement beyond my own door couldn't be transmitted to my family. With them I became secretive, mumbling a terse "Yes" or "No" to dinnertime questions. It was a way of striking back at Durham and my mother: if they could have secrets, so could I, and if they were worried about me, that was fine. While they dissected the bad news from abroad, alarmed at the growing number of British boats being sunk, I sailed off alone to devise plans for saving Shirley. When my mother mentioned rationing, and Doug his hockey team, I'd be thinking of ways to eventually break through Shirley's frustrating reserve. Sometimes I wondered if this preoccupation showed on my face, like a telltale birthmark.

In a way, I was lucky that Pinky was simultaneously preoccupied because it spared me his taunts. After all, normal, busty and cooperative Betty Pibschel presented no problems for him. Whole-heartedly she took his blatantly frontal attacks, giving as good as she got and correctly interpreting his physical assults as love. But habitual restriction had made Shirley Upshaw practically immobile beyond the classroom. She still had to endure the baby-wave of her shawled, watching grandmother as she left the house for school. So it was up to me to approach her, though she never made it easy for me when I tried.

Seeing her ahead of me on the way to school one day, I ran to catch up, but when I reached her she glanced over her shoulder, eyes wide with fear.

"Someone might tell her. . . ."

"Nobody'd do that," I replied. "She doesn't talk to kids. Can't you go out after school at all, ever?"

"No. She gives me ten minutes to get home, that's all."

"What about Saturdays? Could you get out then? Some of us skate at Strathcona, up on Christie, or go to a movie. Wouldn't she let you do that?" It was a relief, a kind of rejoicing in my own candour which she did not share. She stepped up her pace, not answering.

"You could go out and get groceries for her, or something. Just tell her it took longer. Maybe not a matinee, but we could skate for a little while. . . ."

"I can't skate."

"I'd teach you. It's easy. . . ." She looked at me then with something close to gratitude, but shook her head.

154

"I can't. You just don't know. I don't like talking about her."

"Neither do I," I admitted, "but it's like she's with you all the time. That's what you're letting her do." She didn't answer. I could sense the resistance between us, the way it sometimes felt before a summer storm when the air thickened, becoming electric and heavy. Whatever it was about our separate worlds—the conditions she lived in that I knew and understood—the knowledge seemed to get in my way rather than close the distance.

I waved a hand around me, trying to make her laugh. "D'you see her here, now? Is she hiding behind that tree, eh? Or disguised as Don White maybe?"

She whirled on me then, white-faced.

"Don't talk to me like that! How do you know what it's like? Just leave me alone! Nobody leaves me alone!"

She ran ahead, leaving me to trudge the rest of the way to school by myself.

At recess, when I tried to talk to her, she turned away and walked over to Ann Kirkpatrick, who was reading her history text with the same absorption most of us reserved for Terry and the Pirates. I was brimming with hurt and a touch of pure cruelty. *Just what you deserve—someone else nobody can talk to.*

"Hey, Jackson!" I bellowed, "I'll race you around the field."

"What the hell for?" He lumbered over to me.

"Because I feel like it, and I can beat you."

We used somebody's limp, lost mitt as the starting point, and plunged on Dick's GO!, ripping through the light, melting snow the length of the yard, around the shed by the hockey rink, across the oak-treed limit where the identical, jagged peaks of houses rose above the eight-foot board fence. Dick's powerful legs pushed him slightly past me on the turn, and he gained a couple of yards. I kept the distance evenly, gulping air and feeling a sting of pain in my nostrils. I could not feel my legs, or the icy slop filling my shoes. As we swung into the last twenty-five yards, I heard Jackson's rasp and knew that he was going flat out. I sprinted with everything in me, caught up, flung myself on purely vindictive willpower past his thudding body, and won by a couple of feet.

My pant legs were soaked, my feet ached, I could have gulped snow just from thirst. Like all people who watched and rarely acted, Shirley and Ann were staring at me with critical indecision. I stood panting heavily, hands on my hips, shaking out my calf muscles the way I'd seen professionals do it, dipping my head in personal indifference, as though I was capable of better things.

"T-t-too bad you c-c-an't spell that well," Ann said.

Shirley turned her back and said nothing.

20

In the dingy, shrinking days of November I felt as if I was tumbling helplessly on the sharp points of confused emotions. I would wake suddenly from a nightmare about shut doors in a maze of black hallways to find my own room just as forbidding, its atmosphere thick, closing around me like a grey, pulpy shroud. I resented Durham so deeply that I could barely be civil to him, and Shirley's rejection added daily thuds of depression. Even when Critchley-Williams had her tack up a newspaper clipping about London's barrage balloons and her anguish at being before the class made her whole body shake, I was only aware of my own hurt.

Eventually these sour silences were noticed by my mother, but she misinterpreted their cause. "Are you coming down with something?" she demanded, then recounted the chances against it like a maternal metronome.

"I thought you were getting enough sleep. Maybe ten o'clock is too late. . . ." She plunked potatoes on the kitchen counter.

"I'm okay—"

"You look tired. . . ."

"I'm not—"

"You seem to eat well, porridge in the morning, and better lunches than most. . . ."

"Look, I'm *not* sick, okay?"

Placidly scraping at potatoes, hardly seeming to hear me, she went on, "You go out of here dressed warmly enough, but are you leaving things off at recess? Your scarf? Or your rubbers? How often do I have to remind you?"

"Damn it all, I'm not sick! Anyway, what do you care? Since when do *I* matter?" The knife in her hand stopped moving; anger flew into her eyes, then a hard outraged look, as if she'd come upon a stranger in the kitchen.

"What is *that* supposed to mean?"

I felt hot and wild, startled at my own recklessness. "You'd go away if you could! I heard you tell Aunt Pru. You could understand Cody—" but I pulled back, afraid that I'd blurt out something more—*you could understand Cody running away because you want to go with Durham!* She stared at me, puzzled, and slowly put down the knife. Then she closed the kitchen door the way she did when she argued with my dad.

"So that's what you think," she said quietly. There was no tenderness in her voice, just relief and a slight note of wariness. Now I was overwhelmed with fresh fear that I had pushed her to admit the one thing I did not want to hear. I didn't like the way she'd closed the door, sealing us in the kitchen, an act I irrationally associated with bad news, or tears shed in private, or my nightmare.

"Did I say that I wanted to run away?" She gave me an uneasy smile. "Well, I can't remember that exactly, but obviously you do. Yes, I do feel that way, sometimes. I guess I'd like to run away from the snow, and the potatoes, and worrying about you and Doug and George. *And* the war, and whether or not England will become Germany. . . . But I guess you feel the same way, don't you, at times? So must your dad, tramping up to the streetcar six days a week. . . ."

"Does Durham?" I'd said it without thinking, but my mother only gave a short laugh.

"Durham? Of course. But he has nothing to hold him back, so running is just a normal way of life for him. For

158

Durham, staying in one place would be unusual! Take the lid off the saucepan before it boils over, would you? No, what I need is a holiday. What we *all* need is a holiday. So what I think we'll do is try to save a little every week, maybe get enough by July to rent a cottage. How does that sound? Lots of swimming, maybe a rowboat?"

"You mean it!? Great!"

The steam filled the kitchen and misted the window so that the ice sealing the outside sash was hardly visible. The rising wind rattled our back door. It was only four-thirty, but night had already closed in on us.

"So," my mother said matter-of-factly, rinsing her hands under the tap, "I won't be running away, and you won't be either, not for a while I hope! Put on your coat and bring in the garbage cans before they roll away. And Keith—" Her voice became level, just a bit heavier. "—don't swear at me again. Ever. I don't like it." I'd have promised her anything at that moment. I felt light, little, childishly grateful. Out of the sauna kitchen into the frigid navy blue night I went, carrying a vision of sunlight and splashing oars, and my parents calling to me across the water.

Despite my mother's assurance, it took a while for me to convince myself that Durham was no longer a threat. Suspicion tended to seed itself whenever he smiled too long in her direction, or offered help with something she was about to do; then I imagined his charm still hypnotizing her like a steadily swinging watch. Gradually, however, I found I was forgetting to worry about them. Not that I suddenly trusted Durham; only that I believed my mother with the same naïvete that made me certain she had always been the blameless victim through the whole episode. At that age, it never entered my mind that she might have encouraged Durham or that anything more had actually gone on between them than that one afternoon I had witnessed. Not until I was much older and a hell of a lot more objective about my parents did I see how my mother might enjoy a secretive and passionate involvement, spiced with a little risk and heightened by the knowledge that Durham would not stay forever. In the end, I decided that it was Durham who was deeply hurt. My mother had coolly weighed his lifestyle against her enduring affection for us, and we had won. That insight didn't arrive until much later. At the time I felt only immediate relief, then a kind of gloating triumph that tapered off into something close to condescension. I could afford to be nice to him, once in a while.

By now, of course, the escalating war had gone far beyond headlines happening somewhere else. My father had seen a garrison parade down Yonge Street, and the re-telling brought tears to his eyes.

"Young fellows," he said gruffly at the table, "*boys!*"

Durham carefully held his voice down. "But that's always been the case, hasn't it, Ed? Old men start the war and boys end up fighting it. Probably someone said the same thing about you, twenty years ago, that you were just a boy." My father's damp, wretched eyes came up to meet Durham's, and for the first time he did not argue. He cleared his throat, sat straighter, and in a firmer voice told us that the street-cars had stopped and the people within had leaned out the windows to wave and cheer at the wind-swept, chill-fingered band. The next day he dug out our Union Jack and supervised as Doug strung it from the front porch roof.

Several of George's Fifth Form friends had left school to enlist, and those remaining lost all urgency about passing or getting credits, since futures seemed to freeze in the air and a uniform of some kind was inevitable. Older teachers who'd served in 1918 warmed noticeably toward upper school pupils, talking to them as equals in the hallways, letting detentions go. If an early enlister turned up at the school in his newly-issued uniform—neck muscles bulging from six weeks' basic training, back like an ironing board, face ruddy and hair slickly clipped—he was lionized like one of the elite corps. Classes stopped dead as teachers stricken with shyness and pride deserted the predictability of algebra for the temporary seduction of spit-and-polish, and what might be a final conversation with someone whose life had no certainty at all. For the classes left suddenly to stare at this scene, there was no poignancy. Most saw only the khaki or navy blue or grey-blue starred with brass buttons, and the hero's welcome, and equated the glamour with freedom they didn't have.

When George told us about these visits his own eyes mirrored envy, the same restlessness he'd described at school, though he knew that no one, not even my military-minded father, wanted him to enlist. "It'll come soon enough and you should have all the schooling you can get," my dad advised. "I just wish I'd had your opportunity. I left school at twelve for a mill in Kent. . . ." and George's eyes lost their gleam as my dad recounted the dreary nine-hour working days again, finishing with his familiar statement: "And there were no diplomas from the School of Life, I can tell you *that!*"

There could be nothing personal for me about the war, not at this point. Some of our classes had begun collections that interested me only for a short time. A slowly-growing ball of silver foil provided the only shine in the dark-oak school hall, and tin cans, bottles and bacon fat were amassed for reasons that remained a mystery to us.

Durham had gotten as close as he was going to in helping the war effort by taking on a job painting posters for the government, which he did up in his room with the open window blowing the smell of his pipesmoke and paints into the upstairs hall. Having devoted many weeks to hating him, never entering his room unless I was sent there, I found I couldn't just bounce in on him now as if nothing had happened.

"That you, Keeter?" I'd been shuffling around the stairs, into the bathroom and back to my room.

161

"Yeah."

"Want to see what evil times and the lure of the dollar have done to my standards?"

"What?"

"Come here and I'll show you what urges the average person to greater efforts in the present conflict. . . ." Bantering. Baffling me with woolly words. I hesitated on the stairs and didn't answer.

"Would you like to see the posters?" he explained finally, his voice less light, but kind. I could sense the power of my own silence to hurt him, right then, while he was close to begging me for company. For a moment the feeling of manipulating him was overwhelming, and I couldn't reply. I thought of saying *What posters?* as though his work no longer mattered, when his next words sounded nearer, and I turned to see him standing in his doorway, leaning against the frame with a perplexed smile on his face.

"Now, is that any way to treat an uncle who may be leaving here in a few weeks? If you don't like posters, you might at least share a Coke with me." With a show of reluctance, I shrugged and followed him into the room. On his table was a drawing of turbanned girls, all grinning teeth with no divisions between them, seated at sewing machines. Underneath he'd printed: My Needle Hums Along The Track, For Hitler's Ears I'm Pinning Back!

"Stupid stuff," Durham said shortly.

"Why do you do them if you don't like the work?"

Durham rubbed his hands together and sat down. "Money, my friend, the easiest money I've ever made. They're not paying for my intellect, or the touch of Rembrandt." He waved a hand toward a stack rolled against his dresser. "Take a look at those, if you like."

THRIFT BUILDS TANKS, said the first, an advertisement for a Royal Bank Budget book. The next was more to my taste:

LOOK! (a caricature of Mussolini with fangs)

WHO'S! (a wild-eyed Hitler with wolf ears)

162

LISTENING! (a seedy little man listening to a sailor who was saying "She Sails At Midnight")

Below, this, Durham had sketched a murky sea with a torpedoed ship going down, and underneath, CARELESS TALK COSTS LIVES!

"How many do you have to do?"

He drew a steady breath and stretched his arms high above his head, flexing his fingers. "Oh, enough to get me to Vancouver and keep me in food until I decide where I'll finally lay down some roots." He was staring out at our barren backyard where little else but roots remained. Leaves flown, bark bugless, dry stalks of dead flowers left from the autumn. The sky flat and stale, the colour of wet newspapers. On a wedge of the street visible behind our house, a slat-sided garbage truck lumbered to a halt. A man wading hip-deep in the refuse reached for a full can held up to him from the roadside, dumped it, trod it down savagely. The truck shuddered out of sight, leaving the sound of cans clattering and a sick, sour smell.

"Vancouver," said Durham evenly, "is warmer, they say. More rain, I believe, but more temperate, too." He looked to me, in the small and uncomfortable space of time, slightly aged. Around his stomach the shirt buttons pulled and gaped, showing a spongy roll not affected by his daily walks. Matching bags of bluish, puffy skin hung beneath his eyes and thick creases marked his face from nose to soft, bristled chin. I supposed he'd asked me in to cheer him up, to divert him from something—a dark mood, the deadly dull work. But his worries weren't mine; I could only see him as a suddenly shrunken and disarmed enemy. When he turned briskly to face me, I felt flustered, thinking he'd caught the disillusionment on my face.

"I'm *boring* you," he said, a host caught in a lapse of manners, "and I almost forgot the coke, didn't I?" He poured some into a used coffee cup and gave me the rest, clinking the cup against the bottle smartly, winking: "Here's to me and to you, men of the world! Listen, I have better stuff for you to look at than this." His hung-laundry look vanished as starch poured back into his movements. Diving into a crate, muttering, choosing and discarding, he finally pulled out a large scrapbook. "Now *this* is poster art, my friend. You'll find an old Harper's Christmas cover in there by Eugene Grasset. Was he Swiss or French? Can't remember. But he was so good he did stained glass windows and tapestries. There's Parrish, too, your mom's favourite. You'd never know by those delicate trees and naked ladies that he once won a prize for an advertisement of a bicycle!" I sat on his bed, turning the pages, hoping the bare bodies would be more interesting than Doug's Moon and Mann biology text, where Reproduction was reduced to X-ray plates of pelvises and dry, dotted diagrams.

"—and there are some Gibsons, the man who created the Gibson Girl and the styles your grandma wore." He sat down before his easel, working quietly while I flicked through the objects of his admiration. What I saw—detailed, lyrical and glowing—was as different from the gross comic-strip stuff on his easel as intricate wrought iron from a curtain rod. I watched him dabbing unreal wigs, boomerang eyebrows, grinning mouths, and remembered the care and softness he'd put into my painting. I felt a rush of sympathy for him that had nothing to do with the rootless fate of a gypsy; what touched me was the gap between what he could paint, and what he now had to paint.

"I think the picture of Shirley and her house is as good as anything in here," I said with all the generosity I could muster.

Durham's face could landslide warmly upwards when he was complimented. He smiled broadly, dipped his brush. "Back to my war effort," he declared pompously, throwing out his chest and tapping the easel where the sewing girls required army uniforms beneath their needles to make any sense of the verse. "Did you know, sport, that all of us can fight in our own way?" I began to laugh at his mock patriotism, which only encouraged him. "The farmer in his field, the simple clerk whose order sheet keeps the wheels turning, you with your bacon fat and me with my brush? Yes! Every one of us! And now all of Canada's six hundred thousand unemployed—including me—have something to do. Isn't that great?"

If Durham had paid his way, I believe he could have lived on in the house, entertaining my mother without a flicker of concern in my father's mind. More than once it looked as though my father let Durham take over conversations and assume the role of companion quite purposely, privately relieved that the burden was no longer his. Often he would get up from the dinner table to sink into his chair with his *Tely*, leaving them alone to talk on for another hour about England, or Brahms, or philosophy. So it came as no surprise to me that he also accepted as natural Durham's purchase of two tickets to Artur Rubinstein's Massey Hall concert, and that my mother and Durham went off together up Arlington Avenue, she in the good green suit buried under a winter wool coat, Durham willingly strangling in a tie and white shirt. Rocking rhythmically on his heels, my dad watched them from the window until they were only blurred legs.

"Good for her, a night out like that," he said into the sheer curtain. "She doesn't get out enough, you know," sternly, as though it required explanation and a shaded reprimand to those of us who took up so much of her time.

I felt sodden with information he didn't have, drenched through with it while he stood, dry and placid, smiling at the disappearing figures. I would never tell him, even when his complaisance irritated me almost as much as Durham's deception. But I had to say something, to show my own relief.

"Durham's going away soon, to Vancouver—"

A glint of pleasure swam through my dad's eyes and evaporated. "That'll be the day! What makes you so sure?"

165

"He said so."

"Durham says a lot of things. Durham says more than he does."

"But he *did*, and he meant it—"

"When? When did he say he was going?"

I fished for an unassailable fact, a date. The lack of absolute proof made me stutter. "Well—I didn't hear—there wasn't—"

"You see?" my dad's voice rose in negative triumph. "He doesn't give a date because he doesn't know!" He went into the hall for his coat and helmet.

"Didn't he tell you and Mom yet?"

"No, he didn't. And he isn't likely to as long as your mother makes everything so comfortable for him here." He was examining the tilt of his helmet, adjusting the thick chin strap. "Don't forget now—get your homework done before you listen to the radio."

When he'd gone, a thumping panic sent me up the stairs two at a time. What if Durham had been pretending? What if the sadness I'd seen in his face was something else—pity for me, knowing that they'd be leaving tonight? I tripped in my haste on the top step, hurting my knee. *Shit!* Hobbled into my parents' room where their ingrained neatness made search so easy. Brush, comb, a tin of dusting powder and a few loose pins on the dresser. A framed photo of George, Doug and me, taken some years ago, when we looked scrubbed and trusting for cameras. She'd have taken that with her, and some of the other family pictures around the room. Still, I had to be sure. Opening the closet door I smelled the musky mixture of polish and pomander. My mother's small leather bag stood next to our old straw family suitcase. Nothing was packed in them.

On the bed her nightgown was folded neatly. My dad's blue suit was now worn by the wooden valet, a headless sentinel in the dim light of the room. Everything looked normal, placid, a place to return to. She wouldn't go tonight, I knew, but still I felt a trickle of fear. Durham told me he

166

was leaving us, so what was this big night at a concert for? Not a celebration certainly. More likely Durham would use it as a last resort. He'd picked the place and the atmosphere they both loved, away from us, and there he'd do everything in his power to convince her to go with him. It would be just like him—no matter how she answered him—to surround her with the high drama of concertos and crashing chords, so that either way he would be the hero of a setting she'd remember for the rest of her life.

21

That weekend Durham got steadily and quietly drunk, locked in George's bedroom. Durham, who roared and laughed and sent echoes bounding around the house when he was sober, got drunk in a private, purposeful way, as though he had suddenly gone into some bizarre type of training that required single-minded concentration. At first the rest of us went around pretending nothing was happening. My mother's face had a sharpened, set look, but she didn't mention Durham and began to cut out a blouse, flattening the onion-skin pattern with swift, curt movements on the dining room table. When Durham had not appeared by late Saturday afternoon, all of us seemed to be moving mechanically, bumping into one another and excusing ourselves with excessive politeness.

"I could hear him from the hall," Doug informed us after his third trip to the bathroom, "he's singing something."

"What's this all about, anyway?" my dad asked mildly. He'd put the question to my mother, but Doug answered.

"He's getting drunk up there," said Doug. "But at least he doesn't throw chairs around, like Halwick. . . ."

"Do *you* know what's going on, Georgia?"

"How should I know? If Doug says he's getting drunk, then I guess that's what he's doing." Her foot sped up on the sewing machine's treadle. "Why must you always ask me everything? Doesn't anybody else around here *ever* know anything?"

My dad's soft, earnest face grew concerned at her anger, which seemed aimed unfairly at us while the cause remained upstairs, well out of range. "Now, now, don't get upset," he said quickly. "It's probably nothing." He dropped a wink at Doug, attempting to lighten her mood with a little teasing. "Maybe it's just a little pacifist guilt, eh? Or maybe he's decided to join up after all, and this is his farewell binge?" When this drew no response from my mother, he sighed and went to the kitchen to fill the kettle, preparing to soothe over his disrupted Saturday with a cup of tea. Doug and I followed him.

"Here are a couple of dimes" he said. "You two can go to the show this afternoon; there's nothing here I particularly want you to see." His eyes looked clear, decisive, innocent. "You were right the other night, Keith. He *is* leaving. That's why he's up there, acting like an idiot. No more free ride. Now he'll have to shift for himself. . . ."

Close to dawn, I was hauled from a deep sleep by a strange, prolonged rasp that, in the misty recesses of my dream, I'd thought to be a car being cranked outside my window. It was Durham vomiting in the bathroom, enduring it alone as no other person in our house would have had to.

That was the night of our first heavy snow. Slow-falling, wet flakes, very large and pierced like doilies, plopped soundlessly against the glass, briefly beautiful. *How do they know no two are alike? How could anyone know that?* Durham retched and coughed, and the blue-white, leisurely snow fell.

I went into the hall and stood outside the bathroom door: the hard, high-arched soles of his feet were toward me because he was kneeling before the toilet, his big head lolling forward. I didn't go in.

169

"You all right, Durham?" He cleared his throat and spat.

"No—but I will be. Go back to bed." His voice was grey and dry.

"Do you want some Wild Strawberry Compound?"

"Christ, no! I've had enough berry as it is. Go to bed before you wake your folks. . . ." The sole of one foot edged backwards and pushed the door shut. "No offense, sport. I'd rather you didn't see me. . . ." There was nothing to be done, no way to help without crossing into the part of his pain I neither understood nor wanted to share.

"Durham?" I whispered against the door. "It's snowing out—"

Somehow I thought he might like to know that.

Despite a hangover that seemed to turn his sunken cheeks to putty, the next day Durham asked me to go with him on a sketching excursion to Hogg's Hollow.

"Do us both good," he insisted, "getting fresh air and a look at the countryside in winter. How about it, sport? After all, I'm leaving in a week. . . ." He had slept in until ten o'clock, but for the first part of the trip he seemed winded and too tired to talk, though he cheered up when we boarded the Yonge trolley heading north from the city limits.

"Your dad wanted me to stay for Christmas, but I think it's time to get along, wouldn't you say? Your father is a kind man, you know. A stable, sensible soul of infinite patience. He doesn't like the idea of me missing a typical Canadian Christmas, plenty of snow and a big dinner. Envisions me in the clammy climate of Vancouver, I suppose, begging on a street corner—" He broke off to look out the window, humming gently to himself. It seemed so easy for him to talk, to spin his thoughts without apology, that his silences too were uncomplicated and warm. I began to relax, almost ready to tell him about Shirley. Still I held back, only able to skirt around the subject.

"Sure is swell up here—I'll bet Shirley Upshaw never came this far out—" It sounded so contrived, clunking stupidly from me, that I immediately wished I'd said nothing.

But Durham just smiled amiably and drifted back into conversation. "Not likely. And what a pity that is! You'll see when we get there. There's a valley behind the Jolly Miller where the stream freezes solid. From the hillside it looks like tinsel dropped through the trees." He nudged the brown paper bag of sandwiches between us as though it were my arm. "Someday you should take Shirley there. . . ." I blushed and he looked judiciously away. "Well, my friend, all that will come in time, and you've got plenty of that. . . ." He took a long swig of bitter black coffee from the thermos and burped behind one big mitt. "First, of course, you should get to know her much better than you do. I don't mean just occasional hellos, or peering down at her from that tree, either. But how she *feels*, what makes her happy or angry—" he yawned suddenly "—the qualities that make her unique. One thing about Shirley would fascinate me: she must be incredibly *strong*." He broke off to see if I was still listening. "But I'm sure you've found that out for yourself."

I remembered her wheeling on the girl in the schoolyard, cracking her cheek in fury. Was that what he meant? It would have been simple enough to ask him right then; he had made it easy. But he was yawning again, his eyelids drooped. "God, how that snow hurts my eyes! Don't ever do what I did yesterday, sport. It's no solution to anything, believe me. I've marinated my stomach. I can't even blink without pain. Your mother is furious. . . . By the way, did I say anything yesterday that I might not remember? Anything stupid?"

"No—you were singing a lot."

He raised his eyebrows. "Ah. 'The Road To Mandalay,' was it?"

"I don't know. It was pretty loud, though. . . ."

He groaned dramatically and muttered, "The *original* words, I hope. . . ." And for the rest of the trip he dozed on and off, his hands falling curled and open on his lap, like a small child's.

The sting of sharp clear air in the silent Sunday countryside brought him roaring back to life. "This is the cure, Keeter!" he shouted over his shoulder as he bull-moosed his way through deep stiff snow. In the white-felted woods, his cheeks reddened, his eyes shone. Behind us, he pointed out the tavern that crouched like a blanketed animal, its stone snout spouting dark smoke, and talked about pioneers who'd taken weeks in winter to cart their produce down to the docks of York. For me, the fun of it was far too short, and even though he was battling down his hangover, I knew Durham had enjoyed it, too.

"Sorry there won't be more of these," he told me with genuine regret. "Why didn't we start sooner?" The following week, he spent much of his time sketching closer to home. He seemed to be deliberately removing himself from us in short, bearable stages.

I had just reached our porch on the way home from school on Monday when my mother thrust her preoccupied, dinner-preparing face through the door. "Don't come in yet, I want you to go get Durham. There was a long-distance call from Vancouver for him—"

"Ah hell, he'll be home soon anyway!"

"Don't swear! Just do as I say. He's sketching at Hillcrest Park and with his sense of time he could take forever. The call seemed important—be sure and tell him that—" and the door shut on her last wisp of freezing breath.

The park was just a few blocks away, sloping up from Davenport Road on the south, bordered by steep, cobblestoned Christie on the east, and providing a lovely view for the elegant stone houses to the north and west. In summer the park's arthritic old apple trees held children like fruit, and the tennis court rang with the bong of expensive balls and the easy laughter of rich people who flipped us a dime when we brought back a ball from a wild shot. I found

Durham perched on his canvas stool at the top of the hill, and gave him the message.

"Not urgent," he smiled, "just business. I'll call back later. Why not stick around? I won't be much longer—" He paused to squint belligerently downhill to the stunted, smudged houses by the train tracks. On Davenport, a convoy of olive green army trucks crawled by, headlights on. "By the way, saw your elusive friend today. Said hello, but she didn't answer."

I started out to defend her, but instead found myself telling Durham everything that worried me: the way she acted in the schoolyard, one day pleasant, the next cold; her stony shyness in class. Finally, with immense relief, I heard myself spilling all the details of our Hallowe'en break-in. I had never been able to forget the horror of those clippings and the pictures of Cody on the living room wall.

"I see," Durham would say now and again. "I see, go on," until I'd housecleaned the whole mess from my mind.

"Well, Keeter, I find myself at a slight disadvantage, not knowing quite how to advise you. Perhaps I should consider what your parents would say—"

"If I'd wanted *that* I'd have told *them!*"

He shot me a look of surprise and respect. "Good. At least we've got that out of the way. You don't want a lecture, or one of Pru's tea-singed proverbs. I guess I'd be a fool to congratulate you on such skilful breaking and entering. But then I'd be a liar if I didn't admit some admiration."

"Breaking in doesn't bother me," I said impatiently. "It's what I *saw*. All those headlines and pictures—"

"—for Shirley to see every day of her life?" he ended my sentence gently. "Well, I know it's hard for you to accept the fact that Mrs. Upshaw's madness isn't confined to yelling out of windows and piling stolen balls in a carton." He began to sort pencils by pawing through the box, looking stumpy and ursine in his large fur cap. "Ah, here it is, the soft grey for the smoke down there. I was in the Upshaw house myself once, you know. *Not* by way of the milkbox, I might add, but invited in by Cody when his mother was out. He couldn't have anyone in when she was home. He'd made a bookcase he wanted me to see. Cody was very clever that way. Now let's see—what do *I* remember about the place? Cushions on the sofa. Ugly satin things, puckered like prunes. Magenta, olive, violet, cobalt blue—positively godawful on a maroon sofa. Did Cody tell me, apologetically, not to sit on them? Yes, he did, and I imagined the three of them at night, standing around admiring and avoiding them, like people visiting those roped-off display rooms at Eaton's College Street."

"Was Cody afraid of his mother?"

Durham looked at me for a moment. "I don't think any of us really knew. She had his baby pictures all over the place, she seemed very fond of him in a cloying sort of way. It's your mother's theory that he *had* to break away, and that his affair with the Appleton girl wasn't so much a way of getting even as it was sheer lack of experience. He'd never been allowed much freedom to mix with other kids, boys or girls. Hand me that rag, will you? Tell me, did you know that your mother was at Cody's trial?"

"You're kidding!"

He shook his head. "I wasn't here when the terrible thing happened. I was in the States. Your mom wrote me explaining as much as she knew, some of it from the radio and newspapers, street gossip, and so on. Claire—that's Shirley's mother—and Cody had been drinking up in the tavern on Dufferin. Beer and cheap wine, no *worse* drunk you can go on, believe me. Someone flirted with Claire, who was only seventeen, remember—out of school and working at Woolworth's. Younger than George, so you get the picture. Anyway, she flirted right back, which enraged Cody. Some reports claimed he went after the other man with a knife and Claire got in the way. Others said he'd meant to kill her in his jealous rage." He paused to clear his throat and hawk into a handkerchief. "Well, they got her to Western hospital, but she died an hour later."

174

"Was Shirley born then?"

"She'd be around a year old, I guess. Thank God they'd had the sense not to take her up to the tavern with them! People do that, you know, the silly buggers. They arrested Cody and kept him in a cell in the Stewart building down on College. When he was told to get a lawyer, he didn't phone home. He phoned your mother." Durham glanced up at me briefly. "It makes some sense, sport. He wouldn't contact his mother. By then, Child Welfare had taken Shirley. Maybe he just remembered the time your mom had given him coffee and treated him like a normal person; I don't know. Well, Georgia got him a lawyer, a young fellow up on St. Clair hungry for business and not adverse to making a name for himself in a big juicy case the whole city knew about. . . ." I suppose I looked stricken with shock, because Durham suddenly grinned. "Don't look like that, my friend! Your mother never was one for staying out of things, you know that. In that way, you're very much like her."

The sun was dropping, bleached and powerless, into the lake we could sometimes see on clear days. Above us, a plane splotched with green and mustard camouflage droned heavily, like a moth labouring to stay aloft.

"Durham, if they don't want war planes to be seen, why don't they paint them blue, or grey?"

"Because they get bombed on the *ground*. God, I'm getting hungry! Did I ever tell you about the girlfriend I had who flew planes? No? Very spiffy lady, with frizzy bobbed hair before it was fashionable and those marvellous unreadable eyes that look like green stones under water. Hilde, a German girl who once flew this ridiculous thing that looked like a canvas canoe with wings over the Alps on a dare." He ran the tip of his tongue over his lips. "I thought of marrying her at one time. But she was too independent, always taking off without saying where she was going." He gave a gruff nostalgic laugh. "Don't get too disdainful of your more eccentric relatives, Keeter. They're the ones you'll remember later on, not the dutifully dull ones. . . ." He blew on his numb hands and began to collect up his things. We started briskly across the park.

"Hilde was quite something. The only time I saw her really depressed was when her father committed suicide. Just walked into his office one morning, said *guten Morgen* to his secretary, and kept right on walking through his window, which happened to be ten floors above ground. Terrible shock to my friend. For a few weeks, Hilde wouldn't answer her phone or her doorbell. Just retired from living. So I took the bull by the horns, broke in one morning and proceeded to make a nuisance of myself, pointing out the mess she had become, until she got so angry she threw a vase at my head! Great therapy. Do you know what I'm trying to say, sport?"

"No."

"Well, I see some link between Hilde and Shirley. Both seem to back away from living because of personal tragedy, and there's some temptation to let them get away with it, isn't there? Look at it this way. Just suppose your attempts to reach Shirley made her realize that sometimes the world has a *right* to barge in on us, and that it can be a good thing. Maybe you stopped her from getting too comfortable in that living room full of her dead dad. Gave her a jolt she needed."

"Now—" he emphasized the word, stepping up his pace as we rounded Tyrrel, "the trick is to keep after her—to get her to throw that ball of hers at *your* head! Who knows? She may fly over the Alps herself, someday."

That evening, Durham found the letter that my mother had written about Cody's trial. "Just give it back when you've read it," he said. Opening the envelope, I found ten pages, crammed from margin to margin. I hurried through the polite opening.

"—children are well. . . .bought Halwick's old bike for George's ninth birthday—quite attractive painted blue. Heard of Vermont's twenty-inch snowfall—did it bury your easel? Ha ha! *Have* to make a joke, bad as it is, because of a

176

terrible terrible thing happening here—I'd have written you earlier but there wasn't enough to tell at that point." I skipped over the next page; it repeated what Durham had told me in the park.

"—it's such a shock, seeing Cody's picture in the papers. Mrs. Collins bought a *Flash*, can you imagine, because they had a photo of poor Claire lying outside the tavern with blood running down her neck and on the sidewalk. It was awful. When it happens close to home, to people you know, it's so hard to accept. Then, almost as big a shock. Cody phoned me! At first I thought it was some sort of grim joke, until I realized who was speaking.

"I asked him if he'd called his mother, knowing that he couldn't—if he was all right, when I knew he couldn't be worse. When I got my wits together enough to ask if he had a lawyer, he was able to make some sense. What it came down to was that he had no one. I said I'd do what I could, and he began to explain the murder, repeating that he'd 'hurt' Claire *instead*, over and over again. Someone came on the line then, telling me the accused was in no condition to talk.

"Though I was able to get him the lawyer, I don't think any of us held out much hope. The trial at City Hall lasted just under eight days and I was there for the last three. The place was packed, of course, and even friendly witnesses like Cody's landlady mentioned the fights he and Claire had, as if murder had been in his heart all along! On the last day, the judge heard the summaries and charged the jury, and the awful wait began. I crossed Queen Street to shop and to get a cup of tea, then went straight back, feeling lightheaded and trying to be hopeful. Only two hours after they'd gone out, the jury returned, and there was a mad rush for seats.

"I had to stand against the back wall, watching the juror's expressions as they trooped back, just like they do in movies. The judge asked Cody to stand, but all I could see was a partial profile and his thin shoulders as he turned toward the jury. 'We find the defendant guilty of murder in the first degree with no recommendation for mercy.' When the judge asked if the prisoner had anything to say, Cody just shook his head. For a moment, I was filled with panic. I heard the judge's sentence as I pushed past the people, trying to get away from the words, but Durham, it was like one of those hideous dreams where you try to run, but can only drag heavy, tired legs.

"The sentence followed me into the hall—'taken to the place of execution and that you there be hanged by the neck until you are dead and may the Lord have mercy—' As I went down the stairs, a young couple ran past me, on their way to get a wedding licence, I imagine.

"*I* began to run then, because I could feel tears in my throat. Something happens to the mind under stress, as well as the body. I remember thinking how beautifully the marble floor shone, and wondering what *Zeebrugge* carved into the back of the war memorial meant! As if a part of my brain remained untouched by what I'd heard and seen.

"This is a terrible letter. Rereading it makes me feel badly again, yet glad in a sense to ease the burden by sharing it with you. Naturally, everybody on the street is saying that they could see it coming, that Cody deserved what he got. People are so damned wise when they don't have to make the decisions."

The last few lines of the letter were about Thea and the family. Then her pen-fattened *Georgia* appeared beneath the words, *as ever*. I folded the pages, put them in the envelope addressed to Barre, Vermont, and slipped it under Durham's closed door.

Reading the letter had a curious effect on me. I discovered a new kinship with Durham and my mother for trusting me with the truth about Shirley's parents. Armed with knowledge she didn't know I had, I felt immense power and elation, as if I'd shoved my way past the last walls and entered an arena that only required open evidence of my love. I thought the word. I whispered it a couple of times against my frost-flecked window, trying it out like a new taste on my tongue. I said it aloud to the indefinite white figure in my painting. I said myself to sleep with it, conjuring up her room and her body with wonder. I love you.

If you are lonely, you have my Sunnyside canary by your bed. His eyes stay open the whole night, because he never sleeps. If you are afraid, reach out and touch him. And remember that he sings in the daytime.

"Our teacher's having us over to his place, the whole class, before the holidays. . . ."

"Oh?" Durham was hunched glumly over a bowl of cracked wheat, stirring in one mound of sugar after another. He did not like the morning. My mother, who loved it, plunked a huge pot of tea in the centre of the table and sat down.

"*That's* going to be difficult for Shirley. She won't be able to go."

"Unless you convince her, of course," added Durham, sliding heavy eyes in my direction. "Maybe you could try talking to her about it. But then, some girls are awfully hard to convince, aren't they?"

"Is she easy to talk to?" my mother asked. "Has she mentioned her grandmother to you?"

"That's just about all she talks about."

"But the old lady doesn't meet her at the gate now—that's something—"

"Because of the icy sidewalks."

Durham had swilled the first cup of tea and was refusing a second. "Have to be downtown early—sending the stuff west."

"When's the party?" asked my mother.

"Monday, after school. We're going straight there."

"Will you need something? Cookies?"

"No. He's giving us hot dogs and ice cream."

"And he's having the *whole* class? Quite a job. That's nice of him."

"Madness," Durham said, but he smiled wanly at me.

"But I think it's just what Shirley needs, don't you? I mean, she has five hours away from her grandmother, five days a week. I think you might influence her, Keith. *Ask* her to go. People never treat her normally, do they? If you show her you expect her to act differently, she might manage it. It's worth a try. Durham, don't you think it might work?"

Durham halved a piece of toast with one savage bite.

"Who knows?" he said. "Sometimes it does." He stood up and carried his dishes to the sink. "Depends on the girl, and the kind of courage she has. . . ."

The sweetish smell of stale dried snow on winter coats filled the cloakroom. I plunked my math books onto the floor and got into my windbreaker. Usually Shirley was out of there at four o'clock exactly, before anyone else, sprinting nervously in her grey coat like a pursued squirrel. Today she'd cleaned off the blackboards for Critchley-Williams, so I waited out the delay in the hall.

"Shirley?" She seemed frantic, anguished, not flattered as most of us were to be chosen to help the teacher. She ran past me, buttoning up her coat.

"What?"

I remembered her grandmother's time limit on getting home. A starched pink hankie fell out of her coat sleeve, and she gave a flustered moan, scooped it up, began to run again with her hood flopping. The whole thing had the look of a Saturday cartoon, and I laughed. "You look like Cinderella, for chrissake!"

Still half-running, she called, "*Don't* swear—"

"—and you sound like my mother. Okay," I added hastily, "I won't swear, but just stop making everything an excuse, okay? Are you going to the party? And I'm not teasing, I want to know."

"No. You *know* that. I wish you'd stop bothering me."

"That's not bothering, it's asking—"

We were running down the last flight of iron stairs, which clanged beneath us like berserk bells.

"Well, are you going to answer me?"

"I just *did*."

"I'll bet you didn't even ask her, your grandma." Stubbornly, she stepped up her jerky pace across the snowduned yard. "Well, did you or not?"

Angrily, she flung her stone-grey eyes in my face. "That's none of your business!"

"Sure it is, because I *want* you to go. What teacher ever did this before? Did Miss Nicol give you a party? Can you imagine old Randall asking kids to *his* place? Pinky says it's a dungeon, that he lives alone with rats for pets! Look, why don't you just *ask* her? Or go without asking her? She can't kill you—"

No reply. Her profile looked like the cardboard cut-outs done while you wait at the Ex, flat and lifeless. We had just two blocks to go before I would have to cross over.

"I want you to *go*," I repeated, "and so do the other kids." I risked the lie. I didn't care.

She'd broken into a funny lopsided run. "You'd better cross now," she said without turning, "She's going to be mad enough because I'm late. If she *sees* you—" She broke off, and I knew that her courage had gone. Suddenly I thought of Durham and his flying girlfriend and his advice about getting Shirley to throw something at me. But now I was too angry. I was sick of her stupid silences, her gutless little-girl run. Didn't it matter to her how hard I was trying? It hurt that she could walk beside me but give me no more attention than a shadow.

"Look," I finally let it go, "I don't care whether you go or not any more! You haven't got the *nerve*, you know that? Maybe you get marks that put you in my grade, but that's all. You should be in with the babies because you can't stand up for yourself! You take all that crap and then run home for more! And you know what else? You'd make *any*body swear!"

I stomped across the road away from her without looking back.

22

All that week, Durham had been putting out peeling canvases, crinkled paint tubes and old splayed brushes for the garbage collection. The work he was sending ahead cluttered our hall, wrapped in brown paper and inked with bold black warnings: HANDLE WITH CARE!! DO NOT BEND OR DROP!!! FRAGILE!!! Exclamation marks like a busbied regiment all over them. For a short time my mother put up with the disorder, but she was planning a dinner for the night before he left and as the day of departure grew closer, she confronted him.

"When are you getting rid of these, Durham?"

"On Friday, luv."

"Why then? Why not today? The dinner is Friday night and I want to clean up the hall. Does it *really* matter if they're sent a little sooner?"

"No, I suppose not. But does it *really* matter if the hall is clean?" He was mimicking her tone softly, not absorbing her irritation. "After all, everyone will be tracking in slush, and Thea is bound to bring at least one dog. All your work will have been in vain. Look, why don't you spend the time you'd use cleaning the hall to play me some Schumann instead?"

Usually my mother would accept Durham's bantering,

sometimes teasing him back. This time her voice firmed and rose, as if she were talking to George or Doug. "I'd like them out of here *today*, right after lunch, please."

By nightfall the parcels and cartons were gone, and I was able to skid the full length of the hall on stockinged feet.

To everyone's amazement, Uncle Gerald had decided to come to the dinner with Aunt Pru, a breakaway from habit no one could explain. I barely remembered him, though there was something familiar about the put-upon jellied eyes and diffident manners. Because they arrived first, they sat somewhat stiffly on the couch, one cushion apart, sipping sherry and making small talk with Durham and my dad. Doug and I were forced to make an appearance which momentarily halted the adult conversation.

"Ah, *here* they are!" my father declared, too loudly, as though we'd been lost and someone had dredged us up. We shook hands awkwardly with Gerald.

"Don't I get a kiss?" pouted Pru.

We had to lean down to touch clamped lips against the powdery half-moon of her face, immersed in the over-whelming vapour of lavender perfume.

As if to mark our courage, the doorbell chimed, and Thea came through the front door George had opened for her with the tense, swift steps of an old woman determined to prove her vitality. She wore a wool cape, and carried what looked to be a fur muff, until it snapped at my father as he reached to put it away in the hall closet. "Naughty girl, Fluff! *Never* bite the host, or you won't be asked again!" And she cackled wickedly at her joke, hurrying into the living room where the men stood as if for an anthem. "Oh, sit down, the lot of you! Nothing annoys me more than a custom that reminds me of my sex and my age!" Pru's face had coloured to deep pink at the bluntness, and Gerald sat down uncertainly.

Thea took a straight-backed chair, settling in with small, spare gestures of grace. "You all know Martin Langley, of course," she said, waving her clanking wrist in the direction of a hammock-shaped man who, my mother had told us earlier, now boarded with Thea. I left with relief to fill the water glasses, grateful that Thea had confined her greeting to a brisk hello and a handshake. Having made a polite appearance to welcome everyone, my mother announced that dinner would be ready in five minutes, and left the room to begin serving.

It proceeded, as all our evening meals did, with my father's prayer, his tightly-closed eyelids jumping nervously, his tone one of command rather than diffidence: *For these Thy gifts we give Thee thanks, oh Lord, for Jesus' sake, Amen*, said despite Thea's agnostic presence and the whimpering of her dog beside her chair. Somewhere past the passing of the mashed potatoes the atmosphere changed from self-conscious politeness to nostalgia. Durham raised the memory of an earlier party, when Thea had apparently shown them all the intricacies of the Charleston. Everyone laughed, and Durham added that Pru's Gerald had joined her.

"Good times," my father declared richly.

"Perhaps," Pru put in severely, "but I never could accept modern dancing," as though the rejection underlined her better breeding. "Frankly, I find it difficult to trust people who no longer waltz. Too *much* of the tried and true is disappearing, to my mind. They've dismantled our lovely *Chippewa* just this past summer, for instance. Oh, the excursions we had on *that*—now gone into scrap, I suppose, to make some awful tank for the war. . . ." She took a radish and her glum disapproval vanished as her face took on the placid satisfaction of a baby silenced with a dummy.

But she had turned the conversation inevitably to the war, and how soon George would be going, and Durham's luck in finding space going west when trains were needed for troops. Through it all, I half-heard the disjointed banter, jarred to involvement only once, when Thea's boarder asked

me if I had a girlfriend, and I told him no, and he ignored me
again.

"Keith? Would you pass Mr. Langley his dess*ert*,
please?" In the flicker of the candles I saw their faces,
gleaming now with light sweat because my father had built
a monstrous coal fire in the furnace; faces patient, amused,
full of celebration and food. I passed the dessert, suddenly
thinking how dull and predictable they all were, retelling
their old tales, raking through the past to unearth a nugget
that made the present bearable, their mixture of English
accents clustering here for comfort and making George's flat
Canadian voice sound foreign.

"Gra-a-nd meal," declared Gerald, a Sheffield man, dabbing at mauve lips, his neck rising above the collar like a
soufflé. Under Pru's frown he belted back his glass of port as
if he'd taken a pill.

For an instant Thea's hand lay on my mother's like a
brown veined leaf on ivory. "Lovely, Georgia, but I shall
consider it an evening wasted unless you play for us later. . . ."

I slept heavily and briefly, waking to bursts of laughter,
sleeping, rousing again to snatches of song and the thick
wobble of someone's baritone—*I'll si-ing thee so-ongs of
Arabeeee*—my father? Durham? Gerald or the boarder?
Drifting away, and back again to the unmistakable hectoring
of Aunt Pru on the upstairs landing. *They go to the bathroom
in pairs*, Durham had joked once, *like bobbies patrolling the
Limehouse section of London.* "—could not *abide* Lydia's
cat! Lydia died last spring, and mercifully did not suffer, but
left us the cat. I've had it put away. Terrible animal, wild-
eyed, always leaping at me from the mantel!" The stolid feet
clumped off, and I fell asleep with the pillow over my head.

I had no idea what time it was when I had to go to the
bathroom.

I could hear my father's breathy snore, the clatter of cold

branches against the window, the pendulum of our wall clock. A lamp burned in the living room, lighting a square of the waxed floor and the smudged paw prints left by Thea's dog.

"You might be able to come west later, when they don't need you as much. They *won't*, you know. In five years, Keith will be wanting to live his own life. . . ."

I pulled my robe closer, huddling at the top of the stairs, well out of sight. There was a light double clink as a cup was placed carefully on its saucer.

"You forget that by then I'll be forty-five years old," my mother said, "perhaps a grandmother a couple of times over if George is married."

Durham's voice, urgent and hushed: "Do you honestly think that would make any difference to me?"

"Perhaps not, but it's bound to make a difference to me. Look, Durham—do you remember telling everyone at the table tonight that you were like a Bedouin, roaming freely? That you chose that life because it suited you? Well, you weren't really joking. It was the truth."

"You're trying to tell me that you don't have the same longing?"

Only a second's hesitation. "No, I can't tell you that because you know better. More than once I've wished I was a man. But what you're offering isn't that sort of freedom at all. I wouldn't be an equal, enjoying your kind of choices. In the end, I'd be as needed by you as I am by Ed and the children, just exchanging one set of responsibilities for another."

A protracted silence, with blasts of hot air pouring upward to me through the black-grilled register by the stairs. The old clock bonged three times, cutting off part of Durham's reply. When I could hear again, his tone had altered, hardened, as though he'd been insulted.

"—never been too attracted to martyrs, Georgia. That's just how you sound to me now, all give and no take."

"I'm sorry you see it that way. But what attracts me most

186

about you scares me off, too. Bedouin women *aren't* free, Durham." The domestic sounds of china being stacked, the thin heels of my mother's party shoes clicking toward the kitchen. "Look, we've been over this before. We can't go on forever. You have to get some sleep—you won't get much on the train. Are you sure you'll be warm enough with just one blanket?" Durham had given George back his room, and would be spending his last night on the couch. The kitchen tap ran briefly, the icebox door clunked shut.

"There's another cup of coffee, if you'd like it." Her chirrupy, carry-on, English, now-that's-over-with voice.

I could hear the plop of the chesterfield cushions as Durham piled them on a chair to make more space for sleeping. "Are you going to come down to the station, to see me off?" I detected self-pity in the question and felt keenly Durham's loneliness. *Why must you hurt him? Why not say yes?*

But there was a quality in my mother that I was beginning to recognize, a deliberate, impartial coolness that predominated once the agony of decision was done. The usual warmth in her eyes would turn to calculation, her generous face would lose expression and close in, as it did in public places, and the rancour of resolve would replace the music in her voice.

"No, my dear, I think not. I can't see how that would help you. Or me."

"Perhaps," said Durham softly, "it would make you regret your choice, is that it?"

I heard my mother begin to speak and then stop abruptly as though a phone had gone dead. I went into my room quickly as she started toward the hall, and lay listening to her tired climb up the stairs, shoes in hand so as not to waken anyone. Not long after, her bedroom door closed, and I imagined her, calm, exhausted and sure, curled against the snoring figure of my father.

Most of Durham's leave-taking was done with the same

187

trampoline optimism he'd shown throughout his visit. As he shook hands with my dad, there were jokes about sending us back gold from the mountains, while my father lied kindly that the stopover had been a pleasure for us all. Doug hung back, then lunged a plate-sized hand into Durham's. George, probably mesmerized by the feel of a mattress under him again, had slept in, and Durham did not want him wakened.

"He'll get enough of *reveille* when he enlists. Let him sleep! But *you*, sport—" he laid a friendly arm across my shoulders, "I was rather hoping I could convince you to come down with me—make it seem more like another excursion than a final farewell. You'll see all the uniforms."

"Sure!"

"Good! Well—Georgia?" He said her name as a blurred, hopeless question that brought a dart of anguish to my mother's eyes. "Georgia, how can I possibly thank you for all your care and kindness?"

Now he saw that his house would be restored to him again, my father began to bluster with generosity. Cheerfully he suggested that Durham kiss my mother good-bye, which Durham did, trying to make it friendly and lighthearted. He held her briefly and strongly against him, while my dad smiled approval, while my mother's face struggled for composure over Durham's shoulder, while Doug stared at his birthday wrist-watch as if this embarrassment had a limit that could be timed. For a moment Durham seemed stuck there, no longer able to say anything funny, or wise. At last he let her go with a soft straight-armed motion, setting her back from him. "I'll write," he said quietly.

The Union Station of that over-wrought Saturday filled me with awe; I felt small again, trailing in Durham's wake through the smothering overcoats musky with mothballs, and new uniforms that smelled like plasticine. The lobby shimmered with sound and a peculiar golden light that bathed everyone in false and noisy radiance. There were carts loaded so high with luggage that they hid the redcap behind, and uniforms from Norway, Australia, the United States and England—men arriving to train in our country while our enlisted men moved out to places shrouded in wartime mystery. Though their accents varied, there was a compact, healthy sameness of expression, a feeling of competition between them. They seemed to me, then, like all the heroes of all the Saturday matinees I'd ever seen collected in one place, carelessly courageous and waiting for a camera to roll.

Durham parked me on a wooden bench in the waiting room, disappeared, and returned with two orange crushes held high over the crowd, like flares leading him back.

"A short wait, sport, but the train will be leaving on time." Beside us, a brick-faced sailor was crushing a girl and her corsage in a lengthy, passionate kiss. Durham glanced at them and took a long glumping swig from the bottle.

"Sure you can find your way home? Your mom'll have my hide if you get into trouble."

"How can she get mad at you when you'll be in Vancouver?"

"Righto," he agreed softly, and stared dimly ahead.

"I just go back the way I came. . . ."

"Right. Nothing to it." Across from us a lady at the Traveller's Aid booth was gesturing earnestly to a couple who tilted toward her, concentrating painfully on instructions they could barely hear. The sailor had stood up, heaving his duffle bag like a dead body over his shoulder. The girl was crying in a soundless contorted way that made her seem ugly.

"Not quite like our other outing together, is it?" I shook my head. "Well, nevertheless, it was good of you to come, and I appreciate it. I suppose I should give you all kinds of advice, since you'll be grown up when I see you again, most likely. *Don't* smoke American cigarettes. Too strong. Something Turkish in them. And don't drink like Halwick. He doesn't enjoy it, you know." He paused to light his pipe. "Well, how are things going with Shirley?"

"Not so hot. She's always scared. . . ."

"Well, don't lose *your* nerve, Keeter. It's not lost all at once, you know. It goes in bits and pieces. No sin in letting her know how you feel—" He stopped abruptly, listening to the garbled announcement echoing above us. "Ah, there it is. Not too many people going west, I hope. May get a whole seat to myself to flop out on!" He would not let me go with him to the platform in so dense and preoccupied a crowd.

"Take care of yourself, Keeter—or is it Doug?" He smiled, remembering his mistake on our first meeting. "I'll write as soon as I arrive, keep tabs on how you're doing. Remember, it's the *Bay* car you get on, going *north*—"

"Okay—"

"Say good-bye again to Georgia. Make her play, won't you?"

He shook my hand in his solemn, ritualistic way, which might have made me ill at ease if the whole station hadn't been so filled with feeling. Just behind Durham, the sailor was edging backwards, sending bleak grins to the girl; then he shouted *I love you*. His voice, harsh and yearning, was swallowed up immediately in the deafening noise.

Durham seemed to interpret the confusion on my face as sadness. Becoming mightily cheerful, he repeated his promise to get me out there someday to mountain-climb with him. And left me with a memory of blustery *cheerios* and the sight of his brown fedora slouched like a spy's, angling sharply out of the sea of blue and khaki caps.

Lunch was waiting for me on the kitchen table when I returned, my mother's usual ploy to loosen my tongue with nourishment. She sat opposite me, pale and wan from the late night, but sharp-eyed, keen, wanting to know how it went. I told her what I remembered, though I don't believe any of it really satisfied her. If I had been twenty years old, as thoughtful as my father, as inventive as Durham, I might have been able to convert the emotional charge of Union Station into a poignant description of Durham's sadness. Instead, I felt uneasy with her, defensive, resentful of the

190

deception that made her form her questions with halting care.

"Did he seem. . .well, happy to be going?"

"I dunno. He sure wasn't as sad as all the soldiers." It was a dirty crack, playing up his pacifism, but I felt manipulated. She bit her lip, keeping her eyes steadily on my face.

"Drink your cocoa while it's hot. Pinky called a while back." Another pause, then, keeping the light tone as though it really didn't matter, "I don't suppose he had any impressive last-minute messages?"

"Nope."

"George was sorry he missed him. Did Durham say anything about that?"

"Can't remember. Where's Dad?"

"Napping."

"Then what's the thumping upstairs?"

"George is putting his things back." She seemed to be waiting for more from me as her fingers drummed a phantom five-finger scale on the oilcloth. I got up to take my dishes to the sink, unable to stay behind with her or add to what I had already said. My mind was on the sailor and his girl. *One arm around the back, the other lower—turn the head sideways and when the lips are together, move your head once in a while—why do they close their eyes?* Whatever my mother said to me as I left the house went unanswered; I was free of Durham and had begun the natural process of freeing myself from her.

And in the act of letting go, I found that I was restoring them gradually to their original places in my life: an eccentric, kind but absent uncle; a sensible, unselfish and, above all, dependable mother. Whatever they'd had together was dwindling in my memory to a hazy affair tinged somehow with musty and dated embellishments, like my mother's yellowing sheet music. Inevitably I began to dismiss them as both old-fashioned and old, always important to me separately, but never again a couple.

191

23

For a time after Durham left, I genuinely missed his presence. The house was comfortable, quiet, orderly, but conversations often lagged as if we all needed the unpredictability and bounding verve of Durham to make them shine again. This feeling lasted only a short time for me, because the vacuum he was bound to leave was rapidly filled with my crush on Shirley. It was becoming intense, but exasperatingly one-sided.

Much later in my life I thought I had developed enough mature insight into my childhood to apply some logic to that time. It became simple enough to explain away most of the highs and lows of bumbling puberty, to even laugh about it whenever the memory of it came up among other men who'd shared many of the same agonies: in a group, after a leisurely lunch, nostalgia tended to be more hilarious than painful.

This wasn't the case, when, sharply, I'd find myself confronted with the old hurt when I least expected it. A new patient who happened to be blonde, too thin and ridden with nerves, jolted me to the same pity I'd had for Shirley. There was the time when I was walking my small daughter through her first snow, and she broke away from me with the startling bow-legged speed of snowsuited children. For an instant, a jab of remembered pain brought back Shirley's unpredictable escapes and returns, and with them, my own leaps from leaden despair to hope. Intellectual maturity was no help to me in those moments: under logic lay emotions that felt uncomfortably like those of childhood.

On the weekend after I lost my temper with Shirley I veered between justifying my anger—wondering why I bothered with her at all—and nursing a kind of anguished guilt. But by that time I was smitten to the bones, as irrational as she was. One glance at her in the classroom made me decide to undo my cruelty of the past week in some offhand, face-saving way. While the class was moaning its reluctant way through "Nymphs and Shepherds" during Miss Berry's music period, I scribbled a note and shoved it at Don White.

"Pass that to Shirley and if you read it first, I'll flatten you—"

Clunk, d-i-n-g went the tuning fork in Miss Berry's dimpled hand. "Do-o-h! Now, all together—" and her fruity soprano bounced on the surface of our rumbling discord like a bottle on the sea.

"Watch her tits," Dick husked into the back of my head, "watch 'em when she breathes in."

Shirley was covertly reading my note, flattening it to the song book.

I really want you to come this aft. That's why I was mad last week. K.

She stuffed it carefully in her sweater pocket and turned her head my way, smiling so slightly that it would go unnoticed by anyone else. I spent the rest of the morning in a state of euphoria.

I burst through the door around six o'clock that night, flinging my coat in the general direction of the hall tree, forgetting my galoshes and tracking damp parabolas down the buff glow of the hall floor.

"That you, Keith?"

"Yeah—"

"Did you put your rubbers on the paper?"

"Yeah—" I backtracked, hastily pulling off my galoshes and tossing them onto last night's *Tely*. I could hear a dripping tap and the shift in the furnace of coal settling, which usually meant the house was empty.

"Where is everybody?"

"Doug's gone to a show," my mother replied, "I *never* know where George is, and your dad has stocktaking tonight so he stayed downtown. We had dinner over by five-thirty." She was settled on the chesterfield, legs stretched out and crossed at the ankles, her small pointed feet jutting upward like dog's ears. Across her lap and curling down to the floor was a dark boa constrictor of a scarf which she was knitting for the Navy. Raising her eyes briefly away from the needles to look at me, she asked, "Well, how was it? Did you leave his place in a mess and ruin the poor dear's reputation?"

"Guess what? You aren't going to *believe* this! She *went* to the party!"

She pushed the wool aside, her eyes wide and peppery.

"Really? Shirley *went*?"

"Right from school on the streetcar, like the rest of us!"

I told how she'd taken a seat, glowing like a lamp in the swarm of kids half-filling the car. It had still seemed difficult for her to make conversation with anyone, so she'd been content to look around, laughing at Don White's antics, overreacting as shy people did to jokes that weren't funny. The conductor, old and Scottish and clamp-lipped with disapproval, had ordered Don back into his seat and was then mollifed by the discovery of Critchley-Williams' ancestry.

"He said, 'What would ye expect of Canadian childrrren?' Like that, the way Mrs. Collins talks—"

"Tell me about the party," my mother interrupted impatiently, "what did you eat, and was Shirley—I don't know—at home, comfortable?"

"Yeah. She liked it. Especially the food."

194

I suppose in the shock of her having gone at all, I saw the party through a mist of magnified hopes. I described her eating of two hot dogs with the awe of a person who's seen someone intensely religious break the fasting rules of the church. I didn't mention that she had spilled her cola and sat through Musical Chairs smiling uneasily, until Dick Jackson suggested Spin The Bottle. Then, with her face burning, she had slipped from the room to go, May McKay said mockingly, to the "little girls' room."

Watching my mother's encouraging face, I left out the details of Shirley's discomfort. Anyway, I didn't think her shyness was any harder to bear than Ann Kirkpatrick's stutter, which plagued her every waking hour and tortured her most when she was excited, or happy, or angry, and most needed words.

"Well, I'm really pleased," my mother said. "It must have taken a lot of courage. And maybe old Mrs. Upshaw isn't the terrible harridan we thought, eh?"

In my room, I concentrated on the ride home along St. Clair, reliving every detail: the darkened stores, except for Lippert's Smoke Shop, where the first signs of Christmas glistened and blinked in his toy-filled window; my nervous, exultant closeness to Shirley, sitting beside me on a double seat; the affection I read into any simple remark she made, my new pride in her quietness, which made Betty Pibschel's lunges toward Pinky seem crass and dated. Shirley did not want me to walk with her down Arlington, this time out of her concern for me as well—but I refused to trail twenty yards behind her, entering into her reasonable fear as though it were also mine. So we compromised, laughing and chattering, brimful of discovery: I went most of the way, then let her disappear around the corner and into her house well before I returned home.

I found it impossible to line up singly the events of that afternoon. There were gaps that eluded me, that I'd hoped to hoard, ordinary as they were. The harder I tried, the less I remembered of actual conversations. But it didn't matter.

What mattered above all was that she had finally broken through and that I had helped her do it.

By the time my dad returned from work, and George was playing "Stairway To The Stars" in his bedroom, and Doug clomped upstairs after hockey practice, normalizing our room with his chapped face and outdoor smell, I felt exhausted, as though I'd written an exam on Shirley Upshaw.

For the rest of that night, I floated around among the family, *there*, but separate, too, inhabiting my own island of peace in the swirling stream of talk.

She was not in class on the following day, which disappointed me, but nothing more. Colds were flitting invisibly from room to room in school, like rumours.

That afternoon, however, she came in minutes after the bell had rung and put a note on Critchley-Williams' desk before taking her seat. This was normal procedure; most of us scarcely looked up.

"Page sixteen, class," Critchley-Williams directed adenoidally, fighting his own cold, peering at us with bloodshot eyes. "Lampman's poem today—" By recess I'd forgotten her morning absence, but Pinky grabbed my arm as we marched, army-style, through the hallway toward the stairs.

"Didja *see* her?" he whispered, careful to keep his eyes straight ahead. The sentinels of silence were posted along the route, ready to leap.

"Shirley? Sure—so what?"

"Get a *good* look, outside—"

I couldn't understand him and he didn't want to explain.

Out in the yard, she had made her way to the far corner, avoiding, I supposed, Ann Kirkpatrick. When I reached her, impatient and eager to talk, she was standing rigidly against the fence, pulling her hood close about her face. It was a damp, deceptive day, though not as cold as last night when she'd walked with me, hood down and hair flying.

"Are you sick?" I asked. "Maybe you shoulda stayed inside—"

196

She mumbled *No*, huddling, still looking off away from me. I walked around her, not entirely baffled by the change of mood because I was used to it, and looked into her face. One cheek was slightly swollen, touched with bluish-tan, as though she'd mopped carbon accidently against her face. Across her jaw, a dull straight red line ran from the edge of her lip to her ear lobe.

"Jesus, she *hit* you! She hit you, Shirley! *Why* did she do that?" Her eyes looked pale and cold, wrung out. "Was it because you went yesterday? I thought she *knew!*'

Numbly, she shook her head. "I didn't tell her. I just went. I was going to lie to her, make up a story that Ann wanted me for supper and they didn't have a phone—" It seemed to hurt her to talk, and she stopped for a second.

"Why didn't you *tell* me," I said, "I could've made up a really good one, one she'd believe."

"It wouldn't have helped. That was bad enough, her thinking I'd gone to Ann's. I had to go to my room as soon as I got home, she was so mad."

"But your face—"

Shirley turned to me, her mouth quivering, and looked away. "You know," she said bitterly, "how *clean* she makes me look. At night, I always give her my clothes and she puts out the dress for the next day. So she got my clothes while I was locked in my room. I could hear the washing machine bumping away, and I was looking out my window. Then I heard her coming up the stairs, making a terrible sound. I thought she was sick. I called out to ask her and she screamed *a liar! a liar, like your father and a cheap tramp like your mother!* I couldn't move, hearing the key in the door." I watched her gulping, helpless, not crying but shaking the words out in spurts. "She had a stick in her hand and even then I didn't think she'd hit me. She never had. Then I saw the note from you in her other hand. I'd forgotten to take it out of my sweater—"

We'd been spotted by Miss Nicol, who minced over the lumpy ice fields toward us. "Move on there! No loitering, you *know* that!"

197

"Come on," I said, "walk toward the school. Nobody will care about how you look. Come on—" I had no words to make it easier. I was shaking from head to toe.

"Keith? Don't tell anyone else. Her note says I fell on the stairs. And you can't walk me home. She *knows*. She's going to meet me at the gate again. She says I can't go off the porch, not even on weekends. I'm even afraid she'll come at recess sometime—she *said* that—to watch when I'm not expecting it."

I burned with anger. "It's my fault! I signed the goddam note! I talked you into it." The bell rang and we had to freeze in place.

In school, I wrote her a note: *Don't worry. She can't hold on forever. Answer on this and return. K.* I underlined *return*. In a moment, making a mouth of disgust, Don White shoved it back at me.

Yesterday was worth it. S.

24

After this, events tumbled one on the other, so hectic and contradictory that they seemed insane against the backdrop of Holy Week and Christmas. The night after I'd spoken to Shirley in the schoolyard, while I was still desolated by the pain I'd caused her, my dad dashed through the front door, his face wrenched with urgency. "Quickly, call the Humane Society! Old Hughie's dog's dying out here on the road!"

I was about to do as he said when my mother took the phone. "No, let me. Sometimes they don't believe children—"

I ran out to find only my dad, Hughie and Pinky, stopped on his paper route by the emergency, there to see. Hughie was sitting on the road, weeping, cradling the dog's big head in his arms.

"Was he hit?" I whispered. We were all whispering. "No, he just went all stiff while he was walking, and turned in funny circles," said Pinky. "Then he fell over—" The dog's eyes, muddy with pain, still would not close. His ribs exploded erratically and caved in as he tried to breathe. His distended tongue hung, drooling saliva over Hughie's pants. My dad went for a blanket to wrap around the dog, but when he tried to unwind Hughie's arms, Hughie would not let go. Finally, my dad tucked the blanket around both of them.

"It's times like this," he said grimly, "that I wish I had a gun. I put a horse out of its misery in the war—" I glanced up at him with new respect, seeing his strong compassionate face, grateful that he did not leave us. By the time the truck arrived the dog was barely breathing, and I could see that my dad was worried sick that Hughie would never let him go, would want to get in with him. At last the truck drove away and my dad and Pinky and I managed to get Hughie back home.

The next day my dad said he saw him walking down the centre of Arlington, smiling away, calling to the dog who wasn't there as though nothing had happened. "It's funny," he told my mother, "how being a bit crazy helps him, isn't it?"

In those few days before our holiday began, the principal attempted to keep classes battened down. His daily bull-horn messages contained the warning that "our school is *not* on vacation until four o'clock, Friday, December twenty-second!" Critchley-Williams got around this by letting us write compositions on subjects of our own choosing.

Pinky's story was read aloud because he'd cannily written about the death of Hughie's bulldog, embellishing it with a few untrue grisly details. When he had finished, Critchley-Williams put it down and removed his glasses.

"Very good, Yorke, good descriptive eye there. But I picked it from many equally good efforts for another reason. We all know that Christmas is supposed to be a time for giving—that's why there's a place to put your white gifts for the poor out in the hall. But, I wonder, as a class, if we might be a bit more personal? Mr. Brown, though he seems to feel and act differently from us, must have suffered a very great loss. We all recall, I'm sure, his joy last September, when he took part in our pageant." He paced slowly up and down before the blackboard, tapping a pencil against his ear.

"Now—just suppose each of you contributed five cents. We have twenty-two pupils here. That would be—" He stopped, smiled, and waited. We were looking around at

each other, mystified. Shirley's ruffled sleeve rose hesi-
tantly above the heads. "Yes, Shirley?"

"One dollar and ten cents," she said, so softly that he had
to lean to catch it.

"Exactly. Good girl. Now—I happen to know of a rather
lovely little dog that can be bought for two dollars. Anyone
want to tell me how much *more* we'd need?"

"N-n-inety c-cents," said Ann.

"Yes, to *buy* the dog. A little more for a bit of food
perhaps, and a bow. It is *my* idea to get the little dog for
Mr. Brown, as our Christmas gift."

Up went Dick Jackson's arm, smartly, like a Nazi salute·
"Sir, what if his old lady don't like the idea?"

"Good point, Jackson, but a *solved* one. I'll take the
liberty of ringing the lady up to see if she would be agree-
able. Now, if you'll think it over for a few moments before
deciding, I'd then like a show of hands. Anyone for whom ,
the nickel poses a problem needn't worry. I shall make up
whatever's required. . . ."

Shirley could not get a nickel, so my mother insisted I take
two. ("How's she going to put up with the ridicule, dressed
in all that finery and not able to contribute? But tell her it's
only a loan, then she won't feel badly.") It took some convincing, but she finally accepted the money and dropped it
into the box on Critchley-Williams' desk.

Every day now, at noon and after school, she again had to
endure the disgrace of her grandmother, whey-faced, wild-
eyed, waiting beyond the gate to walk her home.

"*I* thought she had more guts," Mary York derided, swaying along beside me on the side of the street Shirley could
not use. "Look't her, scared of that old bag o' bones! What
you see in her I'll never know!"

"Oh, shut up! How'd *you* like being the only kid? It's okay
for you with that big bunch at your house. Who'd pick on
you?"

"My father is who!" she swung back belligerently. "Only
I don't just sit there mewlin' like a swatted cat!"

I knew it was Mary's way of surviving, being chippy and proud, trying somehow to stand out any way she could from a family that made her its second mother. But she embarrassed me, so I told her to get lost and ran off toward the guys having a snowball fight half a block ahead of me.

We'd just tugged our Christmas tree home along Tyrrel when the doorbell rang. Since my dad was in the basement hammering an X of wood for a stand, my mother answered it. I was in the living room, putting newspapers where the tree would go.

"Where is your son?" The voice was cracked, dry, like the unused voices of the old suddenly driven to speak.

"Why do you want him, Mrs. Upshaw? Is it something I can help you with?" My fingers prickled, clutched the paper. There was a terrible sensation in my ears, the way I felt underwater when I held my breath too long.

"You have never helped. You have *never* helped. Raising hooligan sons!"

Even in my numb condition, I heard the calm words of my mother with astonishment. "Perhaps if you'd like to step inside, we could—"

"Never! Cody was here. You think I don't know all these things? How he came here, getting odd ideas?"

I wanted to get my dad, *move*, go into the hall to help. There was the cold thought that she'd harm my mother as I remembered the red welt across Shirley's face. But I had no strength, as if illness had struck.

When my mother tried to say something, the rasp cut through her words. The old woman's voice had risen, burying all logic and my mother's habitual manners. "He'll go to hellfire, that child of yours! He's been after my Shirley, talking to her alone! He's written a note, tried to make her as evil and cunning as he is! I *know* these things! He's the one who writes those filthy words on the school fence—" She broke off, spluttering, gagging on her hate.

I heard Doug's feet stomp to the top of the stairs and he called down, mystified, "Mom, who the hell *is* that?"

Faced with insanity, my mother had decided to contain it. Sternly she said, "It's all right. *Don't* come down—"

"No, don't come down," screamed Mrs. Upshaw, "don't come near me, you foul devil-ridden Keith! And don't come near Shirley—" her voice plummetted horribly, like a rock hitting a head, "—because I'll fix you if you do. There'll be no Christmas for *her* because of you, no tree—we'll go to church and pray—" She seemed unable to stop. Even as she backed down the porch, and our walk, I heard the ugly gibberish fading away, until my mother closed the door and ended the litany of revenge.

She came into the living room, shaking slightly, very white, and methodically helped me spread the papers. From the basement my father's hammer banged and rang. We could hear him, between blows, singing "Jingle Bells." I began to cry. I had not cried for a long time, and the pain in my throat was agony.

"It's all right, Keith, it's all right to cry. I don't blame you. She can't help it, but it doesn't help much, knowing that." She put her arms around me and I leaned against her, bawling like a kid, until it had gone and I could move again.

"Now dry your eyes and get the decorations. And don't worry about Shirley. She's survived this long, hasn't she?"

The last day of the fall term flew by with the school choir singing carols in the main hall, lined up in suppressed merriment beneath our Union Jack and beside a rapidly growing ball of shining silver foil.

Critchley-Williams brought the new pup to our classroom in a cardboard carton, where it slept for a short time, until our voices roused it into bounding curiosity, and it escaped the box to ramble the aisles in idiotic delight. There was a thin leash and a collar with a red bow. Our card was signed by everyone: *Merry Christmas to Hughie Brown, from Room 307.* May McKay worried that it wasn't exactly like Hughie's old dog; it was lighter, and the flat nose was pale brown, not black.

"That's because it has a few imperfections. Legs are a little long," mused Critchley-Williams, hastily pulling the pup from his wastebasket, "and the colour of his nose would not make him breedable by thoroughbred rules. He's called, in fact, a Dudley. Somehow I can't imagine Mr. Brown worrying much over that. Nor would I! Lovely little chap." Immediately, we named him Dudley. He waddled from desk to desk through the dwindling, darkening afternoon and peed warmly in the cloakroom before we wrapped him in an old towel for the trip to Hughie's house.

Shirley did not go up to the door, but managed to linger long enough to see the small ceremony Critchley-Williams had insisted upon. We had to sing *Merry Christmas To You* (Critchley-Williams sang *Happy* instead of *Merry*) and he gave a little speech about Father Christmas coming early this year. Into Hughie's soft child's face came a heroic struggle to understand.

"Say thank you, Hughie," prodded the woman behind him.

And he did, probably without knowing why.

My father had corralled George, Doug and me in the basement Christmas Eve. "Want you to see what I got your mother—" and he removed four big planks propped against a sheet-covered ghost. Triumphantly, going *ta-ta-ta!*, he swept off the sheet, exposing the gleaming white enamel of an electric refrigerator. "How about that, eh? A Kelvinator! Reconditioned like new, hums like a Rolls!"

Christmas Day itself seemed hazed over, removed from reality, so that it had no name like Saturday or Tuesday. Durham had sent a cheque with which my mother was to get the piano tuned. She liked my Cutex Colour-Wheel, and the free sample of Rose polish I'd sent for with a magazine coupon. My brothers and I got a book each and socks, and my dad had had my first long pants made in his own department at work. There were socks hung on our bedposts to open, wool gnomes misshapen with oranges, nuts, a hockey puck and pocket games. During the King's broadcast, delivered in a measured, mournful voice, both my parents dabbed at their eyes and said, "Poor man," because Edward had left him this unwanted job.

Some of the gaiety was dimmed for me because I knew that nothing like it existed across the road. But from the melancholy, as though it were dark earth, was growing something defiant and dissatisfied within me.

I'd seen Shirley going off to church with Mrs. Upshaw very early under a low, desolate sky, no hint of wind or sunshine, and everything—the houses, the sky, even last week's stale snow—tinted the colour of heavy cream. An odd, uneasy day. *Will you have to go up to the front and kneel, and say you are a sinner? Will the old lady cry out, Lord, forgive her? Because of me, is that your Christmas?*

After dinner, when my father lapsed sleepily into his chair, filled with fruitcake and wearing new slippers, and my mother made her annual pilgrimage "back home" by pressing her ear to the hour-long broadcast of greetings in unintelligible accents from every corner of the Empire, I went outside to play a little hockey on the street, trying out the new puck with my old stick. The sky, even late in the day, glowed a deep pea-green, and fragments of a thin east wind eddied around the early-lit lampposts. In the Upshaw house, one dim lamp gloomed from the living room, another behind the shut blind of Shirley's bedroom. Anger rose in me, not guilt now, or regret or self-condemnation.

Again and again I slammed the puck into the curb, gearing myself for something. Maybe it was the expectation that something new might turn up, that a glint of hope might just be there, waiting on the other side of the night.

25

Whatever whimsy it is that remakes the world and lifts our gloom began in the night by transforming everything outside. I sat up in bed on Boxing Day blinded by glare. I'd slept late, without dreaming, without hearing the sleet storm that my dad told me had struck before dawn. Trees, telephone wires, clothes lines and eavestroughs dripped silver. Wire fences were glass lace, all our wooden fences moulded into giant popsicles; our garbage can, permanently stationed by our front porch, was now gift-wrapped and tasselled festively in blue-white ribbons of ice. Even the rope left trailing over Mueller's fence for his dog was a glittering coil that shot sparks of coral, like some exotic necklace.

Most of the kids on our block were already outside skidding on the road's natural rink when I rushed out to join Pinky and Don.

"Hey!" Don pointed across the street, looking like an animated teapot in his new Christmas toque. "Look who's comin' out! Why don't you go over and give her a big fat kiss, eh, Gillies?"

She'd come cautiously through the door carrying an ice-chopper almost as tall as she was. Maybe she'd had no holiday, but the Children's Aid must have given her the white angora mitts and Sonja Henie bonnet that tied under the chin. She stood looking soberly across at us, gripped by self-conscious panic. The curtains on the wreathless door parted, and we saw Mrs. Upshaw's knuckle rap sharply against the glass. Immediately Shirley began to jab at the arctic porch, not strong enough to do much more than raise tiny shards of ice around her white boots. Above her head where the roof joined the porch, stalactites of blue-glinting ice were unevenly suspended. In a swift, graceful impulse, she put aside the chopper and reached to snap one off.

This brought no crack of knuckles, but rather the wrenching scrape of the door being jerked open. "PUT THAT DOWN! They're dirty!"

Beside me a little kid from a couple of doors down gaped at her, his arms bristling with captured icicles. "No they're *not*," he hollered. "My mom says they're jewels!"

The few kids who'd bothered to hang around to see this diversion, who hadn't skidded further down the street to watch the arrival of the Salvation Army band now circling near Hillcrest Avenue, burst into laughter. They hooted Mrs. Upshaw back into the house, and Shirley was left alone with her humiliation on the ice-bound igloo of her porch.

What if she went inside, too? Wouldn't it be the old lady's final and perverse triumph if she saw that Shirley chose to escape back into the house rather than endure the taunts outside?

I couldn't take the strain anymore, the cackles of laughter aimed at the closed door but pelting Shirley, all those ugly guilt-ridden days that had soured this holiday. Throwing back my head, I gave a vaulting, glorious, ear-shattering Tarzan yell that flew out and rebounded against our glass houses. Then I turned and drove a flat, merciless shove into Pinky that sent him skittering backwards. His eyes narrowed, his face darkened in fury. "Okay, Cheeta," I dared him, "see if you can catch me!"

I tore away from him, hearing his salty blast that he'd kill me! his thick Irish oaths hitting my back as I flew full-tilt

down the road while he thumped menacingly on my heels.
Past swiftly-parting children and the Halwick's place I ran,
past Hughie's pup, steaming a yellow hole in the ice with his
urine, still hearing Pinky's persistent clumps and the band's
"Deck The Halls" clanging through the clear air. I knew I
could beat him. Despite my puffery and practice, he played
better baseball. He could outswim me. His school marks
floated steadily above mine like unreachable pennants. But
I could *run*, and if using his one weakness would draw eyes
away from Shirley that's all I cared about.

The flaps of my leather cap snapped back like knight's
colours as I began to pull away from him, feeling that I could
fly. Above my head the huge frozen trees tipped to touch
each other like fan vaulting, and the sound of Pinky's boots
faded behind me. I turned then to pump smoothly back,
feeling the exhilaration of seeing her there, still outside.

I headed for my maple tree, as I'd done all summer,
shinnied with difficulty up the slippery trunk and squirmed
along a jutting branch while the icy tree sang like a mammoth wind bell. *This is for you, Shirley, your Christmas
present*—and I swung outward. But I was heavier, and the
glass branch glided away under my mitt. I had a sense of
profound surprise as it let me plunge in a shower of crystal
to the sidewalk below.

My leg snapped, briefly burning beneath me. I had a
moment of anger as I lay there, limp and twisted like a
discarded toy. Through the pain I heard my name, unfamil-
iar because it sounded so far away. I recall distinctly a dead
wet leaf plastered to my cheek, the jagged edges just visible
beneath my eye, like extra lashes. And Pinky, my insult
forgotten, advancing and receding in a bronze blob, dropping tears on me and wailing that I was dead, I was dead.
Then the private throb of a headache that eased as someone
placed a rolled coat beneath me. And replacing Pinky was a
blur of white angora, Shirley's grieving face, no longer hidden from me on this street by hedges and curtains and

window glass. She was shivering, smiling when I recognized her.

"Hey!" I cried, "you must have crossed the road!"

And I passed out.

Pinky told me about it later, as I sat like Critchley-Williams with one stiff, plastered leg propped on a footstool, thumbing through a fresh batch of comic books he'd brought over. He told me that she'd slipped and slid down her glassy porch and across the rink of a road to get to me while her grandmother's hands pounded uselessly at the window. "And when you passed out, the old woman opened the door and was shriekin' loik a banshee, 'Get back here, you bad, bad girl,' like she was two or somethin'. Holy Mary, I'll tell you it was like the movies an' all! But she paid no heed, just stayed there 'til your pa and ma came. . . ." Matter-of-factly, he got up. "Well, I have to go now. See ya later."

Friendship, as I'd discovered when I raced him, had its limits; there was a triple feature holiday matinee, and if I'd been in my death throes, it wouldn't have stopped him from going.

When I could return to school, hobbling in heroic good-nature along the familiar route and amiably allowing everyone to sign my cast, I noticed the change in Shirley. Her walk, its rhythm and stride, struck me strangely, as though a familiar march had suddenly changed its cadence. Day by day she discarded her silence a little more, cautiously joining other kids at recess. One day, when another boy said hello to her in the hall, I felt the first pang of jealousy. Sharing her was the most difficult part of the transformation, because for such a long time she'd been as much a prisoner of my imagination as she had of her grandmother's tyranny.

At the same time, something was happening to the old lady. She gave up the walks to school and, according to Pinky, was becoming more absent-minded every time he called for the *Tely* money. Sometimes she ranted that she'd paid him, that he was a thief, but more often she just placed money in his hand, staring blankly, as though she'd forgotten why he was there. Once, she called him Cody.

As Mrs. Upshaw's grip weakened, Shirley became more independent. One night after dark I was on my way to St. Clair to get some Player's for my dad—he would not patronize Meuller's store because Meuller was German—when I saw Shirley walking down the driveway.

"Hi."

"Hi." I felt disoriented, confronted with her new normalcy. "Well, I'm going up to St. Clair for my dad—"

"I'm just going for a walk." She hesitated, looking as uneasy as I did. This wasn't school, or recess. Or daylight.

"Well, d'you want to come with me?" Bound to habit, I found myself quickly scanning her house windows for a sign of the inhibiting shadow.

"Don't worry. She's asleep. She's been doing that a lot, falling asleep. I think she's sick." We began to walk, stiffly at first.

"Will you get a doctor?"

"I guess so. She wants me to write her sister and tell her. She lives in Aurora. I met her a couple of times. She's nice. . . ."

We both fell silent as I mulled over the idea of Mrs. Upshaw having a sister who was nice. We saw Hughie struggling with his leashed Dudley, trying to keep him in the centre of the road. But the dog kept pulling and tugging with his broad shoulders toward the sidewalk and the trees.

"Look what's happening," Shirley said. "He's getting closer to the sidewalk! Maybe this dog will get him over it, walking in the middle of the road all the time."

We crossed Benson to the dark patch near a lane where I'd run fast in fear when I was small, thinking of hooded men and sudden, seen horrors. I took her hand, and she left it in mine. I wanted to kiss her, too, the way the sailor had kissed his girlfriend at Union Station. I'd practiced it on Mary

Yorke once when we were playing hide-and-seek, but I couldn't do that with Shirley. Instead I stopped, and turned mechanically, and planted my winter-chapped lips against her cheek, briefly and ecstatically feeling the tickle of angora on my ear. She did not draw away, and because she was Shirley, that was her supreme compliment. My senses soared into joy; I fixed in my mind the ice-coated night, the sting of the air and the brilliance of the stars around her, making a shrine to return to when growing up would, even for an instant, no longer be exciting.

We began to walk again towards the lights of St. Clair and the smoke shop. But now she had taken *my* hand, and I felt old enough to invade the Dive, or smoke all my dad's cigarettes, or even join George when he went downtown to enlist in the Navy.

A few weeks after New Year, Shirley began to walk back and forth to school with me, no longer afraid of the consequences. We had, at last, what we wanted, but neither of us knew quite what to do with our new freedom, until we slowly began to talk, exploring each other's likes and dislikes, or just lapsing happily into natural and comfortable silences we'd never known before. Not once did we mention Shirley's past or Mrs. Upshaw.

Then, suddenly, Mrs. Upshaw died. That evening, the house blazed with light.

"How she would hate that," my father said, watching through the curtains, "all that light, and neighbours calling." My mother took over some stew and a cake, as though it were a party. There were, she said, many church members going and coming.

"And Shirley's all right because her great-aunt is there. From Aurora. They were taking down the pictures when I went in."

For three days, Shirley was away from school. When she returned, it was to tell Critchley-Williams that she'd need a transfer. She would be leaving Toronto with her aunt. And

211

the teacher went with her to the office, talking quietly to her, carrying her coat.

On Saturday morning I was in my room when my mother called to me, her voice touched with the urgency of someone who insists on good manners. "Keith? I think Shirley must be leaving today. You can see from your window. They're putting suitcases in the car." I craned my neck and saw the big blue DeSoto, trunk yawning. "Don't you think you might at least say good-bye?"

It isn't that easy, saying good-bye—it's only been a few weeks since we said hello. How the heroes of matinees deserted, how the cocksure military men evaporated when you really needed them! My adult slick of damp hair, newly mastered, my schoolyard swagger, now fully justified, didn't help much when I knew she was going.

But I was determined to give her some sign that it mattered to me, and I had begun a swift run down the stairs when the doorbell rang. I warned my mother back hastily: "It's *okay*, it's for me—"

Shirley stood a foot back from the door, smiling uncertainly, like a canvasser. For the first time her hair had no curl, but hung in lank pale skeins over the shoulders of her coat.

"Hi—"

"Hi—"

"Well, I guess I'm going now, so I came to say good-bye—" she back-stepped lightly, flushing, at a loss for anything wise or memorable to add.

"Yeah, well, I guess everything will be better—" I glanced over her shoulder at the younger version of Mrs. Upshaw waiting by the running board. "Is she okay?"

"Yes, she's really nice." A dark flicker of humour touched her eyes. "She just *looks* like my grandmother." We both laughed; we were both hugely uncomfortable. "Oh! I almost forgot. I owe you this." She probed into her pocket and held

212

out a nickel. "For Dudley," she explained, "remember you loaned it to me?"

I took it without saying anything and held it, my heart thumping. I had no present for her, nothing to give, nothing to say that would make any difference. She would go.

She smiled nervously in the direction of her aunt, who was not hurrying her.

"Well, I'd better go. She'll be cold, waiting there—be seeing you—"

"Ya—"

She crossed the road and got into the car, the front seat this time, and waved as they drove away. The next day a man arrived to pound a FOR SALE sign into the Upshaw front lawn, advertising the end of my childhood.

EPILOGUE

"Good heavens, still here?" Biggs' mini-skirted secretary pauses briefly in the office doorway, pretending dismay. I am momentarily numb, staring back at her as if she'd dropped from an alien planet, inflicting an odd neutrality on the room. I have no idea of the time and expect the comforting clunk of a childhood clock.

"It's raining," she says accusingly, shaking herself neatly like a blocky little pug. "Wouldn't you think they'd put a post office in a place as new as this?" With great care she removes a clear plastic bonnet that guards her unmoving globe of hair as if it were a salad.

"I suppose it would help. By the way, have you the time?"

"Quarter to one."

"I'd like to make a phone call."

"Sure—" she is buffing her white plastic boots. "—go ahead, but dial eight first."

Before I can get out of the chair the telephone is ringing.

"*I'll* get it," she says hastily, as though *I* would have. "—'d afternoon, Finlee Biggs 'n Upshaw? Yes, he is. One moment, please. It's your office, *Doctor* Gillies. *You* didn't tell me you were a doctor!"

"A dentist." Her expression instantly cools, a reaction I am used to after all these years. "Hello, Gillies here—"

214

"Hi. What's going on?" She is a nurse of the sixties, irreverent, placid, sympathetic with patients, yet she exudes a sense of transientness. "Look," she says brightly, not waiting for my answer, "the root canal for two has cancelled. And the Scott boy—you know, the chipped tooth—broke his ankle playing football this morning. So you're free for the afternoon."

"Any emergencies?"

"Not so far. People don't tend to have emergencies on a lovely Friday, right? If you're so tied up there, there's really no point in coming back." The thought of an afternoon off is seductive. This nurse is changing me. "Still there? Look, I can handle anything that comes up."

"Okay, I'm convinced. But I'll call in around three, just in case—"

Biggs has suddenly burst through his door, shrewd face contorted with contrition, brown hair carved like the thatching on an English cottage. "Gillies, for chrissake come in! Debbie, get the doctor some coffee. Cream and sugar? Black? Black, Debbie. Jesus what a day, one thing after another—"

Despite the long wait, he makes small talk as if it were expected, witless meanderings about his cottage and his cases. Finally he hands me his gold-plated Sheaffer, using it to indicate three X's by spaces that require my signature on the mortgage.

"There, there, and there. Smart, getting rid of old houses. Not a bad price, twelve thousand. Should buy a few drills, eh? A helluva lot more than your folks paid for it—"

"I'm not sure that they had to. My grandfather built it—"

And suddenly I see Durham's shaggy presence looming stolidly around the fringes of a small group of people, cap tugged down over long wiry grey hair. In an effort to dress up for my mother's funeral, he had worn a brown suit jacket over his denim jeans. The cycle of fashion had caught up with him. Pinky Yorke was there too, in his late thirties still a stocky, russet figure, as if someone had bronzed all of him as

215

a keepsake, not just his infant shoes. There was no trace of an accent when he told me that he'd become an architect. "—designing houses instead of breaking into them!" And we'd both laughed, drawing a look of reproof from ancient Aunt Pru who had shrivelled to a handful of fur and powder, roused to enthusiasm only by funerals.

"—honestly thought you'd have to settle for less," Biggs is saying, sounding like a realtor, rising brusquely to shake my hand.

On my way out, I glance one last time at her closed door. What questions could have been answered in such a short time? It's possible that dredging up that grim and disrupted childhood would only hurt her. And even after five years I have my own divorce-bruised ego to manage: what I thought would be freedom felt like failure. Above all, I do not want someone I loved so much not to know me.

Outside in the hallway, surrounded by a bleached choral version of "Blue Velvet," I think vaguely of a restaurant and food. The DOWN light flicks over the elevators a few yards away and I sprint for them, glad to move fast and enjoying minor satisfaction at slipping in sideways before the doors thud gently closed. I straighten my tie, puff out my cheeks. I have an afternoon off. That is something.

"The only person I ever knew who could run like that was Keith Gillies."

Within a space of time I cannot measure there is a swift, keen leap of pure joy, which I'd always thought was reserved for the young. I have a split-second and stunning realization that she is *here*, that she not only knows me but wants to tell me so. When I turn to look at her I feel overwhelmed with images: her oddly touching angular posture, the clean cut of her grey suit, a half-expectant but tentative rim of happiness around her eyes—

"Shirley, for God's sake—" I blurt it out, uncaring, scattered, too old-fashioned to try to shake her hand. Then, inevitably, I remember that I am going bald, that I am

216

self-consciously sucking in my stomach muscles.

"You didn't press the button for your floor," she says, her voice echoing some of my agitation. "Do you want the main, too?"

"Yes—yes." This music box that plummets us through the centre of the building will soon settle, then spew us out into the lobby.

Now my own tense silence magnifies details and pummels down all my intentions. *If only you meant nothing to me— then how easily I could make conversation!* I notice the grip of her hand on the brass railing, a growing smudge of pink across her cheekbones. My muzzy, marbled reflection stares back at me.

"The walls are mirrored. I suppose it's an illusion of space—to help claustrophobics—" Her head turns quickly toward me with what I hope is gratitude.

"Yes," she says very smoothly. Putting *me* at ease? "I like them. They're flattering, for one thing. The veining re-moves wrinkles—" Suddenly she is smiling, warmly, broadly, a strong smile. "Isn't this ridiculous, this whole situation? Talking about mirrors and wrinkles when there's so much to ask?"

With a mixture of relief and discomfort I realize *she* has taken the situation in hand instead of me, and the reversal bothers me. It's a bit like hearing Ann Kirkpatrick tossing off the old, cruelly elusive consonants without a sign of a stutter.

"But I suppose we never had time for small talk, did we?" she is saying. "And this isn't the sort of meeting I'd imagined."

"No. I thought I'd see you again, but it would be in a park, and you'd be walking a dog."

"Did you marry?" She is asking it the way my nurse would, casually, as if any answer would be equally accept-able.

"Divorced—" *Ping.* Main floor.

The lobby is swarming with lunchtime crowds. A fountain

spurtles over a pond of submerged pennies, watched by men and women with plastic coffee cups and hot dogs in their hands. As two men with attaché cases circle around us, she murmurs, "Let's move over there," and in a graceful motion that doesn't widen the space between us, she's found an undisturbed place to one side of the elevators.

"I'm sorry about your divorce," she says without cynicism or false pity. "There's always some trauma, at least there has been in the cases I've taken. Since I didn't marry, I can't really know how it feels to break up." Her voice has risen; we're both talking too loudly. Around us wafts the smell of frying hamburgers and floor disinfectant. I can't seem to relax, having to make conversation over the infernal music, the clamour of noon voices. It strikes me as ludicrous that we're trying to renew our friendship while standing beside a robot-like plastic litter bin.

"Look Shirley—I haven't had lunch yet. Have you?"

"No."

"Would you have it with me?"

"Yes."

No equivocation, no feminine moment of hesitation. She has caught the look of surprise—or censure—on my face. It's this new bluntness, where once everything between us was contrived and oblique, and I was the blunt one. Something in her expression clouds momentarily, withdraws.

"Are you so sure you *want* me to, Keith?"

"Of course! I can't think of anything I'd like more."

"Ah," she smiles, "gallant as ever. But I'm not the same. I've had to change, more than most people, probably. I think you've noticed."

"It doesn't matter. We've all changed. We can talk about all that. . . ."

A woman, cheek still bulging with the last of her lunch, reaches past me to pop a paper bag into the litter bin. Shirley doesn't seem to notice; she watches me steadily. "It *does* matter. I try not to think too much about the past. For me, now is a lot better than then. Do you understand? So much of it was like the Dark Ages, and I had to work my way out of it. The process wasn't easy. Maybe you won't like me now."

She has spoken lightly, but beneath it I sense a warning, as though she must let me know that she is glad of her impact on me, but that she will not relinquish independence so dearly bought. Like me, she knows that her old infirmities had their attraction for me, that her helplessness was as much a lure as her mystery.

There is something else. If that part of Shirley no longer exists, then the armour I flaunted has outlived its usefulness. Somehow its symbolic clank to the ground is a profound relief. Did I really expect her to talk to me as if we were still stumbling shyly around the schoolyard?

Suddenly I want to wash the concern from her eyes. "Listen, Shirley. Let's go and have lunch together—and we can compare transformations. For all I know, you may not like me either. . . ."

I see a smile around her mouth now, and her eyes glint gently with something that always made her shut doors and drawn blinds irresistible: challenge.

There are still some unknown roads to run, a few colours left to fly.